The Burning of Juniper Slaide

JOHANNA HANDLEY

THE BURNING OF JUNIPER SLAIDE

Published in the UK in 2016 by Rudling House.
A CIP catalogue record for this book is available from the British Library.

ISBN 978-1-910957-16-5

Cover design and typeset by Karen Ronan
coversbykaren.com

www.rudlinghouse.com

RH

For Darcy

CHAPTER ONE

I'M trying not to think about the empty chair next to me. I stare straight ahead at the wall, focusing on a spot just above Mr. Baines's head, forcing my eyes to stay put. Most of all, I try to ignore the anger, the one that's been simmering away inside me for days now, that I just can't seem to get rid of.

Our teacher is huddled over his desk, still wearing his winter coat. He doesn't look up, not once, not even when he calls out James's name and is met with silence. He sighs, picks up a different coloured pen. I picture the bright red cross next to James's name, loud and angry against a neat row of blues.

I mumble "here" when Mr. Baines asks me to, and then, like everyone else, I wait for the bell that tells us it's time to get to the first lesson of the day. I pretend to listen as he gives us his standard pep talk, the one about impending exams and future decisions. This speech again. These words that manage to seep through to my brain, thunder around in my blood, make me feel sick. *Not long before it's all over. We'll be thrust out into the world of adults. College and university applications should have been sent a long time ago*. Gulp. Oops.

My eyes hit the clock on the wall every few seconds. Ten minutes to go. I doodle. I draw absent-minded pictures of my classmates on my sketchpad.

Rob Lewis. Rugby Lump. Social Bulldozer. School Joker-slash-Joke. Likely to be wasted all day long but always happy to state his greatest achievement: I've-never-touched-drugs-in-my-life-man. I draw his face with big bear features, huge, enraged. I add a big bear body, with two cans of beer in his big bear claws.

Natasha Shelby, my nemesis. Or at least she would be if I

even existed in her world. I vaguely remember being popular like her once, but not anymore. I draw her with legs up to her chin, blonde and pinched, with an exquisite resting bitch-face.

Carla Jackson, a Quiet-One, like me, but not like me. Takes time over her perfectly-styled hair, her throwback 1950's outfits. I draw her surrounded by singing flowers, her Quiet-One rockabilly friends happily trapped inside the petals.

Ugh. I spread the faces out in front of me. Nothing's working today; all my drawings are wrong and they've been wrong for days. It's the eyes. Vacant. Devoid of expression. My heart sinks at the empty space next to me again, and I can't stop myself from shuddering. *Think about anything except James*, repeats the voice in my head, the same voice that's preventing my hand from working properly. The same voice that's stopping my pencil from doing what I want it to. The same voice that's blinking James's name into my eyes in big red flashing letters.

I'm about to rip up my soulless faces when I think better of it, fold them into the front pocket of my bag. I'll deal with them later.

The clock again. I've got art next so I force my mind to go there. I love everything about art lessons at Shackleston School. My space, tucked away in the corner out of sight. My teacher, Mr. Stuart, who long ago gave up trying to teach me anything and left me in peace to get on with it. The only thing I don't love about art is that it's all the way over on the other side of school, across the football pitch. I spend some time thinking about how to get there, what's the best route, how to avoid the crowds and not get in anyone's way, not draw any attention to myself. *The dilemma of my everyday life.* Usually, I'm good at staying in the shadows.

But not today.

Because it's not the bell that jolts the classroom awake,

bringing us back from wherever our minds had gone. The new school speakers, high in the corners of the classroom, start to splutter. Everyone stirs, looks up, startled. When the voice speaks, it's loud and unsettling even though we were expecting it.

And it's my name being blasted around the classroom. "Juniper Slaide, to see the Headmaster please," says the muffled but undeniably nasal voice of Jackie, the school secretary.

Heads turn. Curious eyes find my face and lock on, grabbing onto me like vultures, hungry wolves, narrowing down on me, probing into my space. Mr. Baines pauses in his monologue, raises a questioning eyebrow at me. Rob Lewis is impressed. He leers, lifts a pretend glass in my direction. Natasha Shelby's cool blue eyes notice me, linger in disgust. Carla Jackson swallows for me, looks away.

I feel the heat spread over my cheeks, covering my ears and then my neck. I burn for my wolf-eyed classmates, unable to stop myself.

It takes me a moment and then I'm up, gathering my things. I'm bright red as I walk out, head down. Someone sniggers when I almost trip over a schoolbag, and I speed up, desperate to get out before my face explodes.

It's cool in the empty corridor, and I close my eyes, lean back against the wall and take a deep breath. In all my years at Shackleston School, I've never been called out. That kind of honour is usually reserved for the louder, more disruptive students. The popular ones. Not students like me, who never put a foot wrong and are determined to go unnoticed.

When the speakers shout my name again, it reverberates all around me. Cringing, I start walking to Mr. Brankin's office in the main building, across the cricket field. As I push open the door to get outside, the cold air hits me, soothes my hot face. I tell myself I don't know what this is about; I haven't done anything wrong. But my stomach twists with every crunch of my feet over the ice-frosted grass, and I wrap my coat tighter around myself. I speed up.

Jackie's withered face nods at me when I get there, barely looking up from her screen. She looks bored, but she's focusing on something, probably Sudoku or Solitaire or some other old-person game. I tell myself to relax. If Jackie's normal, there's nothing wrong. But still, it's like there's a hand inside my stomach, grabbing at me, twisting my gut. I take another deep breath as I walk to the headmaster's door. I knock.

He's at his desk. His smile is gentle, but I can see something troubling the usual kindness in his eyes. It stops me from going any further, and I linger in the doorway, not sure what to do, afraid to step inside, afraid of what he's about to tell me.

And then I notice *her*. Lucy Creed. James's Mum is here.

She's sitting on the sofa, across the room. She looks up at me as I step inside and our eyes meet. I'm taken aback, not just because she's here but because of how. Her hair is in greasy tangles around her face. There's no perfect makeup, no glittering jewellery. Her immaculate clothes have been replaced with grey jogging bottoms, a shapeless jumper. Her eyes, which are usually the kind of bright, piercing blue that can make a person blink several times in a row, are dull and red inside. She's been crying. She's still crying, I realise, as my heart thumps.

I have to look away. She's always been the beauty queen of this town, all icy blonde and gliding. Everyone loves her. She's one of those perfect cake-baking mums, a standout community member. She smiles with flawless teeth, laughs the perfect tinkle-laugh. To me, she's always felt a little cold, but then, no one ever approved of my friendship with James. Our families, the Slaides and the Creeds, were never supposed to be friends.

Mr. Brankin clears his throat, but James's Mum gets there

first. "Where is he?" she barks, her voice faltering, but I can feel the anger coming off her in waves.

I flinch. My face burns again and I hate myself. I look straight ahead at my headmaster because I don't want to look at her anymore. "I don't know," I stammer. I beg him with my eyes. *Help me. Believe me.*

He frowns as Lucy slumps back down further into the chair and covers her face with her hands. She makes a noise, a low howl, and I know she's crying again.

I don't know what to do and no one asks me to sit, so I just stand there, inside the safety of the doorframe. I tell myself I haven't done anything wrong. I try to stick my chin out and force the guilt away, but it's there, spinning around in my gut like a furious tornado, trying to flip me inside out so everyone can see the truth.

"Juniper," says Mr. Brankin. He's trying to sound reassuring, but the anguished noises coming from James's Mum are freaking him out. I can tell by the way his eyes keep darting from me to her, and his eyebrows are having difficulty staying on his face.

My personal tornado intensifies.

"Mrs Creed is worried about James. He hasn't been home since Sunday. Have you heard from him at all? Do you have any idea where he might be?"

I swallow. *Sunday?* It's Wednesday now. James has never been gone this long before.

I shake my head. I prepare myself for speech again, something I usually try to avoid. "I don't know where he is," I tell him, forcing myself to look at him. *Don't look at her. Don't look at her.*

Mrs Creed, Lucy, as we were always encouraged to call her when we were little, keeps up the desperate sobbing. She shouldn't be going through this. James shouldn't be doing this to her. He shouldn't be doing this to me. I grasp at the sudden flash of anger, trying to get it back. Even anger is better than this terrible guilt. I've got nothing to feel bad about, I tell myself. James is the one who's doing this. James is the one who should feel bad.

The crying noise stops for a moment, and I glance at Lucy before I can stop myself. Her nostrils flare as she glares at me. "Oh, come on, Juniper," she says. "You two are joined at the hip. If anyone knows where he is, it's you." She practically spits the words out, like they're poison.

I shake my head again, embarrassed to find myself welling up now. I rush to get the words out, before I start crying too.

"James hasn't been talking to me," I say. My voice breaks. I don't sound like myself. I sound like a whiny little girl. "He stopped. Two weeks ago."

This, at least, is true. It's a James-thing. When he decides not to talk to you, that's it. You're dead to him until he changes his mind; he manages to make everyone feel his contempt. He's just as likely to do it to his mother, a classmate, a teacher, or anyone. Even me.

I watch some kind of realisation dawn across Lucy's face. She knows what it's like to be on the receiving end of James's silent treatment. Something's made sense to her, and I can tell she believes me, at least a bit. But then she puts her head in her hands again and starts up that awful weeping. The noise is sickening, like her spirit's being ripped out of her with every agonizing moan.

Mr. Brankin gets up from his desk and walks around to her. He sits and puts his arm around her, and she leans into him, sobbing properly now. He looks up at me, nerves and worry in his eyes. "Juniper, if you can think of anywhere James might have gone, or if he gets in touch with you at all, please talk to one of us, OK?"

I nod at him, a silent promise, already broken.

He nods back, satisfied, before turning back to Lucy. I'm dismissed.

The minute I'm in the corridor, I break into a run, heading for the nearest toilet. I lock myself in the cubicle, sink down against the door and hug my knees to my chest, waiting for the panic to pass. I try taking deep breaths, but it's not going to work, so I rummage around in my bag, my fingers closing around the one thing that can help me to calm down. I pull out the matches and breathe. I focus on the tiny box, listening to its contents fall about inside as I pass it from hand to hand, running my thumbs over the rough edge, then the smooth.

I listen for a moment to make sure the bathroom's empty. I need to do this now, no matter what. I take out a match and scratch it, lighting it straight away. It flickers, gently at first, but then the flame takes hold. It breathes, and I breathe with it. It's beautiful. It wavers, growing, picking up speed until it swallows the whole length of the match so I have to blow it out, just before it touches my fingers.

I reach over and drop the used match in the toilet. Then I light another one, staring at the flame, letting it take me all in, calm me down. I light ten matches in the same way, each tiny bit of heat taking me closer to feeling normal again.

After some time, I'm able to think straight. I don't know how long I've been in here. I've missed art, that's for sure. I'll have to make it up later.

It's going to be OK, I tell myself. *Everything will be OK.* James has run away before. He does this, then he comes back. I try not to think about Lucy Creed, about how she looked, distress trembling through her. I try not to think about how I lied to her, I lied to my headmaster. Because of course I've seen James. I was the last person to see him before he left. And I'm pretty sure it's my fault he hasn't come back.

CHAPTER TWO

APRIL 2, 1985, Marisberg, Kentucky,

Everyone has a Story, right? One that belongs only to them, defines them, dictates how they live their lives. My mother's Story was 'Cancer'. She coddled her illness, cradled it in her arms and let it take over her life. My brother's Story, I guess we'll call it 'Drugs.' I have no idea where he is now, but I'm sure his Story is consuming him, and vice versa.

Before today, I thought my Story was this: 'Philip Creed, small-town boy grows up to become a famous writer.'

But I was wrong.

My story, is 'Lucy'.

When I walked into Tally's Bookstore this morning and saw her at work behind the counter, my heart stopped. I'd known Tally wanted to take someone on, but I had no idea her extra pair of hands would change my life. The world shifted. There she was, my Story, right in front of me.

Tally gave me a knowing look and whispered in my ear. Lucy, she said, and I breathed in the name, letting it wrap itself around my heart. The girl in front of me had lived in my head for years, but I was stunned to find her this beautiful. There was an air of quiet mystery surrounding her as she dealt with customers, delicate hands passing books and receipts over the counter, piercing blue eyes that never allowed themselves to linger on anyone for too long.

As I watched, I saw something else, something deeper. The smile plastered on her lips was a lie; it had shattered into a million pieces by the time it reached her eyes. There was a sadness in her, so strong and so real that I felt it wash over me, and it was unlike anything I'd ever felt before. I needed to know her, to know everything about her. I wanted her Story. I wanted to make it all better.

I moved towards her, and we stared at each other, without speaking. I shook my head because I'd been silent for too long, and I didn't want her to be the first one to speak. But I was stuck. What could I say that would do the moment justice?

So I took out my pen, and I wrote the only words that came into my head.

Let me fix you.

She took the note, and when she turned those blue eyes up to me again, I could see that somewhere inside her, she wanted me to try.

Now, as I write the same words down in this diary, I know it's going to be my life's mission. I will fix her, I promise.

CHAPTER THREE

EVERYONE knows playing with fire is wrong. We've had lectures from the firemen, we've seen the videos, heard the stories. We've been told countless times. We're supposed to be afraid of fire; it's not a toy. It's not a game. It's dangerous. It kills.

I'm supposed to know this better than most people. I have first-hand experience of how fire destroys things. Wrecks homes. Shatters lives.

But I can't help it. Ever since what happened to me, there's something about the flame that helps me, calms me down. There's always this moment, a tiny speck of life, where it could go either way. Die or destroy. And that's my moment. It's under my influence. It's as though because of what happened, I need to tame fire somehow. I control it. It's mine.

I read somewhere about people who become obsessed with the thing that destroyed them. It's like I'm suffering from a kind of Stockholm Syndrome, but with flames taking the role of the kidnapper. Like I want to get to know fire, I want it to love me. It's weird, I know. I'm weird.

I keep it a secret, even from James. And if Kata knew, she'd be horrified. Kata hates fire more than anything. She's even had all the old fireplaces in the gatehouse boarded up in every single room, which is understandable, I suppose. She'd go crazy if she knew I had a stash of matches; she won't even have them in the house.

I'm careful. Usually, lighting a match or two is enough. Sometimes, when things get so bad I can't breathe, I light more. Papers, card, sticks. But I'm always careful. I stay safe.

After school, I sit on the window seat in my room, looking out at the castle that used to be my home. Or rather, the shell of the castle, its walls black and charred, housing nothing but air. Nine years ago, I lived in that castle. Nine years ago, a fire destroyed it and with it, my parents and my wonderful grandfather.

I was eight years old when it happened, and since then I've worked hard at erasing all the memories. A coping mechanism, they said. When I got out of hospital, my Aunt Kata and I moved into the gatehouse, and we made it our new home. Kata loves me enough for three parents, she says, and I know it; I feel it every time she smiles at me. And James was always there. He was my best friend before the fire, and he was my best friend after it.

Everyone tried to separate us, but it was useless; we always found a way. After a while, people accepted it. Eventually, Kata gave up and welcomed him into our home. The old guys around town stopped staring and tutting at us in the street. His mother left us alone whenever I was at his house. She'd bring us cookies and cupcakes, but whenever she spoke to us, it was always to James, like she'd do anything to avoid looking at me.

Always, *always* together. James and me, me and James. We've heard the word inseparable used in conjunction with our names so many times that it's become *our* word. It belongs to us, it's attached to us, like we're attached to each other.

But sometimes, not often, just sometimes, James stops talking to me. And every time, it's like I'm lost. I wander around school, not sure where to go or what to do with myself. And it hurts. Usually, the silent torture only lasts a few days, and then he turns up, jumps through my window and collapses onto the window seat, all smiles and laughter. Life goes back to normal, James and me, me and James, always together, like nothing ever happened.

Some of what I'd told the headmaster and James's mum

was true. He *had* stopped talking to me. For two weeks and two days, to be precise, and it was beginning to feel like forever.

But it was strange. There was something different about this time. I had no idea what I'd done, which was normal, but I could tell something was weird. He wasn't doing what he usually did. He wasn't parading girls around in front of me in the playground, a stupid, fake smile plastered all over his face as he glanced over at me to check I was watching. His laugh wasn't extra loud in registration, and he wasn't passing notes to new best friends over my head in English. He was quiet. He was alone. His dark blonde head was down, stuck in some old book I'd never seen before. I'd plucked up a bit of courage and tried to talk to him a week ago because he seemed so out of place here, so unlike himself, so awkward. But he'd ducked into a toilet to avoid me, and I'd felt bewildered, even more lost than usual.

So I'd resigned myself to it. He'd turn up, at some point, when he was ready. And when he did come tumbling through my bedroom window, late on Sunday night, I felt that familiar rush of relief wash over me. Finally, he was back. Finally, he was talking to me again. Things could go back to normal.

It was late, and Kata had gone to bed early. I'd been sketching at my desk when I'd heard the window slide open, and I'd jumped up to make sure my door was properly closed so as not to wake her.

I turned around to him, unable to stop the grin of relief on my face, my heart pumping with excitement and something almost like delirium at his return. I couldn't wait to hug him, to see that sheepish smile, know that he was ready to tell me he was sorry without ever saying the words out loud.

But something was wrong. He wasn't laughing. He wasn't

happy. His eyes were red, and they were looking at everything except me. He had two bags with him, his sports bag and an old red rucksack I'd never seen before, and both looked heavy. He stood there in the middle of my bedroom, clenching his fingers around the straps.

Panic rose up in my throat. I felt my knees give way a little and I sank onto my bed, waiting for the words, whatever they'd be. I had no idea he was about to change every rule our friendship was based on.

"He's innocent," he said, his voice breaking.

I didn't understand at first. "Who?" I whispered. "What are you talking about?" I wanted him to get that he was being too loud, that he'd wake Kata up, and we'd be in trouble.

He said it again, quieter this time, but still not whispering enough. "He didn't do it, Joo."

I frowned. I didn't want to understand what he was saying. All I could think about was that any minute now, Kata was going to walk in and start shouting at us. I wanted him to be quiet. I wanted him to shut up. I didn't want him to be saying those words, and I didn't want my thoughts to be flying away ahead of me to places they shouldn't be going.

In nine years, James and I have never talked about what happened. It's the rule. It's the deal our minds made with each other. We were best friends before, we'd be best friends after, no matter what. Nine years ago, we needed each other more than ever. I'd lost my home, my parents, my beloved grandfather. I needed my best friend more than anything.

But James also needed me. He'd also lost someone close to him, his father, Philip Creed. His father didn't die, but he was gone, and gone forever. He was banished from James's life and locked away.

He's still locked away now, in Gilford Prison, serving a life sentence for arson with intent, and three counts of murder.

CHAPTER FOUR

NOVEMBER 29, 1985, Marisberg, Kentucky,

On our first date, we went to O'Grady's in Jadesville. Lucy smiled a little when I pushed open the heavy door, and I knew I'd been right to choose this dark, quiet hole of a bar. We sat in the corner, her back to the wall, facing the door.

I ran off my questions straight away. I wanted to know who she was, where she was from, what was she doing here in Marisberg and everything, everything about her.

But it was a mistake, and one I regretted instantly. Lucy froze and closed up. Her eyes went to the door, and I could tell she was wondering how she could escape without being rude.

I rushed to fix my error. I understood her a little then, on that very first date. It was obvious she was running away from something painful that she wasn't ready to share. I started talking about myself, rattling off information, anything I could think of to stop her from leaving.

When she realized I wasn't going to pressure her into talking about herself, she began to relax. She stayed.

Since then, we've been on five more dates, and I'm no closer to knowing her. Everything I learn, every tiny piece of information she parts with, I write down in a list that isn't even a page long yet.

She's English, twenty years old.

She always wears dark clothes that are pressed and perfect, and cover as much of her up as possible.

She loves silence, Jane Eyre, pretty sceneries and fried chicken.

She hates noise, small spaces, darkness and cheese. Yes, cheese. Even the sight and smell of it makes her gag. (Thankfully,

I am also not a fan).

Wherever we go, her eyes mark all the exits. She looks first at the doors, then the windows, then the people. She's on edge until she's looked every single person in the eye and decided she's safe.

She takes my breath away every time I look at her.

She's terrified of something, but I don't know what. One day, she'll trust me enough to tell me. One day, she'll trust me enough to know that I'll never let anyone hurt her again.

CHAPTER FIVE

HE'S innocent.

I'm trying to sleep, but I can't stop the words from swimming around in my head. James has been gone for over a week, and I can't switch my brain off anymore. The anger I felt before is still there, under the surface, rising up every time I think about his words, but it's more than that. It's this restless fist in my stomach that's keeping me awake, clenching and unclenching inside me, an uneasy threat. I reach for my phone under my pillow again and look at the time: 2.37 am. *Ugh.*

Since I was called into the headmaster's office last week, James's disappearance has been made official. On Friday, in a special school assembly, Mr. Brankin made the announcement. He used the word *missing*. Seven hundred and twenty-three students gathered in the main school hall as he delivered the news and told us not to worry, that James would be found and returned safely. He asked us to come forward if we knew anything about James's whereabouts, anything at all.

Seven hundred and twenty-two pairs of eyes turned towards me, and I felt wide open; my heart raced, my face burned. Everyone thinking the same thing, asking the same questions, while they stared and stared. Did I know something? Was I hiding something? I was bright red, but I looked straight ahead and tried to think about art, about my final project. About fire. Kata. Anything.

Missing? It's ridiculous. He's not missing. He's playing some stupid game that I don't even want to think about. He does this. He disappears, makes everyone worry, and then comes back. *Right?*

But this time, I know where he's gone, and I haven't told

anyone. I haven't told his mother. Guilt curls itself around the fist in my stomach as I think about her.

She was there, in the assembly. She stood in the corner of the hall, and after everyone had finished looking at me, they moved their questioning eyes toward her. Lucy Creed, looking like some other-world version of herself. Lucy Creed, lips chewed and raw, eyes bloodshot, terrified.

Because of me.

I could say something. I should say something. I should talk to someone, tell the truth. I should tell Lucy, at least. But how can I possibly repeat James's words out loud? How can I tell someone else what he was saying? That his father's innocent? The thought makes me shudder.

I think back to the last time I saw him. I vaguely remember him saying he'd found something, discovered something that belonged to his father, something that meant he couldn't have started the fire that killed my family.

I vaguely remember him saying we'd been wrong all this time, and he needed to go and make it right with his Dad, to tell him he was sorry for never visiting him, for leaving him all alone when he didn't even do it.

I don't remember much else after that, but I know I couldn't listen to James anymore. My pulse started racing, pounding hard in my head. How could he be bringing all this up, saying these things? We'd never spoken about it, not once, not ever. We were never going to. Our friendship, the most important thing to me in the world, had survived because of this fact.

We don't talk about the past.

It's in the past. His father did what he did to my family, and everyone suffered because of it. And we all worked hard to forget: Kata, me, James... the whole town. To put it in the past and leave it behind.

Anger was bubbling and building inside me as James spoke, hammering in my ears and overtaking his words so I couldn't hear them at all anymore.

I stood up from the bed and faced him. "He confessed," I blurted out, interrupting whatever James was saying. The words out of my mouth were too loud, but I couldn't help it, I needed him to know, to remember. *His father pleaded guilty.* How could he forget that?

It was James's turn to tell me to be quiet. "Shhh, Joo, please... you'll wake Kata." He looked at the door when he said my aunt's name and I frowned. This was new. I'd never seen him look like that before. It took me a moment to realise it was fear on his face, and that was weird too. James had never cared about waking Kata up before.

"He confessed," I hissed at him. I was still too loud, but it didn't matter anymore. If this was a joke, it was horrible, cruel, twisted.

But James shook his head. "I don't know why he did that, Joo. I don't know why he confessed, but it's not true. He isn't guilty. He didn't kill your parents. He didn't kill Papou."

Papou. The mention of my grandfather's name crowded my vision with tears and unwanted images. I hadn't thought about him in a long time.

"Joo," said James, bringing me back, pleading with me, even though he still couldn't look me in the eye. "You have to believe me. Please. I've got to go and see my dad, figure out how I can get him out of this. I need to know the truth. I'm so sorry."

That quick flash of surprise again because James had never apologised for anything in his life. But then the rage overtook. I felt it thrashing around in my head, burning under my skin. He was apologising, but for what? For changing the rules and talking about the past? For saying his dad wasn't guilty when the whole world heard his confession? For telling me he was leaving?

"Joo..." He whispered my name, looked at me properly for the first time. Our eyes locked on to each other, his: bloodshot, unhinged, terrified. Mine: scowling, hurt, confused.

James. My mirror image. My best friend. My soulmate.

"You can't tell anyone, Joo..." he was saying as he undid his eyes from mine and glanced towards the door again. "You can't tell Kata. You can't tell anyone. Promise me, please. My father..."

All of a sudden, someone started screaming. "Get out, get out, get out." The screaming seemed to go on for ages, and it was so loud I had to cover my ears to stop hearing it and cover my eyes to not see James throwing his bags back out of the window and jumping out behind them. It was only when Kata flew into the room, and her arms were around me, and she was rocking me back and forth on the bed, that I realised it was me. I was the one who was screaming like that. I was the one who had shouted out those words, along with a whole load of other words that I can't remember now. And James was gone.

Kata held me against her until I stopped shaking. She shushed me and stroked my hair and tried to say things to make it better, even though she was shaking herself. When I was calm, I pulled myself out of her arms. Her beautiful olive skin had turned pale, her grey eyes, tired and marked with worry, blinking away at me, waiting for me to talk to her.

She unglued a strand of my hair from my face and tucked it behind my ear. "Joo," she said. "What's going on? What happened?"

I shook my head. There was no way I could tell her. No way I could bring myself to repeat James's words. I didn't want anyone else to have to experience that kind of pain, especially not Kata. Saying *his* name, *Philip Creed,* out loud, in front of my aunt? Not possible. I couldn't hurt her like that; we've worked too hard to forget.

"I'm OK, Kata," I said, taking a deep breath. "I'm sorry. I didn't mean to scare you." I was starting to feel the urge to spark something. It was itching in my fingers. I needed Kata to leave now, so I could be alone, so I could do what I needed to do to calm myself down.

"Joo, you're not OK," she said, her eyes wide and troubled. "What happened? What did James do to get you so worked up like that? And why was he here anyway, at this time?"

I heard the note of annoyance creep into her voice. I pulled away from her; the last thing I needed was a lecture.

She sighed next to me on the bed, and her voice switched back to concern. "You know you can talk to me, right? Whatever it is?"

I looked at her. Her perfectly round face, so similar to my mother's, so similar to mine. The barely-there lines at the corners of her eyes were deepening as she tried to read me, tried to understand what was going on.

I felt myself clam up, shut down, close the door inside me. Kata was wrong. I couldn't talk to her. Not about this.

"I'm OK, I promise," I said. "You know what James is like." I sniffed for good measure, hoping that appealing to her love/hate relationship with James would work.

It did. My aunt tutted and rolled her eyes, and I could tell I was getting somewhere.

"I'm exhausted, Kata," I said. "I just need to sleep now."

She pursed her lips. "OK, Joo. You get some sleep. We'll talk in the morning." She gave my head a stroke as she got up but then thought better of it and leant down to kiss my forehead.

I held my breath until I heard her door click shut across the hallway.

I waited. I thought I'd give it half an hour or so, and she'd be asleep, and I could spark something. But it was too much to bear, and after ten minutes, the urge to set fire to something was too strong. I paced around my bedroom, watching the clock, too wired to do anything else. I needed to be able to lose my eyes in the flame, let the heat burn James's words out of my head.

The sound of Kata padding around outside my door made me stop my pacing. I heard her tread down the stairs. I heard the front door open and then shut quietly. Where was she going? It was well past midnight... But it didn't matter to me as much as sparking did. I raced down the stairs to the little guest toilet at the back of the living room, the one that we never use. I locked myself into the tiny space and leant back against the door, ignoring the freezing cold, ignoring how the brick floor was seeping through my socks and soaking up my legs as though I was standing on a lake of ice. This was where I needed to be. I pulled some toilet roll off the holder and I used my matches to light it over the bowl. The flame, beautiful and soft, started small, licking the edge of the paper so delicately, like it was almost afraid of itself. And then it got a taste of its own power, and it was off, tearing into the paper, flying up it so fast and so angry, devouring it in one go.

I felt the incredible rush through my whole body. The flames rose up high, and just before they could touch me, I dropped the paper into the toilet, panicking for a split second that it wasn't going to go out. And then I watched it die, its black ash crumbling into the water. I banished all thoughts of James's words out of my head. I'd screamed at him. I'd told him to leave me alone, to go away and never come back. And right then, I'd never meant anything more in my life.

But now, over a week later, I'm lying in bed watching the daylight start to creep in around the edges of my window. Another sleepless night. My brain is refusing to be quiet, those two words keep barging into my mind.

He's innocent.

For hours, I've been trying to tell my head to stop, to forget, to put the words away and lock them up with everything else that we don't talk about, that we don't think about.

And when I do manage to stop seeing the words, stop hearing James's voice throw them at me, I'm assaulted with the image of Lucy Creed. Her, in Mr. Brankin's office, looking like she'd been thrown out of her own body. Her, in the assembly, looking like a favourite doll that had been abandoned and left out for days. I pull the duvet over my head and groan.

Under the covers, another word floats around in the darkness. *Missing*. I squeeze my eyes shut to make it go away. He's not missing. *He's not.*

It's no use. I lose the battle with my mind. Surely James should have been back by now. Gilford Prison is only two hours away; he should have been there and back in a day. So where is he? What's he doing? Why isn't he back?

If he really went to see his father, he would have got the confession straight from the devil's mouth. So the only reason I can think of that he hasn't returned is because of me. Because I, his best friend in the world, screamed at him and told him to never come back. What if he takes me at my word? What if he never comes back at all?

That thought fosters a panic inside me so tremendous that I have to come up for air, clutching onto my duvet and putting one foot on the floor to stop the room from spinning.

Get a grip, Joo. I groan again. I know what I have to do. I let the realisation sink in, cursing James and desperately missing him at the same time. I'm going to have to figure out where he is and make him come back. I'm going to have to apologise. So that all of this can just stop and go back to normal. No one ever needs to know where he went. No one needs to bring up the past. I can find him, talk to him, apologise, beg him to come home, and then everything can go back to normal. The words can leave my head alone, Kata can stop looking at me like I'm about to break into a thousand pieces, James's mum can return to her normal pristine self, people can stop staring at me in school, and everything can be like it was. *Right?*

Except there's that fist again, swirling this time, playing with me, laughing at me. You're wrong, it's saying, as it pulls me apart. You're totally and utterly wrong.

CHAPTER SIX

NOVEMBER 29, 1986, Marisberg, Kentucky,

Something strange, something so weird and frightening has happened, and I don't know how to deal with it.

I decided to surprise Lucy tonight with a dinner at O'Grady's, celebrating the one-year anniversary of our first date. It's been an incredible year, the best of my life. Meeting her, falling for her, feeling her fall in love with me too... She's been more relaxed recently and it's been wonderful. The light she gives off when she's not being wary and mistrusting of everyone and everything is blinding, beautiful and infatuating.

Dinner was a success, but there was something different about Lucy, something off. She jumped whenever I put my hand on hers, and many times I caught her with that look, the one where she's staring at me but not listening to what I'm saying. She's so far away in her head I could be anyone.

When we got home, she was nervous. I felt a strangeness in the air, like the whole world was on edge, waiting for something to happen. When Lucy kissed me, it was different, urgent, relentless. There was a need in her that I hadn't met before, and, stupidly, I thought I knew what she wanted. I thought she was finally ready. She took me into the tiny den and reached around me to turn the light off. I could sense her undressing in the dark, and I started to do the same. I tried to touch her, but she brushed my hand away, and I held my breath, trying to get my eyes to adjust to the darkness so I could see her, see what she was doing.

She pushed me down onto the couch and held my hands down, leaning against me, making me feel incredible. I was desperate to touch her by then, and as soon as she released her hold on me, I couldn't help it, my hands were all over her.

It was a mistake.

I hadn't realized she was holding my hands down so I couldn't touch her. I hadn't realized she'd turned the light off so I couldn't see her. My hands were only on her for a second, but I still felt the grooves, the marks all over her body. I felt her tense up, and she pulled away, shielding herself from me. I couldn't understand what I was feeling, so I reached back and turned the light on, without thinking.

She ran from the room, enraged.

I stared after her, shocked at what I'd seen, not understanding it, not quite believing it. The scars, ugly and glaring, are all over her body, angry red gashes, right up to her neck. She was gone, out of the room in seconds, but I know what I saw. The thought that someone could do this to her makes me feel sick. This is the pain she's running away from. This is the suffering she's been hiding from, trying so hard to forget.

I heard the bedroom door lock behind her, and I have no idea when she'll open it again. I've betrayed her. This is her secret or at least part of it, the one she never wanted me to know. All I want is to make it better, hold her, tell her that with me, she'll be OK. I'll fix her, I promise. I just need her to know I'll make it my life's mission to never let anything or anyone hurt her again.

CHAPTER SEVEN

I'M sitting in an empty classroom, waiting for hell to start. Hell is going through school without James. Hell is the dizziness, the nausea, every time I think I can feel someone looking at me. Hell is being gripped by panic whenever I find myself in a crowd. Or it's sitting here, wondering where James is, when he's going to come back, and how I'm going to get through these last few days of term without him. Wondering how it's possible that I can still be so angry with him but need him so desperately in my life.

I try James's phone again for what must be the hundredth time this morning. My fingers shake as I listen to his voicemail tell me he's not around and to leave a message if I can be bothered. I've heard his voice repeat those words so many times now that it doesn't even sound like him anymore. It sounds like someone pretending to be him, winding me up, making me crazy. I shove my phone back in my bag, grasp onto the anger again, furious with him for not answering, even to me.

I left early for school this morning so that I could stake out James's house. I walked there, a walk so familiar to me, so natural, that if it wasn't for the stupid fist pounding inside my stomach with every step I took, I could have just imagined I was going to see James, like any other normal day.

I walked up the hill and past St. Augustine's College, its big gothic buildings casting shadows on my way. There's something about St. Augustine's that has always given me the creeps and not just because my father taught there. I can't explain it. I've always felt an intense need to avoid it, and I've learnt to ignore the deep chill that crosses through me whenever I get close by. I hurried past the school without looking at it.

James's house sits alone past St. Augustine's, in the corner of a recreation ground that no one uses. It's surrounded by a huge wall of fir trees, and I walked around the back and slipped through my favourite gap. I'm not sure what I was looking for, exactly. Signs of life. Signs that he'd come home.

I walked around to the front of the house, being careful to stay within the lining of the trees. I looked up at James's window and saw a flicker of the curtain, the back of a blonde head, a bare neck… My heart raced, I held my breath. *He's back, he's back, he's back* was coursing through my blood, making me hot, making my face burn. But then the curtain slid open all the way, and I saw it was Lucy.

My heart plummeted straight into my gut. All the heat left me, and I felt the cold then, biting at my face.

She looked different from how she'd looked in the headmaster's office, how she'd been in the assembly. She didn't have that same air of crumpled rag about her, that wild look of terror in her eyes. She was looking out in the direction of the castle, her chin high, her face tight and set into a look of hard determination. But I could still see the sadness in her eyes.

And I knew James wasn't back. I crept away to school.

Now, sitting at my desk in our empty English classroom, I reach for my phone again. If he's not answering my calls, at least I can text him. I write *Please come back,* and then I watch the message disappear on its invisible journey. Then, on impulse, and because now I've started, I can't seem to stop, I call him again. I listen to his voicemail, again. It's infuriating.

This time when I chuck my phone back into my bag, I get out my pad and start sketching James's face. I draw him in quick, sharp strokes, his caramel-blonde hair too long over those dark blue eyes full of trouble. I draw him a little rounder, his ears a little too wide, his hair a little less coiffed than he'd like. I smile, thinking about how annoyed he'd be if he saw this picture. He'd try to rip it up or force me to change it. *Serves you right,* I think to myself.

And then I think about how much I need him back. How much I miss him, and how bad I feel about screaming at him. So I fix him up. I make his jawline strong, tidy up his hair. I put the defiance back in his expression, make the boy shining out of his eyes look hard and tough. I make him as perfect as he always wants to be. I smile. He'd like this version of himself. When I'm done, I sit back and stare at him, at his face, staring back at me.

Oh James, what have you done? Where are you?

I curse him again and pick up my pencil. I draw myself next to him, looking at him. I draw myself tinged with fire, flames in my light grey eyes and under my skin, like a faded tattoo. I draw fire coming out of my dark brown curls, smoking up into the air, swirling all around my best friend. I draw myself angry, a she-devil, ready to take on the world. I draw the person I wish I was, rather than the person sitting inside my body.

When the bell rings, it's so loud it startles me, and I end up breaking the end of the pencil on my pad.

Damn it. The voices start, far away at first, then closer. My skin prickles with the sounds coming from outside the empty classroom. Trainers scuffing on lino. Excited voices. Locker doors slamming shut. Classroom doors banging open. Loud shrieks of laughter that pierce my brain and shatter my nerves. I need to get a hold of myself. *Calm down.*

Then they're here. The door flies open, and my heart rate speeds up. I can't calm it. I put my bag on my desk in front of me, a barrier, my protection. I get out my phone again and stare at it on my lap, pretend to type something to a non-existent friend.

They've been asking me questions since the assembly.

"Where's James?"

"Come on, you must know."

"Juniper, tell us, go on. Where is he? What's he done this time?"

Me, the one who no one ever speaks to. Me, the one who hides behind James at every opportunity. Me, who's never been noticed, never been looked at. Suddenly, I'm the centre of everyone's attention. *Damn you, James.*

Here we go. Students tumble in, noisy, chirpy. Chairs scrape against the floor, and desks are pushed together. When they see me, they stop. They stare. They whisper.

I stay, head down, focus on deep breaths. Remind myself that I'm fine, I'm OK, I'm ready.

The comments come. Words like "Juniper, are you OK?" and "I wonder where James is" are thrown at me in passing. Natasha Shelby and her Bitch-Queen disciples smile sickly sweet smiles my way, relishing seeing me shrink every time someone talks to me. I jump when Rob Lewis slaps a hand on my desk. He looks at me with milky eyes and a smile that stinks of booze before he moves on to his own desk.

I don't look up, and I don't respond, and no one says anything about the fact that I've turned bright red.

They start to settle, and eventually so does my face. But no sooner has the redness gone than I feel it creeping back up again. There's an invasion of my space, something's not right, there's a shadow over me. Instinct forces me to look up, but I don't get very far. Yep. There's someone standing in front of my desk, staring straight down at me. My face glows purple. Whoever it is, I hate them. *I hate myself.*

"Hello Juniper," he says, and I cringe.

My eyes flicker up to his face and immediately widen in

shock. It's Rory Bryan, the new guy.

I look down again straight away and start typing gibberish on my phone, anything to look busy. I'm twice as flushed as I'd normally be because it's *him*. It's Rory Bryan. Cricket God. Science Geek. Drama King. All shoulders and cheekbones and freckles. The kind of eyes that never stop sparkling, like he's always just two words away from sharing the best joke you've ever heard in your life. And tall… so tall… I don't know how anyone could look at him and *not* melt into a puddle of mortification.

I'm pretty sure he's never noticed I exist before now. *What does he want?* Is he going to ask me about James? Why? They're not even friends. In fact, James despises him, hates how he's managed to infiltrate himself into school so easily. I see how James clenches his fists every time Rory's around, how those blue eyes turn to thunder every time he walks past.

Please go away, I beg in my head. *Please don't talk to me.*

No such luck.

"Hi?" he says again, drawing it out. He's too loud. Too tall, too smiley.

I want to respond like a normal person, but the words get stuck in my throat, and I make a ridiculous gurgling sound that doesn't quite sound like "Hello." I'm furious with myself. I pull my bag down from the desk onto my lap and start rummaging around in it for something, anything. My fingers close around my box of matches. I breathe. I force myself to look up at him again, devastated by how red I must be.

He's staring at me, frowning. The sparkle in his eyes wavers a tiny bit. God, those eyes are green. Bright green, with specks of yellow, like someone put a field of sunflowers in his head. And he doesn't look mean exactly… just curious. *What does he want?*

He clears his throat. "Can I sit there?" he asks, nodding at the space next to me. His voice is too bright, too cheerful, and everyone can hear him. Everyone's listening. Everyone's watching.

I feel my eyes expand like balloons. *Sit here? Next to me? Why?*

I need to get a grip. *Errrrr no* is the answer. That's James's chair. I try to turn my face into a scowl, try to glare at him. I want to shake my burning head and say "No. No way," but the words get stuck in my throat again, and I make that awful gurgling noise. I'm pathetic.

Natasha-Bitch pipes up from behind me. "Why are you talking to her?" she says, in a sing-song voice that's laced with malice. "You know she's a mute, right?" Cue the idiotic giggles from the swarm of Mini-Bitch-Queens who surround her.

The heat intensifies on my face, and I want to die. *A mute?!* I'm not a mute. I can talk. I'm obviously struggling with that right now, but I can. I just… choose not to. I glance around me and am met with eyes, everywhere. Wolf eyes again, like they've just caught the scent of their prey. I can hear their minds ticking away as they stare, wondering what the new guy is doing, talking to the weirdo. *Doesn't he know she doesn't talk? Doesn't he know James Creed does all her talking?* And then, puzzled… *Where is James anyway? I bet the weirdo knows where he is. I bet she could tell us, or at least tell his mother. Poor woman. Did you see her in assembly last week? She's frantic…*

The door slams shut and Ms. Martin walks in.

Rory shrugs. He turns around and walks to his own desk towards the front, a few rows along. *Phew.*

I grip my matches and let my mind flee over to setting this wooden desk on fire, how beautiful it would be to see it blaze. Stupidly, I allow myself to think that whatever that was, that ordeal with Rory Bryan is over.

But it's not. Not really. Because as soon as Ms. Martin starts the lesson, a note lands on my desk.

Hi Juniper. I thought you may feel more comfortable writing to me. Ro x

They're only written words, but the colour still creeps over my face and ears, covering me completely. My mind races. *What does he want? Why's he doing this?* He hasn't been here long, but he's already one of the popular ones. He slid right in and became an immediate part of *them*, the ones who own the school halls, the sports fields, the playgrounds. Bitch-Queens with supermodel legs and their Rugby-Lump counterparts.

I decide to answer. At least with written words, I may be able to put him off trying to talk to me again. I guess he's right about that.

What do you want?

I fold the paper and cross out my name, replacing it with his. I throw it on the desk in front of me and watch it travel upwards towards Rory.

It lands back on my desk in a heartbeat.

I thought I might keep you company, since James isn't here. Ro x"

I stare at his note for a moment. What can I say to that? *Thanks but no thanks?* And *keep me company?* What for? I grit my teeth. This kind of thing would never happen if James was next to me, where he's supposed to be. All of a sudden, I miss him so much it hurts my insides. It doesn't matter what ridiculous things he was saying about his father. I just want him to come back. I close my eyes to stop the tears. I need to text him again. *James, please come back. I'm sorry I screamed at you. I'm so sorry...*

"Miss Slaide?"

My eyes snap open, my cheeks burn. Has Ms. Martin actually called out my name? *No, no, no.*

"Since your sidekick isn't here today to prevent me from doing my job and giving everyone a fair chance, perhaps you'd like to read the next passage?"

I feel sick with shock. The silence in the room, my silence, is so thick and deafening, it's like I can't even breathe through it. My eyes fill with tears. I want to disappear. No one asks me to read in class, ever. I don't do this sort of public speaking, the school *knows* this. As long as I work hard, which I do, they leave me alone. And then there's James, who's always here to make sure it never happens. If he was here, he'd laugh at Ms. Martin right now. He'd scoff at her, shake his head, cause a scene. He'd squeeze my hand and force me to look at him, and his eyes would tell me everything's OK. Then he'd just read it himself.

I blink back the tears. Muffled laughter begins to ripple around the room. I look at the book, the pages from *Rebecca* taunting me, as though the words themselves are the very incarnation of *Mrs Danvers*. There's no way I can read out loud. The ridicule and shame penetrates me, right to my core. The silence is excruciating.

A voice breaks through. From somewhere up ahead of me, I hear the words, lyrical and soft, mimicking the voice of the quiet, nameless narrator.

Ms. Martin frowns and purses her lips. She's about to sigh and say something, but then, like everyone else in the room, she becomes transfixed by his voice, by his walk as he strides across to the front of the class and sits back against our teacher's desk.

When he looks up from the page, he fixes those bright green eyes right on me. And then, he does something so utterly absurd it confounds me. He winks. Rory Bryan winks at me. *What the hell does he want?*

CHAPTER EIGHT

FEBRUARY 2, 1987, Marisberg, Kentucky,

Finally, a turning point in our lives. Something has happened which changes everything for us, gets us out of this terrible rut we've been stuck in since we got married. I'm so excited as I type this. I need to be quick so I can make plans, make decisions for us, for our future.

Things have been difficult for us recently, and I admit I'm to blame. The fact that I'm still unpublished has gotten me down, gotten the better of me. I watch Lucy try to hide rejection letters from me every day, and it's been embarrassing, depressing. I've been unresponsive, selfish even. I honestly felt that if I could only get her to tell me her secret, I'd be able to write something worthwhile, something mind-blowing, that publishers would pick up straight away. I know it sounds stupid, but somehow, knowing Lucy's Story and my success have become inextricably linked in my mind. It's like I can't have one without the other. And for that, I've resented her.

I'm ashamed to say it, I've pulled away. She's had to take on more and more shifts at Tally's to make ends meet for us, and what have I done? I've sulked. I've pulled back. I've been so ashamed and embarrassed at our situation that I can't even be close to her anymore. What if she was to get pregnant? I can barely provide for two of us, let alone a baby.

But tonight, Lucy's managed to change everything. She sat me down on the stairs in our narrow hallway and stood in front of me. She was nervous, I could tell, wringing her hands, those blue eyes darting around everywhere. She told me not to talk until she'd finished.

I felt nervous myself. This is it, I thought. This is the

moment she tells me about her past. And she did, a little, although not in the way I was expecting.

My mother has died, she said.

I tried to get up, to take her in my arms and comfort her, to tell her how sorry I was for her loss, but she frowned and pushed me away. It wasn't what she wanted. I sat back on the stairs and remembered to stay silent, even though I had a million questions. She carried on.

I'm the only child, she said, unable to look at me.

My mind was racing. She didn't seem sad at her mother's death, but there was certainly something that was making her miserable. Something big was draining the colour from her beautiful face. She carried on.

My mother has a house, she said. In England.

I felt my heart start to swell.

She turned away from me then, her face twisting like she felt sick at her own words. It's our house now, she said. In a place called Shackleston. It's mine. It's… ours.

My mind ran away to the future, to our lives, to our destiny. I felt the flickers of hope, of excitement, like pinpricks all over my body.

Lucy stopped talking. I asked her when her mother had died but she refused to tell me. She only kept repeating that we could do what I wanted. That it was my choice. She said it didn't have to change anything, it didn't have to change us.

But it does change everything. It gets us out of our sorrowful lives in this sorrowful town, in this miserable country. We can go to England, to where Lucy was born, where she grew up… I can get a job there, we can start again, we can be happy… And maybe, we can fix the pieces of her past that are slowly destroying her. She has to confront it, whatever it is. She's with me now, surely, after almost three years together, she knows that

I won't let anything happen to her?

Somehow, I know we're meant to go back to her homeland. We're meant to start a new life together, in England. We'll face her demons there together. We'll destroy them, together.

CHAPTER NINE

IT'S funny the effect that Rory's voice has on our class. Everyone sinks back in their chairs. Note-passing stops. Whispers stop. No one taps their pens on their desks, their feet on the floor. A sense of peace descends on the classroom, even on me. It's weird. I can feel the tension leaving me in waves with every word he says.

As he starts to wrap up, Ms. Martin walks around us, handing out assignments. The words FINAL PROJECT are written on the top sheet, and I get a sudden flash of panic when I see IN PAIRS written underneath them. *And James isn't here.* Surprised, I realise that Rory's voice managed to make me forget, for a few moments, the turmoil into which James's absence has thrown my life.

I swallow down the fear. It'll be OK. No one will ask to work with me anyway, and I can pair up with James like we always do. When he comes back.

If he comes back, says the voice in my head. I tell it to shut up and start packing up my things. I'll get hold of James. I'll talk to him and tell him I'm sorry and make him come back. Everything will be OK. The bell shrieks into the room, and the classroom comes alive again.

Out of the corner of my eye, I spy Rory striding over to the teacher. He points at me, and Ms. Martin nods. Then he walks towards me again, and my mouth dries up, my face burns.

I start shoving things in my bag as quickly as I can, I need to make it out of the room before he gets here... *oh no. No, no, no.*

His smile is lopsided and cocky. There's mischief in that sunflower-sparkle now, and I'm stuck, he's blocking my way out.

"So," he starts.

I hold my breath, fear the worst.

"If it's OK with you, Ms. Martin says we can partner up on this project," he announces, his smile getting wider, his eyes positively glowing.

My heart pounds in my head. I grab my bag off the desk and push past him to our teacher. She has to do something. She has to fix this. She knows I couldn't possibly work with someone else, right? She knows I only work with James. The school makes allowances for me; they always have.

"What is it, Miss Slaide?" she says with a visible sigh as I approach her desk. She's not smiling. Her glasses sit on the edge of her nose, and she squints at me. She looks mean.

I falter. "I... uh..."

She pushes her glasses up and sighs, leans back in her chair, lank, colourless hair pasted flat against her head. "Well?" she says, crossing her arms. "What is it? Come on."

I swallow. She's always been like this, impatient and full of scorn. She's never liked me. She's never liked James.

I stutter. "I'll be working with James," I manage to say, thrusting the assignment towards her.

She shakes her head. Then she changes the subject, and it throws me. It's that question again. "Juniper, do you know where James is?"

I'm taken aback. "No, I..."

"Then how can you be sure James will be back in school before this assignment is due?" She purses her lips. Her eyes narrow at me as she leans forward again. "If you know where James is, you have to tell someone," she says. "I hope you're not keeping his whereabouts a secret from his family. Because his mother needs to know where he is, and I believe you know something about that. I know it's difficult for you to work with another student, but frankly, I don't care. Until you tell someone what you know about James, then you'll be treated like any other student in this class, no more favours. And you'll be working with Rory on this assignment. Whether James returns or not. Is that clear?"

Her words are final. They leave me open-mouthed and gaping at her, but she leans over her desk again and starts reading the papers in front of her.

I blink back tears and walk out, ignoring Rory who's still hanging around, that idiotic grin still on his face.

It's fine, I lie to myself as I walk down the corridor, holding the tears in. James will come back, and he'll fix this. He'll never let it happen. He'll go crazy when he finds out I've been partnered with Rory.

I break into a run. I need to get to the nearest bathroom. I need to light something up, watch it burn, burn the feelings, the images, the words right out of my mind. Once I'm locked inside the safety of my cubicle, I reach into the front pocket of my bag. I light up my soulless faces, one by one, watch them burn over the bowl. Rob, Carla, Natasha, all of them, all the students at this school who I can't talk to, can't breathe next to, their faces crumbling up, disappearing inside the flame. I burn James's face next to my own, cursing him, missing him, watching us turn to ash together, then flushing us away.

I wait right up until the last bell of school. When it's quiet outside, and I'm sure the crowds have left, I step out of the cubicle and walk outside. It's starting to rain, I realise, as a cold drop smacks me on the back of the neck.

To my horror, Rory Bryan is there, leaning against the wall just under cover. His dark hair curls over his eyes as he plays with his phone, and when he sees me, he stands up straight. He throws me a smile, and my stomach does a backflip.

"Hi," he says as I attempt to walk past him.

I have nowhere to turn, nowhere to run. I walk on, down the steps, the rain falling urgently now, like it's as desperate to get out of the sky as I am to get away from Rory. I need him to get the message and leave me alone, but he follows me.

"Are you going home?" he says behind me, his tone light. "I thought I could give you a lift. As it's raining…"

I swallow and keep walking, speeding up. I just want to get away from him. And because of that, I end up marching straight into a puddle that I hadn't seen in time. I'm in it up to my ankles, I can feel the cold water soaking up my jeans, getting inside my favourite Converse. This could only happen to me.

I can hear Rory chuckling, and I want to burst into tears. I step out of the puddle and keep walking, my feet squelching water out of my trainers.

"Sorry," I hear him call after me, laughter in his voice. "I just thought we could talk about our project."

I break into a run, leaving him behind, only half caring about how ridiculous I must look. I don't want him to talk to me anymore. I don't want to have to think about him anymore. *I just want James to come back.* Where the hell is he? Why isn't he answering his phone? Why isn't he here, next to me, making sure no one like Rory ever gets close enough to talk to me? And what does Rory want? I don't want anyone in my life other than James. I don't need anyone else.

I've got to find James, find out where he's hiding and make him come home. Because if I don't, I'm going to have to tell someone that I saw James before he left. I'm going to have to admit that I've been lying. And I'm going to have to say those words out loud. *He's innocent.* Two stupid words that I know and everyone knows can't possibly be true. *Right?*

CHAPTER TEN

JULY 9, 1987, Shackleston, England,

And so we're in England. Six months we've been here, and I still don't get tired of saying that.

I'm in love with this big old house, hidden behind its wall of great fir trees, in the highest, most secluded part of Shackleston town. I love this quaint and noble village and its lovely, friendly people, even if they do seem slightly stuck up. I love the fact that there's a butcher, a baker… hell, I bet I'd find a candle-stick maker if I looked hard enough. I love that there's no dust around and that everything around me is green. The air smells like history, like a Dickens novel. There are no trailer parks, no fried chicken, no expressway. And there's a castle! A real, English castle. No one lives there at the moment, but it's a castle nonetheless. The whole town looks like it belongs in a fairy tale.

And I love Lucy, even though she's been mostly silent since we got here. I know it hurts her to face her past, but she needs to see the positive side. We have a home together. I've managed to get a job, a well-paid one, so we actually have a chance of a life here, a future. We'll have money, an income. I start as an English teacher at St. Augustine's College in September, and I can't wait. I'll finally be able to take Lucy out, to wine and dine her, to treat her like the princess she deserves to be. And, it's at her old school… The headmaster there, Simon Cooke, was Lucy's house master years ago. Perhaps, finally, I'll get a glimpse into her past, into the secrets she's so desperate to hide.

I'm trying not to be frustrated by her silence. She spends most of her time locked away inside her mother's old room, and nothing I can do or say will coax her out.

I wonder if she's hurting. I wonder if she wishes she'd been with her mother, been there for her when she died. I wonder what she died of... I wonder all these things, and I'm so desperate to ask, but I can't.

Mr. Ash, the butcher, by far the chattier of the locals, told me that Lucy's mom didn't even live in this big old house when she died. I pressed him for more, but he closed down on me.

Other than him, no one parts with information. It seems the whole town wants to keep Lucy's secret, whatever it is.

When she ventures out of that room, I watch her shrink every time she walks past the locked door in the kitchen. It's obviously a basement down there, but I know instinctively that I mustn't open it. I can't help wondering what's there. Perhaps it contains all her mother's things? I dream of a library of old books, some furniture, some art... But I can't ask her, and I've promised myself I'll leave that door alone. Still, I'd love to know why Lucy left this place, this glorious house, this beautiful countryside.

Tomorrow, maybe we'll go into the village. I'll ask her to show me where she used to hang out. It must have changed a little in the years she's been gone... Who are her old friends? Boyfriends? Why do I feel like these questions would cut her and leave sharp marks in her heart just like those awful ones on her body if I dared to ask them out loud?

CHAPTER ELEVEN

I'M almost home and totally drenched when it stops raining. Just my luck. As the rain slows, it's replaced by a voice, getting clearer and louder as I approach the gatehouse. It's Kata. She's singing.

Despite everything, despite James, despite Rory, I feel a smile almost reach my lips. Whatever the song is, she's giving it the full force of her voice. I can't make out the words, a mashup of English and Greek, whichever enters her mind first, I suppose. It's so out of tune I find myself thinking I'm glad we don't have any neighbours.

I pause outside our front door. It's wide open, which isn't unusual even if it's like there's been a cloud-army, hurling tanks of water onto the earth. My aunt is a great believer in fresh air. Apparently it clears out the cobwebs of the soul, a mantra she likes to repeat to anyone who'll listen. But really, since the fire, I think she just can't stand the thought of being locked in anywhere.

I watch her, through the doorway. She's warbling away with her back turned, her long dark plait swinging with her hips as she washes up.

I sigh. I've managed to dodge her questions and ignore the concerned looks for a week now. I've stayed late in the art room after school, eating dinner in my room and claiming too much homework. I've been up and out before she's even seen me in the mornings. On the few occasions we've crossed paths, she's tried to broach the subject of what happened with James, but I've managed to get out of it, with promises that I'm OK, and I'll talk when I'm ready.

As far as I know, Kata has no idea that people are even

saying James is missing. And why would she? If she goes into town, she minds her own business. There was a letter from school, letting parents and guardians know about James's disappearance and advising vigilance, but I didn't give it to her. It's hiding upstairs in my desk drawer, under all this week's newspapers that I've been stashing away every morning before Kata's had a chance to see them. Ready to be burned when needed.

But Kata hasn't noticed any of that. I was half expecting her to find out about James when she went to church yesterday and saw some other people from town. I thought she'd come back screaming at me, but instead, she came back singing. Nothing was wrong.

I'm not going to be able to hide from Kata for much longer, I know it. I give it a go and try to creep past her towards the door on the other side of the kitchen, but my wet trainers give me away.

She turns, stopping midsong, eyebrows raised to the ceiling. "Juniper Slaide," she says, pursing her lips. "You're soaking wet, and you're avoiding me."

It's a statement, and it makes my shoulders slump. I turn around to face her, feeling the heat on my face as I lie. "Kata, I'm not avoiding you… I need to get out of these wet clothes, OK?" I turn around again and walk to the door. I cross my fingers, hoping that's it, she's going to let it go.

"Joo," says Kata, stopping me again. *Uh oh.* "We need to talk. Something's going on with you, and I need to know what it is. I've been waiting for you to come to me, but instead you've been avoiding me and hiding from me, and that's not on."

I half turn around to face her. "Not now, Kata, OK?" I need to think. I need a way out of this. I need to burn something.

But Kata frowns at me. "Go and get yourself dry," she says. "Then we'll talk." Her voice is set; she's not giving up this time.

I swallow and give her the tiniest of nods before turning and running up to my room, kicking the door shut behind me. I'm not going to get away with it.

I pull out of my wet trainers and my sodden clothes. I dry off before putting on my oldest, most out-of-shape jumper and comfiest lounge pants. Then I settle in the window seat and wait for Kata to come, feeling the dread heavy in my body. While I wait for Kata, I look out at the castle grounds, the massive black slab of castle in the distance.

The grounds are badly maintained but expansive, and there are secrets hiding everywhere amongst them. My eyes find the concealed spots, the hidden treasures dotted around the gardens: my father's statues.

There were never fairy tales and fables for me, growing up. No handsome princes and beautiful princesses, no fairy godmothers or toothy wolves. Papou with his thick Greek accent was a master storyteller. We'd sit in the castle library, and he'd tell me the ancient myths of his home country. I lapped them up, these incredible stories of angry, jealous gods and powerful, beautiful women; huge warriors and great, evil beasts.

The world he created for me within the castle walls was fascinating, full of vibrant colour and life. And my father, also drawn in by Papou's stories, recreated them in stone and wood and scattered them all over the castle grounds, much to my enchantment. As we grew up, James and I ran around the sprawling greens and trawled the woods, searching for new hidden gems, placed somewhere overnight, as if by magic.

Soon, the world began to watch. People heard of us, the Slaide family at Shackleston Castle and our life-size, 3-D encyclopaedia of Greek mythology. For a while, the grounds were opened up to visitors, coming from all over the country to see the mystical place my father had created. Papou and Kata gave talks, walked people around the grounds, telling the stories as they went. Back then, the castle was alive. But after the fire, everything changed.

The statues are still there, but no one visits anymore. I can see some tiny flashes of stone peeking out from the tall grass on the lawns. Down by the lake, there are wooden sculptures carved amongst the overgrown weeds. And in the woods, there are eyes everywhere, even though fallen trees have damaged most of what my father created. I know all their hiding places. I feel them now, staring back up at me, and I take a deep breath, trying to gather strength from them, some sort of sign. *Tell me what to do.*

I get my phone out and stare at it on my knees. Before I can change my mind, I call James again. This time, it doesn't even ring. There's no dial tone, no gruff, arrogant voice telling me to leave a message if I can be bothered. *What?* I try again, but the same thing happens.

The door of my room bursts open, startling me. Kata's standing in the doorway, her jaw set, her lips pressed together. She sits opposite me on the window seat, where James usually sits. I'm struck by how strange it feels when someone else is in James's spot. It's like looking in the mirror and finding your reflection has completely changed.

"Joo, just tell me one thing," she says, eyeing me with soft, grey eyes. "Are you OK?" she asks.

I'm not sure if it's her question or the concern in her eyes, but something breaks inside me. I feel myself split open under the weight of her words. *Am I OK?* I don't even know where to begin to answer that. I look at Kata, and all I can see is how much she cares about me, the strength of her love. I've been deceiving her, and James is gone, and Rory is terrorising me, and my whole world is upside down. I feel my face crumple, and all the tears I've been trying to hold back all day, all week, are suddenly here, streaming down my face. I try to hide them with my sleeve, but it's no use; they're out, they're ugly and they're loud.

In a flash she's next to me, waving me across so that I can make room for her on my side of the ledge. She squeezes next to me, puts her arms around me and says nothing. She just lets me cry.

It feels like a long time before I manage to get myself under some sort of control. I pull back from Kata and see her looking out at the black and burnt form of the castle in the distance. Like James, Kata and I have the same deal. We never talk about what happened. We never discuss the family members lost inside the castle walls. I remember Kata's strength, her force, her protection. I remember her being adamant that we should move on from the past and teaching me how to lock it all away in the part of my brain that I never go to.

What's done is done.

We don't talk about the past.

Right now, her face is lost in memories. I can't help wondering if she's thinking about them: her sister, her father and my dad. Maybe I've been stupid to assume she never thinks about it. Of course she does. Kata never asked to be my guardian. She just inherited the job.

She turns to face me and gives me a gentle smile. "Come on," she says, getting up and grabbing my hand, pulling me up with her. "Let's make some tea and you can tell me all about it. OK? No more avoiding me now, Joo. Whatever it is, you'll feel much better once you've told me."

I nod. I have to tell her. James has been gone too long, and even if I know he's not missing, I need to tell someone where he went. Saying words that bring up the past will hurt Kata, but at least she'll know what to do. Alarm rises inside me. I'm going to have to admit that Lucy Creed is frantic because of me. I'm going to have to tell her why I was so upset with James. I'm going to have to bring up *his* name, *Philip Creed*, say it out loud in front of my aunt, who only ever wanted to forget what he did to us.

CHAPTER TWELVE

JANUARY 4, 1988, Shackleston, England,

Lucy is opening up to me, little by little. Every day this house seems to get brighter, the dark cloud that's been hanging over us is parting a fraction, letting through some light. I don't think I'm imagining it. She's losing some of the hardness that's found her since we got here.

I can tell she's pleased with the work I've been doing on the house. Small changes, a lick of paint here and there, some new doors, new rugs. I watch her when she comes downstairs, how her eyes linger over the transformations, no matter how small they are. She notices everything. And she approves. It's like I'm changing her past before her very eyes, and it's saving her.

I'm beginning to understand this strange town, with its discreet local people who never quite look me in the eye. Everyone knows Lucy, and they ask about her every day. But when I start to answer them, their eyes glaze over. They turn away and change the subject. It's like they're ashamed.

Still, I manage to piece together little snatches of knowledge, little shards of information that I get from her, from the school, from the town. Every day, a small bit of her puzzle falls into place.

Mr. Ash talks from time to time, the occasional comment thrown at me in passing, that I take away and analyze for hours. Yesterday, I asked him about the castle, which I'm desperate to visit. He surprised me. Just ask Lucy, he said. After all, it's owned by her best friend, Roger Slaide.

I'd never heard his name before. Of course Lucy never mentioned him. Mr. Ash went on to tell me that he's an artist, no less, who left Shackleston at around the same time as Lucy. Apparently they were joined at the hip, Lucy and this Roger. He used the word inseparable.

I was almost frightened to bring it up with her, but curiosity got the better of me. When I got home, I asked her about him. I was expecting her to retreat, to run back into that room and lock the door again, but to my surprise, her eyes lit up at the mention of his name. She smiled for the first time in a long time, and she even talked a little. She told me about this boy, her childhood friend, and about how she spent all her time running around the castle as a child.

I wasn't jealous. I actually found myself wishing for his return. I would love it if Lucy had someone who could make her smile like that. I'd love to see her with a friend around here.

It's as I put her together in my mind that things get better between us. I think we may even be ready to start a family soon, and perhaps that's exactly what she needs. She's almost laughing again. I can see it, just under the surface.

We'll get there. I'm fixing her, just like I promised.

CHAPTER THIRTEEN

KATA always knows what to do. Kata always makes everything OK. I repeat the words to myself as I follow her out of my bedroom, pausing to grab the school letter from my drawer before we go downstairs. The weight of what I'm about to tell her is heaving inside me with every step I take, and the fist in my stomach is pumping like crazy.

She makes two cups of tea and sits opposite me at the kitchen table. She's ready to listen.

"Kata," I begin, but I don't know to go on. I don't know where to start.

She smiles at me, and it lights up her face. She looks so calm, so happy that I'm about to share something with her. She wants to help me, I can see it. "You can tell me anything, Joo. You know that. So come on, spill it. Why haven't I seen James for days? What happened last Sunday? Why were you so upset?"

I gulp at her words and then decide to just tell her straight. "Kata, James hasn't been seen since that night," I say, staring down at my tea. "When he was here," I add.

She frowns, and the light disappears from her face. "What do you mean he hasn't been seen? He hasn't been in school?"

I nod and take a deep breath. "Kata, people are saying he's… he's missing."

Her eyebrows fly up. "What does that mean? Who's saying that?"

"Well… there was an assembly at school." Gingerly I hand the letter over.

As she reads, something happens to Kata's face. Her skin loses its beautiful colour, and she turns pale. When she finishes, she puts the letter down and squeezes her eyes shut, her hands gripping the edge of the table. The fist in my stomach starts pulling at me as I watch her fingers turn red first, then white.

When she snaps her eyes open, they're blazing. *Oh no.* I knew she might be a bit cross with me for not telling her, but I'm not sure what to expect from her right now. "Juniper. I can't believe you've kept this from me," she says, her voice quietly shaking. Then she eyeballs me, hard. "Do you know where he is?"

I try to meet her gaze, but I flinch when I see how dark her eyes have become. She's not just a bit cross. She's furious. I look down again. I nod.

"And let me guess: you haven't told anyone?" Kata's voice rises as she says the words. She already knows the answer.

"Jesus Christ, Joo" she says, and now I know without even looking at her that she's crazy mad. "What about his mother? Does she know where he is?" She's getting more and more high pitched, more and more shrill. I can hear the panic in her voice, and it's not helping mine at all.

I shake my head, the guilt making me feel sick.

"Well, where is he then?" she asks, getting up and grabbing the house phone off its perch on the wall. As she starts to dial, my panic escalates.

"Who are you calling?" I can hear my own voice, as shrill as Kata's. *She can't.*

"I'm calling Lucy. She must be frantic. I can't believe James has done his disappearing act again, and you know where he is, and you haven't told anyone." Kata turns her eyes on me again and I can see the shock in them, like she's disgusted with me. But I can't let her call Lucy Creed. So I blurt it out.

"James went to see his dad," I say.

It stops her. She holds the phone mid-air and stares at me, her face white now.

"He what?" she whispers.

I swallow, trying not to cry again, trying not to panic. "Philip Creed," I whisper his name and watch the effect it has on Kata. "James said... he said his father was innocent," I tell her.

Kata sits. I can hear the sound of the dial tone, the phone forgotten in her hand. I didn't want to hurt her with those words. I didn't want to tell her what James was saying when he left, but I had to. I tell her the rest, or what I can remember of it. That James had found something. He was going on some sort of mission to prove his dad's innocence. That he made me promise not to tell anyone.

Kata covers her mouth with her hands as I talk. She's not looking at me anymore, and she's incredibly still. For the first time since I can remember, my aunt is lost for words.

There's a sound outside, a car on the gravel. Kata's eyes snap to mine again, both of us switching gears - *were you expecting someone?* - and both of us shaking our heads at the same time. And then we're up and out of our chairs, leaning over the sink to look out the window. My mind goes straight to James. *He's back, right? This is him, coming back. Finally. This will all be over.*

But it's not James. It's a police car, with two officers getting out, a man and a woman. I freeze, ice cold. Next to me, I feel Kata do the same.

Then, she's moving again. She turns to me and grabs my shoulders, forces me to look at her. The colour is back in her face, and she looks like herself again. Strong. Determined. "Go up to your room," she says.

I dart out of the kitchen, but I don't go to my room. I stay there, at the bottom of the stairs, leaving the door ajar, just a tiny fraction. I need to see. I need to hear. I need to know what they're going to say.

I watch Kata open the front door. I hear her say hello, and it surprises me how she can make her voice sound light and breezy like that, compared to the panic I heard in it a few minutes ago. From behind, I can tell her shoulders are too tight, her back is too straight. Other than that, she seems normal.

She opens the door to let the officers in. The woman looks familiar. I've seen her before. She looks friendly, if anything, and I get the feeling she and Kata know each other, which wouldn't be a total surprise. Everyone knows everyone in this town.

The man doesn't look friendly at all. He's huge, far too big for our tiny kitchen. I definitely haven't seen him before. He shifts around on his feet, his eyes studying everything. They linger on the gap in the door, my gap, and I hold my breath, terrified of moving. But then he looks away, and they all sit down.

The female officer talks first. "Kata, is Juniper around?"

Here we go, I think, feeling the panic rise in my throat. I'm going to have to go in there. I'm going to have to talk to them.

But Kata does something I never would have imagined possible. She leans back in her chair, head up, chin high. And she lies. "She's not here, I'm afraid."

Thank you, Kata, thank you. I'm shocked that Kata would lie but so grateful it almost hurts. It's disorientating. It's like the world's started spinning, and it's going the wrong way.

No one says anything for a while. They all stare at the two still-steaming cups of tea that are right there in front of them on the table.

In a swift movement, Kata's up, grabbing the cups and taking them to the sink. She puts the kettle on. When she turns around, I see her face, expecting it to be bright red, full of shame at being caught in her lie. But she looks normal. Unfazed. Totally

Composed.

I swallow. I have to be still. I can't let the police know I'm here. I can't let them find out that Kata's lying to them. I know she's doing this for me, so I don't have to face them.

Kata places a teapot, milk and sugar on the table. She pours tea into three cups before sitting again.

The female officer talks. "This is Detective Pastelle," she says, nodding at her colleague. "He's from the Missing Persons Bureau. We're here about James."

Detective Pastelle sits up straighter in his chair. *Missing Persons Bureau?* I swallow hard. I can't believe this has gotten so far.

I can't see her face, so I can't tell if Kata has registered the words or not. She doesn't move.

The female officer goes on. "Kata, I'm sure you know that Lucy Creed reported James missing last week. She hasn't seen him since Sunday, the 4th of April. We know Juniper and James are close, so we just wanted to ask her if maybe she's seen James or heard from him at all? We're asking all his friends, of course." The female officer smiles at Kata while she talks.

Detective Pastelle twirls a spoon in his cup.

Kata doesn't say anything. She nods and takes a loud slurp of her tea, waits for the officer to continue. I guess she hasn't been asked a direct question, so she doesn't need to talk. It's a trick I recognise.

The female officer frowns. "Kata," she says, clearing her throat. "When will Juniper be back?"

A direct question, so Kata answers. "I don't know, I'm afraid," she says. There's no hint of worry in her voice, nothing to suggest anything's out of the ordinary. Once again, I'm shocked at how calm my aunt is.

There's another awkward silence, and then Detective Pastelle speaks. His voice is so quiet I have to strain to hear it.

"Given the current situation with James, Miss Panos," he says, addressing Kata formally, "I'm frankly a little surprised that you don't know where your niece is, nor when she'll return. We're advising people to be extra vigilant regarding the safety of their children at the moment," he says.

I see Kata stiffen, and I can tell his words have riled her. She puts down her cup. "Detective Pastelle," she says, and any warmth in her voice has disappeared. "James Creed has a habit of running away. On top of that, he enjoys wasting people's time. I'm sure, when he returns, because he always does, that he'll be pleased to see he's managed to waste your valuable time, and mine." Then she turns to the woman. "Becky, come on. You know this as well as I do."

The female officer, Becky, frowns. "All the same, we'd like to talk to Juniper. Mrs Creed is very worried." She glances over at her colleague, who doesn't look back at her. He's staring at Kata, the frown on his face deepening.

Becky continues. "Look," she says, "I'll leave my card here. Perhaps Juniper could give me a call when she gets back? Please reassure her that we just want to talk to her." She gets up to leave.

Kata nods and gets up too. As she turns around, I see her face, a momentary flash of relief; the ordeal is over.

I almost let out my breath, but not quite because Detective Pastelle is still sitting. "Ms Panos," he says to Kata's back, his voice casual.

I watch her freeze, then swallow, then put on her mask of composure. She turns around. "Yes, Detective?" she says, cool, cold.

"Just out of interest, when was the last time *you* saw James Creed?"

From behind, I see Kata tense up, but it's almost imperceptible. I realise I'm not breathing, and I try to gulp down my own dread. I have no idea what Kata's going to say.

"Me?" she says. As soon as I hear her voice, that fake smile in it, I know she's going to lie again. "I haven't seen James Creed in... oooh... a few weeks. It's been a while, anyway." She picks up the other officer's card. "I'll be sure to give this to Juniper when she comes back." She turns around again, closing the matter.

Detective Pastelle gets up. He follows his colleague out the door, that strange frown still on his face.

I run up to my room and shut myself inside, hugging my knees close to me. I want to light something, watch something blaze. Those newspapers I've stashed away are gagging to be lit up, to burn, to turn to ash... But I expect Kata to come in here any minute. She's going to want to talk. She's going to want to finish our conversation from before, to talk about Sunday night, to talk about James, about Lucy, about the police... *and about Philip Creed.*

So I sit, and I wait. I chew my nails. I tidy my desk. But Kata doesn't come. And all I can think about, all I can see in my mind, is how my aunt, the most honest person in the world, could lie with such ease, without batting an eyelid. Like a pro.

CHAPTER FOURTEEN

AUGUST 9, 1989, Shackleston,

We're having a baby!

Everything has changed again, and I'm pretty sure it's all because of that basement door.

I'd been thinking about doing something about it for a while. Every time Lucy walked past it, she'd tense up, her chin would tremble, and she'd get this wild look in her eyes, just for a second. I knew I needed to get rid of that door.

A few weekends ago, while she was hiding up in that room, I finally did it. I plastered over the door, and I painted it, blended it right into the walls so no one would ever know it was there. I was convinced it would please her, and I was right.

Things have been better ever since. We've become close again. We've spent evenings together outside in the garden, eating dinner and talking, even laughing. Light seemed to have returned to her eyes, a weight lifted from her shoulders. And today, two years after we moved to England, she's made me the happiest man in the world.

She looked so nervous when I came home from work, sitting at the bottom of the stairs, chewing her nails. I was a little shocked at first; she caught me off guard. I'm not used to seeing her out of that room before dinner, and she looked different. She'd made an effort. It was a dress I'd never seen before, and her hair was washed and up, away from her beautiful face. She was looking at me right in the eyes, but she was biting her lip. She had something to say.

She told me she'd been to see an old friend today. I was surprised and almost a little hopeful. She'd actually been out of the house, left that room and seen someone, spoken to someone other than me... Then she told me his name: Dr Banner. And she smiled a smile so genuine and honest, it took my breath away.

I'm pregnant, she said.

I think she must have been scared of my reaction, nervous about what I'd say. Surely she knows it's all I ever wanted for us. A family!

I took her in my arms and danced her around the house. I held her, I laughed, and I cried. We're having a baby. A baby to cherish, to love, to join us, to make us complete. This is it, our lives, finally getting underway, finally we're living what we deserve. I love her so much right now I could explode. This is what will fix her, what will fix us, what will make everything better. I can't wait for our future to start.

CHAPTER FIFTEEN

WHEN I wake up, I feel fuzzy, like all my edges are blurred. I must have fallen asleep while I waited for Kata last night, but my head is pounding like I haven't had any rest at all.

Now, I can hear her downstairs, pots and pans clattering around in the kitchen. I've been lying in bed, waiting for her to open my bedroom door, balancing tea and toast, wanting to talk to me, wanting to talk about James, about what I should do. But she hasn't. Since we were interrupted by the police yesterday, I have no idea how she's feeling. All I can see is that terrified look on her face when I told her James had gone to see his father and that he thought his dad was innocent. I need to know what she's thinking. I need her to talk to me.

There are thoughts that I've been blocking from the back of my mind, things I've been too afraid to think about. I need Kata to confirm the truth that everyone knows: *there's no way James could be right. Philip Creed is a monster, and he's guilty.* I need Kata to tell me that, to repeat it. To get rid of this tiny niggling doubt in my mind that's been there since James left. I decide to stop waiting for her to come to me. I'll get ready and go to her.

But as I'm towel-drying my hair on the way back from the shower, I hear something strange that makes me pause on the landing. There are voices downstairs. My heart skips a beat, and my body goes into panic mode. *Have the police come back?*

Confused, I hear a note of laughter, a male voice. *Is it James?* My pulse races. I lean over the banister in my towel, peering over the top of the stairs, straining so I can see into the kitchen. And then my heart does a triple flip as I spot the curly head of brown hair, and I recognise the voice.

I turn bright red and run back to my room. *What the hell is Rory Bryan doing here?* I slam my door shut just as Kata pokes her head out of the kitchen and shouts my name.

I grab my bag and reach for the matches, lighting one quickly, not caring about the smell, not caring about Kata finding out. I let the flame calm me down, and then I blow it out, tuck the dead match back into the box. I start shoving things around on my desk, looking for makeup that I must have somewhere. As I grab hold of some mascara and brush it over my lashes, the evil voice in my head asks me why I'm doing this, why I'm putting makeup on, making myself look pretty. The evil voice makes me feel sick to my stomach. *What am I doing?*

I put the mascara down and shake myself. *Come on, Joo. Get a grip. Breathe.*

I change my mind again and find some lip gloss, cringing to myself as I put it on. I brush at my ridiculous hair, trying to detangle the stupid mess of dark curls and failing, cursing Rory for turning up like this. I give myself another pep talk and remind myself to lift my head up, shoulders back, stop being such a loser, *come on, Joo*. Another deep breath. And when I pull open the door, I march headfirst into Rory, standing outside my bedroom, his hand poised to knock.

"Whoa..." He beams at me, lowering his hand and taking a step back. "Hi."

I cringe and turn into a beetroot. He's so loud. He peers around me into my bedroom, so I slam the door behind me and push past him down the stairs. I glare at Kata, but she turns away and won't look at me. *Fine*. I march outside into the daylight with no intention of talking to Rory, and no matter how much I need to talk to Kata, I'm annoyed that she even let him in.

The wind hits me as soon as I step outside, and I realise I've walked out without my jacket. *Damn it.* The sun's high and bright in the sky, but it's still icy cold. I wonder for a moment if I could get to school without my coat, but after two seconds of walking, my body feels like it's going to split apart, and I know I have to go back. I turn around and charge straight into Rory for the second time. He's right behind me, holding my coat out in his arms.

I snatch it from him.

"You didn't let me drive you home yesterday," he says, laughter in his voice. "So I decided to drive you to school this morning instead. But then, it's such a nice day, and I was up super early, so I walked here, and I thought we could walk together."

In that moment, everything about him infuriates me, no matter that the sun has turned his eyes from bright green to the clearest emerald colour I've ever seen. He smiles his widest smile, and despite my stomach doing somersaults, I force myself to scowl at him.

I can see Kata in the doorway, looking reproachful. I glare at her, but she doesn't meet my eyes. She turns around and shuts the door, shutting me out. *With him.*

"Come on, then," Rory says, moving past me. "Let's get going. We don't want to be late."

I stand there, dumbfounded for a moment, wondering why, in the space of a week, the whole world is upside down. I have no choice but to follow him.

Rory walks fast, which is good. No one can possibly talk and walk this fast at the same time. Maybe he won't talk at all, and we'll make it to school in silence.

No such luck. "So, Juniper," he starts, his voice brimming with amusement. "Did you put makeup on just for me?"

My face turns into a ball of fire despite the cold, and before I know it, I've blurted out, "No!" I don't want him to think that. Even if it's kind of true, I realise, as the heat of shame spreads through my whole body.

Rory stops. He turns around to face me, his mouth falling open in mock surprise. "She speaks!" he exclaims, grinning.

I stop too. I'm so embarrassed I can't look at him. I try to use my hair to cover as much of my face as possible, then I realise I look ridiculous, so I start walking again, trying not to think about the stupid tears threatening the back of my eyes.

But Rory clears his throat and grabs my arm, holds me back. "Wait," he says.

I turn towards him, feeling weird now because his hand is on my arm, and I don't like the fact that it seems to be shooting a different kind of heat right through me. *Whoa.*

"You know, Juniper, has it occurred to you that I might just want to be friends?"

I look down at his hand on my arm, willing it to go away. *No, it hasn't occurred to me,* I think as he lets go of me and strides off again. I follow after him, wondering what he really wants. Rory and I could never be friends. He has his own friends. The popular ones, the attractive ones, the likes of Natasha and her Bitch-Queen buddies.

And... *I have James.* Right now, the thought of James is so overwhelming that I have to stop again and swallow back the tears. I can't believe he's not here.

Rory stops and turns around. *Please don't ask me if I'm OK,* I think. Not now. I don't want to fall apart in front of him.

He doesn't. Instead, he marches back to me and takes my arm again, gently this time, pulling me along with him.

I feel that jolt of heat from his hand, and I cringe, hoping he can't tell. *What is wrong with me?!* He lets go as we start walking in sync again, and I tell myself for the hundredth time to get a grip.

"Come on," he says. "We really don't want to be late. And don't worry, I have loads to talk about. You jump in whenever you feel like it." He's looking straight ahead, but I know he's teasing me again.

At least he does exactly what he says. He talks. He doesn't stop, in fact. He talks the whole way, over the bridge, down the road and right up to the school gates. He doesn't even pause. He manages to answer every question I've ever wondered about him: why he transferred from St. Augustine's (something about a disagreement with a student), why he's doing science (he wants to be a vet), and English (a love of words, which is clear from the amount of talking he's doing). He tells me about his family, (Police Force Mum, Doctor Dad, exemplary older brother studying psychology at Oxford), his dogs (who he adores) and finally, why he's talking to me.

"I just thought, since James wasn't around, you might need someone. You've been stuck to him like glue since I got here. I've never seen anything like it, to be honest. I've never heard you talk, well, until you yelled at me a minute ago, which doesn't count."

I keep walking, and he catches up with me. I don't believe for one second that he's talking to me because, what, he cares about me? You can't care about someone you don't know. It's not possible. And I'm right because after a pause, he tells me the real reason.

"Also… I'd love to see the statues. At the castle," he says, his voice quiet now.

His words shock me, and we both stop. So this is why. The statues. This is the real reason he's been stalking me, plaguing me at school. My father and his infamous Garden of Gods.

Rory's talking again, something about a love of art, about having wanted to see the statues since he was little, but I have to get away from him. I break into a run, leaving him behind. I don't care how rude I'm being. I hear him shout after me, but it doesn't matter.

All I can think about is the matches in my bag. I run straight to the bathroom and lock myself in a cubicle, pulling out the box and holding it close. There're only a few left now, and the urge to give in and use them all, use them properly and set something alight, is stronger than ever. I hold my breath, trying to make the feeling go away, trying to push through it and not give in, but I can't. Rory's words, his real reason for talking to me, have rattled me too much.

It's no use; I need the flame. I pull all the toilet roll out and swirl it into the toilet bowl. I pile it high so that the bottom layers form a cushion between the water and the rest. I grab another roll and do the same again, adding layers and layers to my snowy mountain. Then I light a match and drop it in. I watch the flames take hold. They rise, high up, almost reaching the top of the toilet itself. And then I get sucked in. The smell, the hot, hot heat, the sound it makes, everything rushes over me at once as the flames grab hold of my eyes. At one point, I start to panic: it's too high, it's too much, and I'm sure there are people outside who can hear what's going on, that can smell it, see the smoke rising to the top of the door… But then, there's nothing left to burn but water. The fire is gone, and everything is OK. *I'm OK.*

CHAPTER SIXTEEN

13th DECEMBER, 1989, Shackleston,

I don't have words for the kind of sorry I feel right now. This shouldn't be happening to us; it shouldn't be happening to Lucy. It's my fault. I've had to work a lot recently, staying late, getting my hours in, and when Lucy got pregnant, I was so happy, so excited. But I couldn't help panicking a little. My wages are enough for both of us to survive but not enough for a family. That's what I was thinking about when I stayed late at work, doing the best job I can for our family. I should have realised it was upsetting her.

But she said nothing. I assumed she knew I was working. I'm not out spending time with anyone else. It's not like I have anyone to spend time with anyway. Sure, everyone's nice and everyone asks about Lucy all the time. But they don't do anything else. They don't invite me for coffee or take me out to lunch with them. No one ever asks me out after work. Simon Cooke can be cruel and cutting sometimes, and he's always looked at me like I don't belong here, like an American should never have been given an English teaching job at a proper English private school.... If I don't get my students to perform well enough, I feel like I could be out of a job. I've been feeling that way for a while now, and what with the baby, I just needed to get my head down. We may have this gorgeous old house, but we still need money, and there's so much to do before the baby arrives.

I can't believe I just wrote that. I'm still in denial.

The baby isn't coming anymore.

When I came home yesterday and saw her in the kitchen, with all the blood... Oh Lucy, I'm so sorry. I should have been here more. I should have paid more attention. I'm devastated at what we've lost.

Dr Banner says we can try again, in a matter of months. He told me it's common, although I never imagined it would happen to us. After everything Lucy's been through in her life, for this to happen now—it breaks me, it really does. And I have no idea what to do or say to make it better.

CHAPTER SEVENTEEN

I STAY in the toilet, breathing in smoky air for what seems like forever and pushing thoughts of Rory out of my head, forcing the disappointment away. Did I actually think he might like me? What an idiot. All he wanted was to see the statues. *That's fine,* I reason with myself. I've never needed anyone other than James in my life anyway. When he comes back, he'll fix this, whatever it is, with Rory. He'll make him stop stalking me like this.

I wait for the school bell to ring before I can move, listening out for the sounds outside to stop, the corridors to be empty, the school to be quiet. And then I do something I've never done before. I leave. I walk right out of the school gates and back towards the gatehouse, my heart pounding, my face on fire, waiting for someone to catch me, a teacher to call me out, to see that I'm leaving school before the day has even started. But nothing happens. No one notices.

I need to go home and talk to Kata. I'm suddenly desperate to see her, to talk about yesterday, about James, about the police. I need to know what's on her mind, and I need her to tell me that there's no way, no way on earth that the wrong man is in jail for the murder of our family. She knew Philip Creed. I need to hear her words: *everything will be OK.*

When I walk into the kitchen, Kata's sitting at the table. She's not singing. She's not even drinking tea. She looks at me with such a blank look on her face, like she doesn't even know who I am. I prepare to apologise, to tell her I'm sorry for skipping school, but she doesn't even seem to notice.

"Kata?" I say, confused and worried about the weird look on her face.

My voice makes her jump. Then she's up, out of her chair and scuttling off, muttering that she'll be back in a minute.

Weird. The fist in my stomach pounds away, and I focus on it, trying to make it stop, trying to control it with breathing. I sit and wait for Kata to come back, but she doesn't, and it's horrible, so I get up. I notice the police officer's business card on the table, and I think about how card lights up differently than paper. It burns slower and stronger. I pick it up and put it in my bag.

I sit down. Then I get up again. I open the front door, then close it. I fight the urge to light something. Kata's always here, always, apart from her precious Church Sundays. Now, she's being so strange… All this time I've spent avoiding her, and now she's the one who's avoiding me.

I decide to go and do what normal teenagers do and watch TV, try to lose my mind in something else. I push open the door to the living room, the one we never use.

It's the biggest room in the gatehouse, always freezing but comfortable, with big old armchairs set around a coffee table, facing an unused TV. Kata says the television is for the depraved. It blackens the mind, destroys the soul and turns people into zombies. I don't even know if it's plugged in.

I look for the remote, trying to not look at the fireplace, filled in with its ugly red bricks. How amazing would it be to be able to sit here and watch the flames burning away? I could watch that for hours, never mind TV.

There it is. I see the remote, jutting out from under a sofa. I press the button, and the TV turns on.

And then I feel a scream reach my throat, blocking my breath, forcing me down onto a chair. On the screen, there's an image that punches me in the gut. It's James.

It's a photo of him, looking happy. Looking proud and fearless and mischievous as hell, his dark blue eyes shining at me out of the TV. I recognise the photo; I was with him when it was taken, last year, outside his house. I'd scrambled out of the frame, just in time.

There's a banner scrawling under the screen.

MOTHER APPEALS FOR SAFE RETURN OF MISSING TEENAGER

It's that word again: *missing*. My fingers tighten around the remote as I watch the screen switch to a room with a long table in it, the banner still scrolling away underneath. It's the local news.

There are three people sitting at the table, and I gasp again in shock. One of them is James, right there, on the left.

But instead of relief flooding through me, I only feel fear. Something's not right. Why is Detective Pastelle sitting on the right-hand side of that table, repeating words like *'missing'* and *'safe return'*?

Why is Lucy Creed sitting there in the middle, looking like she hasn't slept for days, eyes darting all over the place, hands unable to stay still.

And why is that banner still scrolling at the bottom of the screen when James is right there in front of me, not missing at all?

I look at him, confused. His hair's not right. It's shorter, cropped close to his head. His eyes aren't twinkling. In fact there's no sparkle; they're dull, and he looks miserable. And… there's a piercing in his eyebrow? When did he get that done?! He looks bigger, not like himself at all.

And then I go completely cold. That's not James, I realise as horror floods through me. It's Trick. James's twin.

Long-buried memories of Trick push themselves into my brain, jumping over each other to barge their way into my vision.

The three of us, Trick, James and I, playing together in the castle.

Racing around the statues, jumping in the lake.

Our parents, watching, laughing, lounging, drinking. Garden parties and dinner parties, staying up late, acting like adults.

The three of us, giggling, poking, playing, joking…

I haven't seen Trick Creed for years. I haven't wanted to. He's not good news. If James takes after their mum, then Trick most definitely takes after their dad.

A shiver runs down my spine. I grab my phone from my bag and try James again. He has to come back now; this has gone on too long. But there's no dial tone, and I just can't understand it.

There's a gasp of shock from behind me, and I turn around to see Kata. Her hand flies to cover her mouth, and her eyes bulge as she stares at the TV. She looks petrified.

Everything feels a little more real all of a sudden.

She looks at me. "Joo, you have to tell them," she says, her voice shaking.

I stand to face her and nod. I know she's right. "I'll go there after school today," I tell her. "I'll go to James's house and talk to Lucy. OK?"

I'm half expecting Kata to say no, to tell me that I need to call Lucy Creed right now or the police. But instead, she nods back at me, weakly. I look at her, desperate to ask her about Philip Creed, desperate to hear her tell me there's no way, no chance that he could be innocent. But something tells me not to. Instead, I find myself saying, "Kata, everything will be OK."

She nods again, pale and swallowing back tears. As she turns to leave, I feel like I need to say it again. "Everything *will* be OK, Kata, I promise," I call after her as she's leaving the room.

She stops for a fraction of a second and then walks out, leaving me there, staring after her. I wonder if she's thinking the same thing as me. I wonder if she's thinking how strange it is, that I'm saying those words to her when she's usually the one saying them to me.

CHAPTER EIGHTEEN

MARCH 4, 1990, Shackleston

Today, I brought home some news which made Lucy's eyes shine again. Roger Slaide is coming back to Shackleston, back to the castle. He called Simon Cooke, out of the blue, and asked for a job in the Art Department, which he was given immediately, no questions asked.

There's an excited buzz around the school, around the whole town, regarding Roger's return. I feel caught up in it even though I've never met the man. The news is promising, and Lucy's reaction to it even better.

More and more, people talk of this man like he's some sort of legend. I'm building him up in my mind as this fabulously mysterious character, clearly cherished by the people of Shackleston and yet different from them. Perhaps I may actually find a friend in him. Surely if he's an art lover, he'll be a literature lover, and then of course we'll be friends. I may even get to see the castle at last, and from the inside. I bet it's got a big old library in there somewhere.

Sometimes I wonder why Roger and Lucy left Shackleston at the same time. Was there a pact? He must be a part of it, whatever her secret is.

Every time I ask her a question, anything personal at all, she looks at me with a hatred so fierce and so raw it makes me flinch. These days, I brush it off. I've taken to asking her more and more personal questions recently rather than holding them all inside me, regardless of the reaction I get. I love her so much, but she can't shut me out forever. If she won't tell me anything about her, after all these years together, then perhaps her best friend will.

CHAPTER NINETEEN

I WALK back to school. It started raining again while I was at the gatehouse, and the rain batters down on my umbrella as I speed walk, sidestepping puddles all the way. Thankfully, I've got art this afternoon, so I can spend the rest of the day there, working on my final project.

I'll go to James's house after school. I'll tell Lucy the truth, tell her where he went. I've waited almost two weeks, holding on to information that could have saved her all of this worry.

Seeing Trick on my TV screen has unsettled me more than anything. What's he doing back here? He hates James. They may be twins, but they're far from close. Trick hasn't been a part of our lives for such a long time, ever since we were little. He was sent away to boarding school a long time ago, and he never comes back, not even for holidays. I'd pushed him out of my mind, blocked him out, like I block out everything I don't want to remember. But now, seeing him like that, I can't help but think back to how it used to be when he was here, the horror of it all.

At first, the games between the twins were put down to harmless, brotherly fun, but even then, it was easy to see that Trick was bad inside. He'd hurt James, fool him, make him cry. He'd do things on purpose to send James flying into fits of rage, just by laughing at him and not telling him why. He'd hide James's things or destroy them. He'd collect ants and put them in James's bed.

After a while, the ants turned into spiders. Wasps were collected into jars and set free in James's room, even though he was allergic. Rather than hide James's things, Trick would break them. Sometimes, he'd lock James away, in that awful basement of their house. I remember a time when James had been there for hours before anyone found him. The memory makes me shudder.

Things got worse. When James was given a cat, it disappeared. When it was discovered that James had a talent for music, Trick smashed the piano to pieces. When James ended up in hospital with broken limbs, Trick smiled.

After that, he was sent away. I think we were six or seven when Trick disappeared into St. Augustine's College and never came back. And then, we weren't three anymore; we were two. Trick was gone, and after the fire, he got erased from my memory, forced out and forgotten about.

But not today. Today, he's back. Back on my TV screen, back in town.

There are irrational thoughts escaping into my mind. *What if Trick has hurt James again? What if James wants to come back but can't? What if he's trapped somewhere; what if he's trapped down in that awful basement?*

I can't think like this, or I'll drive myself crazy. I get to the art room, relieved to find it empty, and I walk to my cupboard to get my things.

I gulp down the panic, force the thoughts out of my head and look at the model in front of me. It's my final art coursework, a double-sided, bronze bust of the Gorgon, Medusa. One side a serpent-headed creature, the other, a beautiful, wild version before she was cursed and turned into a monster.

I chose Medusa because, as a child, I loved her story. She fell in love with the wrong man, and the wrath of his jealous wife turned her into a monster, this creature that could never be loved again. The story always spoke to me for some reason, and I remember the way Papou told it. Love can make you do terrible things, he used to say. When it seeks you out, it makes you crazy, turns you into something hateful and then punishes you for it, changes you forever, so you can never go back to who you were before it found you.

I start working, moulding the wax, fixing the pins in place, creating the Medusa I want. I lose myself in my work, my hands working automatically, my brain switching off, my body relaxing into my task.

A sound breaks me away from my model. It's Mr. Stuart, my art teacher, my favourite teacher, the only one I don't mind having an actual conversation with. I stop and look up at him. He's leaning back on a desk to my right, staring at my model, rubbing his stubbly chin with his hand the way he always does when he appraises my work.

Like me, he seems lost in my model. His lips are moving as he stares at Medusa, and I get it. He's talking to her, like I do when I'm working. All of a sudden, he snaps his attention to me. His face breaks out into a bright smile.

"She's superb," he says, nodding.

I return his smile and look back at Medusa. I know he's right. If I don't have anything else, at least I have this, my father's talent. Mr. Stuart calls it a natural talent, but I know that's not true. I have my father's talent because I learnt it. I watched, and I listened, and I absorbed everything that his hands did.

"I'd love to display her," says my teacher. "When she's finished." He looks at me, then back at the model.

I shake my head straight away, like he knew I would. My work on show for everyone to see? I feel myself swell with pride, then deflate again immediately. I'd hate that kind of attention, and he knows it. It's not the first time we've had this conversation.

He rolls his eyes, and I know what he's thinking. Never mind Medusa's tragedy. What about an artist who can't let anyone see her work for fear of being talked about? Or worse, talked to?

I wait for him to say something else, to try to persuade me, talk me into it. But he seems to change his mind. He goes back to his desk and picks up a stack of papers and then returns, sliding them next to my model. He has a sheepish look on his face, and I go cold as I realise what the papers are. Names stare up at me.

London Academy of Fine Arts, Dresden University of the Arts, Moscow State Art College…

All applications for the best art schools in the world. I look back up at Mr. Stuart, but he's not looking at me. He's fidgeting with his fingers, very interested in something on one of his nails.

"Juniper, I know you haven't applied to any colleges yet," he says, still not looking at me. "I don't know what your plans are for next year, but the application deadlines are all over. I took the liberty of calling some of these schools, and I sent them pictures of your work."

My face heats up, and I watch Mr. Stuart's face redden too.

"I asked them for an extension of their deadlines. You show so much promise, Juniper. Any one of these schools would be lucky to have you."

I'm gritting my teeth as he speaks. Art school. It's all I've ever wanted. But leave Shackleston? Leave Kata? Leave James? My heart sinks at the thought of him. We were supposed to apply together. I've been waiting for him to decide, to tell me where he wants to go, so I can apply to the same place. I could never go anywhere without him. He's been next to me my whole life, I can barely get through two weeks of school without him. How would I cope in a whole different country?

I start to shake my head, but Mr. Stuart interrupts me. "Juniper, it's OK," he says. "No pressure. But it would be wonderful for you, and I just want you to think about it. I'm here if you need to talk, OK?"

I know he's trying to be kind, but I can't do anything except look at the ground. I want this conversation to be over. I don't want him to be here anymore.

He senses it and turns to walk away. Students are arriving, and he's about to start another class. But I can tell he's disappointed. I can see it from the slump in his shoulders, and it makes me feel guilty. He's never been anything but wonderful to me, and the last thing I want to do is disappoint him.

A thought hits me. "Mr. Stuart," I say, and he turns around, looking hopeful. "Do you think I could stay late after school today? I'm just... I'm not done working, and I'm kind of on a roll here..."

He sighs and walks back over to my desk, taking a set of keys out of his pocket.

I can tell he's still upset, so I try my best to look him in the eye. "Thank you," I tell him, hoping he knows I mean it, and it's not just about the keys.

"Anytime, Juniper," he says. "And as for the keys, you can hold on to them. You're here so much anyway. I'll use the spare set. Just make sure you lock everything up."

I nod at him, glad to be able to stay late, glad to be able to spend more time working on Medusa and glad he trusts me with the keys. And deep down, I'm glad to be delaying the inevitable trip to see Lucy.

I turn back to my model. She's so familiar to me now; it's like I'm creating a face I know. I'm aware of bells sounding out around me, other students coming and going, Mr. Stuart walking around me, amongst others. I vaguely remember hearing him say goodbye as he left, telling me not to stay too late. But I'm so focused on Medusa now, on the details of every part of both of her faces, that I push everything out of my head. Everything that's happened, all the panic, the fear, disappears into my hands. I focus. I let the work absorb me, wait for it to take me off somewhere else. And then, everything else fades away.

CHAPTER TWENTY

APRIL 29, 1990, Shackleston,

I'm devastated to write that another catastrophe has befallen us. I'm gutted to my core. I feel the shame throughout my entire body. Where did we go wrong?

Dr Banner tells me that it's less common for it to happen twice, but it can still happen. He's reassured me that there's nothing physically wrong with Lucy. She's fit and healthy. It's all just sad, sorry bad luck.

Lucy has retreated back into that box room that now smells of the dead. I can't get her to come out.

My reaction to her words were difficult for her, but I just don't understand her. I hadn't even known she was pregnant. And then for her to say those words… It was like a double blow. She knows that starting a family is my deepest wish, and I've been talking about it a lot recently. Not to put pressure on her but just so that we can talk, plan, dream…

Last night, as we sat in our chairs outside, looking at the world, she laughed. It was a strange sound, almost cruel. I'd never heard her laugh like that before. She was laughing at me.

I thought your deepest wish was to be published? What happened to that deepest wish? I thought your deepest wish was to know all my secrets? To fix me?

Her words were mocking me, and I've never felt so ashamed. Of myself and of her. And then she said the words that left me cold:

It looks like I killed another baby today.

Who says that kind of thing? I was taken aback, horrified, even before I realised what they meant. I slammed my book down and jumped up, startling her. How can you be so cruel? were the first words out of my mouth.

The guilt came immediately after that. Her face fell. I think perhaps she was just trying to protect me by not even telling me we were going to have another child. She was trying to save me from the wonderful anticipation, the horror of loss.

She thinks she killed our child, but surely she must know it's not her fault. These things happen to the best people in the world, for no reason whatsoever.

When I got home from work today, I knocked on her door with some news that I thought she might like. There is a date for Roger's return. He's coming back next month. He'll be starting at the school in September.

I heard her move around a little when I told her, and I heard the click of the door as she unlocked it. I waited for her to come out, but she didn't. I guess it was an invitation for me to come inside. Perhaps I should have taken her up on it, but I didn't feel ready. I turned around and walked away.

I think I will regret that for the rest of my life.

CHAPTER TWENTY-ONE

A NOISE startles me, and I launch myself back in my chair, knocking over a tin of pins. I'm confused for a moment, groggy, not sure where I am. I take in my surroundings, the familiarity of my desk, my model in front of me. I must have fallen asleep, right here in the art room. Once everyone was gone and the place was quiet, I remember putting my tools down, my head in my hands and taking five minutes, just to readjust, to clear my head, to rest my eyes before going to James's house.

But now, daylight's disappeared. Apart from the rain pounding on the roof and beating against the windows, there's no noise, no buzz, no one around me. I rub my arms, wondering why the air is so cold all of a sudden. I look up to see the side door open, the one that leads out onto the sports field, sending in an icy breeze.

I get my phone out to check the time, shocked to see it's almost five o'clock. I get up, start gathering my things, still a little dazed and disoriented from day-sleeping. How could I have slept for so long? The voice in my head tells me it's too late to go and see Lucy Creed now anyway. Maybe I can avoid it for another day. Maybe I can just go tomorrow.

There's a noise again, and it stops me. I'm hit with the instant realisation that I'm not alone. There's a sound, the shuffling of feet, coming from near the open door. That part of the room is dark, the fading light outside playing tricks with the shadows of various students' models. I shiver again, but it's not from the cold. I know it; there's someone there.

The shuffling again. Panic starts coursing through me as I see the cupboard door waver a little. *Is someone watching me?*

Each individual hair on the back of my neck sends a prickly tremor down my spine. I stay still, waiting, not sure what to do. The air around me has changed; it's charged somehow, alive. I'm holding my breath. And I'm afraid.

The shadow moves, and I see him. He runs out of the side door, into the darkness and the rain. I feel that familiar rush of relief take over, the tension leaving my body in one long breath. I'm not scared anymore. I know who it was. I saw him. I saw his face as he ran out into the cold.

It was James. He's back. *Thank God.* I almost want to cry.

I go and close the side door and rush to finish packing up my stuff. I make sure I lock everything up, and then I leave, immediately warmer in the light of the corridor. There are a few students milling around, attending some after-school activities. Carla Jackson gives me a smile as I walk past her, but I notice too late and don't manage to return it. I'm still a little on edge, but I can't help this ecstatic, wild feeling washing over me. *James is back.*

I smile despite the rain. I can't wait to tell Kata. She's going to be so relieved. And now, I don't have to go to the Creed house at all. I don't have to admit I lied. I don't have to tell Lucy anything. *He's back. Phew.*

When I get near the bridge, I catch a movement out of the corner of my eye, and I know straight away it's him. He must have waited, hidden somewhere in the shadows, and now he's playing a game and following me home.

I turn around, hoping to catch him, but each time I try, he darts behind a tree or a bush, fifteen paces behind me. Through the rain, I can't make him out properly, and after a while I give up, frustrated. *Fine*, I think. *Play your stupid game.* I start to run towards home, any relief I felt at seeing James replaced by annoyance. This is so typical of him. Disappearing and making everyone worry and then coming back here and being weird, spying on me, then following me home. I know what he wants. He wants me to tell him I'm sorry, to beg for forgiveness for screaming at him before he left. The anger starts bubbling up inside me again, and I speed up. I don't turn around again.

Kata's in the kitchen as I walk in, standing with her back to me, staring out of the kitchen window. She turns to face me, that same strangled look still on her face, a question in her eyes. I notice the dark circles. She looks so tired, so low.

I smile at her.

"What's the matter," she says, alert. "Why are you smiling like that?"

I can't help but laugh. "Kata, everything really *is* OK. I saw James. He's back."

For a moment, Kata stares at me, like she's not sure whether or not I'm telling the truth. Then she lets out a huge breath and makes the sign of the cross on her chest. She looks up at the ceiling and closes her eyes.

When she opens them again, I recognise *my* Kata. The light is back in her face, the shine back on her cheeks. She's herself again, and now she's annoyed. "That boy!" she exclaims, swearing in Greek. "He's so bad! He doesn't care about anyone except himself. Where's he been? Honestly! He's had everyone worried sick!"

I can't help but laugh as I let her fuss over me, pull me out of my soaking coat, tutting at me about wet hair, scolding me about flu and getting sick. I'm pushed down into a chair and she places a steaming cup of tea in front of me that I can only look at while she attacks my dripping hair with a towel.

"What did he say?" she asks, coming around to sit opposite me. "Where's he been all this time?" Then she looks down at her hands and reddens a little. Her voice goes quiet. "Did he… did he see his father?"

I shrug. "I didn't talk to him," I tell her. "I just saw him now, at school."

She frowns and looks up at me again, right in the eyes this time, and it makes me squirm. Then she gets up and reaches for the house phone on the wall. "You call his mum anyway," she announces.

I freeze. *What? Why?* James is back. James is fine. He was here. I saw him. He's probably gone home now, getting screamed at and hugged by his mum at the same time.

When I say as much to Kata, she shakes her head, and I know I'm not going to get away with it.

"You know what he's like, Joo. Just because you've seen him doesn't mean his mother has. You need to tell her he's back. It's the least you can do." She raises her eyebrows at me, letting me know I'm still in trouble for lying.

I'm about to protest, but right then the phone rings, and it startles both of us. "It can only be for you," says Kata, with a small smile as she hands me the phone. Then she walks out, leaving me alone with the ringing phone in my hands.

I sit back down. I know it's James on the other end of the line, and I can't help but grin, no matter how annoyed I am with him.

"Hello?" I say.

There's a pause on the other end. A sharp intake of breath. Suddenly, the fear is back. I'm torn between feeling ecstatic that he's back and afraid of what he's about to say. What if he really has been to see his father? What if he starts spouting rubbish about his innocence again? What if it's not rubbish, and he really did find something out, something life-changing? *What if Philip Creed really is innocent?*

"Juniper?" says the voice. My heart shatters into pieces. It's not James. It's his mum. It's Lucy.

I swallow. I can't say anything back. I want to put the phone down, throw it away, hide it in a drawer, never see it again. What does she want? Why isn't he calling me himself?

"Juniper, I know you're there," she says. I hear the anguish in her voice. I hear the strain, the worry. *Oh, God.*

I gulp and try to say yes. I hear her sigh.

"Juniper, we need to talk to you," she says. "Please, could you come over here? Tomorrow? After school?"

I wasn't expecting that. James *has* found something out about his dad. And it's something so bad that he can't even bring himself to speak to me; he has to get his mum to do it for him. *Oh, God.*

"Juniper," she says again. "Tomorrow? After school?"

I manage to whisper yes before she puts the phone down. I'm going to have to go there. I have to hear what they're going to tell me, no matter how bad it is.

I sit at the table, trying to control the shaking.

My first instinct is to spark something. To burn the newspapers I've got stashed away upstairs. It's the only thing that can make me feel better, that can take the panic away. But with Kata here, there's no way I'll manage. Instead, I get my phone out of my bag. Trembling, I prepare myself to do something I've never done before, something Kata would hate. It's like my fingers are working on autopilot as I open up the search engine and stare at the blank space.

Can I really do this? I listen out for my aunt, knowing how angry she'd be if she knew what I was doing, not least because using the Internet on my phone is too expensive. I've never looked this up before. I've never wanted to know. Now, I feel like I need to be prepared. My fingers shake as I start typing his name, *Philip Creed,* into my screen and press 'search.'

The list takes ages to load. There's hardly any reception out here at the castle, and when the words come, they stare up at me, making me wince, making me want to stop, to run away. I force myself to stay and look properly. Shaking, I click on the first item on the list, a reference from something called the 'UK Crime Crypt.'

I take a deep breath. And I read.

Philip Creed, triple murderer, 1965-present

Philip Creed (born 4th April, 1965) is an American triple murderer, also known as The Castle Killer. He is currently serving a life sentence in Gilford Prison for the arson attack on Shackleston Castle, and the subsequent murder of its owner Roger Slaide, his wife, Sofia Slaide, and her father, Christophe Panos. The killings took place in August 2005, and Creed was found guilty in June 2006.

Early Life

Creed was born in the village of Marisberg, Kentucky in the US, the second child of Jeanette Creed (nee Williams), father unknown. He has an older brother, Paul, presumed deceased. His mother died in March 1983 of breast cancer.

He met his wife, Lucy, (nee Jones) in Marisberg, where she worked at a local book store. Creed and Jones were married in Jadesville, Kentucky in 1986, shortly after meeting.

In 1987, the Creeds returned to Shackleston, UK, his wife's hometown, to inherit her mother's assets and live in her family home.

That same year, Creed began working at the prominent

private school St. Augustine's College as an English Literature teacher, despite having no qualifications. Lucy Creed gave birth to twins, James Edward Creed and Trick Creed on 14th August, 1994.

Creed had dreams of being a writer but was unsuccessful. It is thought that this, along with his difficulty fitting into life in Shackleston, caused him to become increasingly jealous of the Slaides of the nearby castle.

Creed was a jealous man who was obsessed with being famous. He was not well liked by the Shackleston community, and it is thought that he was angered by his wife's ability to be accepted back into her hometown after years of absence.

His only friend was Roger Slaide. Slaide became an overnight success in the early 90's, creating a stunning array of Greek mythological statues. It is widely believed that Creed became so jealous of Slaide's success that he purposefully started the fire that destroyed Shackleston Castle and killed his friend. He had no criminal convictions prior to the murders.

THE CASTLE KILLER

On 5th August, 2005, Philip Creed crept into the castle while the family slept and set light to a book shelf in the castle's library. The fire spread quickly to surrounding rooms. Roger and Sofia Slaide and their only daughter, Juniper (born 12th August, 1994), were all asleep in the Castle at the time.

Although the events of the night of 5th August 2005 are uncertain, it is believed that Mr. Christophe Panos saw the blaze from his home at the castle's gatehouse. He called 999 and then, ignoring orders to stay away until the fire service arrived, it is believed he went inside the castle to rescue his family. Juniper was found lying on the grass outside, unconscious and suffering from severe smoke inhalation, but with no burns. It is thought that she was rescued by her grandfather.

It is likely that Christophe Panos then returned into the castle to attempt to rescue his daughter and her husband. The fire service arrived 12 minutes later, but Christophe, Roger and Sofia were nowhere to be found. All three perished in the blaze.

Philip Creed was arrested at the Forrest Inn in Bramsley, a neighbouring village where he had been hiding, two days after the murders on 7th August, 2005. He had disappeared from Shackleston just after the fire. This, along with witness statements from his wife, a colleague and some local townsfolk, afforded the evidence needed to arrest him.

THE TRIAL

The trial began on 31st January 2006. In a shocking move, the defendant changed his plea three days into the trial. He pleaded guilty to the crime of arson with intent, as well as for the murders of Roger Slaide, Sofia Slaide and Christophe Panos.

Creed was sentenced to life imprisonment with no parole, in Gilford Prison, on 15th June, 2006.

I'm aware of the silence around me as I read. Everything feels weird, like I'm disconnected and this isn't about me, it's not about my family. I already knew a lot of this story, but that's all it was, a story. One that I'd pushed so far away into the locked part of my mind that taking it out now and dusting it off feels so strange, like I'm almost numb inside. I don't remember the night of the fire. I don't remember anything.

Some of the information I read wakes things up inside me.

I didn't know anything about James's father. I had no idea that he was American; I'd never thought about him as coming from anywhere or having any family of his own. I hadn't known about his nickname, *The Castle Killer*, which makes me shudder. And I hadn't known that Lucy Creed had provided evidence against her husband. I guess it makes sense that he was jealous of my father's art although, somehow, it wasn't the reason I was expecting. But then, I don't know what I was expecting. I had no idea that Philip Creed had changed his plea, that he'd started out pleading not guilty before his confession. I wonder what made him tell the truth in the end?

I take a deep breath and scroll through the rest of the titles in the list. There's nothing here to suggest that Philip Creed is innocent. Relief starts to make its way through me. There's just no way. Someone wouldn't confess to a crime they didn't commit. Whatever James and his mum want to see me about, it can't be that.

And I'm OK, I realise. Nothing bad has happened to me from reading about the past. I haven't broken down in a heap of tears. I haven't turned into a ball of panic or caused a scene; nothing bad has happened at all. *I'm OK.*

CHAPTER TWENTY-TWO

JUNE 1, 1990, Shackleston,

This afternoon just after lunch, everything was quiet. I was sitting in the dining room marking some papers while Lucy was locked away in that room upstairs, doing whatever it is she does up there. The house was silent and still.

I was shaken from my marking by voices outside, and there was a short, sharp knock at the door. All of a sudden they were here, all of them, Roger Slaide and his family, a family no one even knew existed. I barely had time to open the door and no time to wonder what was going on before they were inside, bringing in bags, bringing in noise.

Roger walked in last, the fourth one in. He shrugged his shoulders and held out his hand, gave me a smile that said 'I'm sorry for what's about to happen.'

We can't get into the castle; Roger's lost the keys, someone was saying. I turned to see a woman, olive-skinned and striking, dark eyes full of fire and wit. Sofia Slaide. It seems Roger fell in love in Greece and married a goddess. The windows were opened, light flooded into the house, noise all around us. I looked up and saw Lucy beaming on the stairs. She came down and welcomed and hugged and kissed and laughed, and I was stunned. This was a different Lucy.

I looked over at Roger, watched him take Lucy in. He seems to be a peaceful man, happy to let his wife and her family take over, bustling around him, while he stays quiet and still. He didn't talk much at all, but glanced over at me from time to time and raised his eyebrows. There's something about his face that reminds me of Lucy, in his expression perhaps. It's like he's witnessed terrible things, things that no one should ever see, and the memory of those things is reflected in his eyes when he thinks no one is looking.

I felt strongly that we'd be friends, but then I didn't have a lot of time for reflection because, well, that family talks. They talk like their lives depend on it. And they laugh. It's a sound that's been missing from this house and doesn't suit it, doesn't sit well here amongst all this old furniture, all these old memories that I'm not a part of.

Along with his wife, Roger has brought her father and younger sister. All three have the same dark complexion, so different from Lucy's pale beauty. And I can't get over how loud they are. Twice, their voices ran off with them, and they switched to Greek, arguing at full volume, so deafening I almost wanted to hide.

It's fascinating to me, seeing how much Lucy has changed in the space of one day. She's invited them to stay for as long as possible, until Roger gets the castle organized. She's miraculously pulled out a set of keys, claiming that one or two of them will unlock the castle gates and the little cottage at its entrance. She had a key all along and never told me.

Roger nodded at her and there was a look that passed between them, one I couldn't begin to understand. I felt they might need some time to themselves, some time to talk.

So I asked the rest of the family if they'd like to take a walk to the castle, see if any of these keys would work. They jumped at the chance. I didn't even have time to grab my coat; they were out of the door and speeding away.

We were gone for several hours because the castle is breathtaking, so beautiful and awe-inspiring that it even managed to silence the Panos family. But what a mess it's in. A complete state of disarray. Everything is overgrown or damaged. It seems that Roger put nothing in place for its maintenance while he was in Greece, and he's been gone for over five years. Still, even if the castle can't be lived in just yet, it's certainly a place of wonder.

When we returned, Lucy and Roger hadn't moved from the dining room, and we brought in noise and disturbed their peace. For a moment, the anger I recognize so well by now flashed over Lucy's face, just for a second. Roger greeted his wife with the warmest of kisses, slight and without any lingering, but soft and full of love. I tried to do the same with Lucy, but we missed and it was awkward. I saw the annoyance in her eyes and, not for the first time, I felt stupid, like a failure.

Still, I'm excited that the Slaide-Panos family will be staying with us for a while, at least until Papou and Roger can put the castle back together again. I'm excited at the prospect of this house having a family, at last, even if it's not my own.

When Roger left the noise to go outside for a cigarette, I saw him glance over at the basement door in the kitchen. I watched him pause and frown at first, then he turned and looked at me. He nodded, once, as if to say he approved of its hiding place, beneath all that plaster and paint.

I nodded back at him, and it felt like we understood something about each other then. We both love Lucy, and we both want to protect her. I don't have a rival in him; I have a partner. Lucy seems to have a silent understanding with him. He brings her a peace that I can't. Whatever it was she went through here, he went through it with her. And maybe, just maybe, he'll be the one to share it with me.

CHAPTER TWENTY-THREE

AFTER school, I set off on the walk to James's house. The cold bites at my ears, and I have to keep sniffing to stop my nose from running, but at least it's not raining anymore. I try to make myself feel brave as I walk across the cricket pitch, taking the back way out of school. At least I'll get to see James again. No matter what it is they have to tell me, at least he's back.

There's cricket practice going on as I walk past, so I go the long way around to avoid being seen and to make sure I don't come into contact with any stray balls. But then I see him, Rory Bryan, waving at me, jogging towards me, that huge grin on his face.

Oh no, I panic, feeling myself freeze and start to burn at the same time. Just what I need.

He only wants to see the statues, I tell myself. He's not interested in me. I won't talk to him; I'll just ignore him. But I hate the fact that my stomach is doing backflips at the thought of being near him, and I can feel my face burning away like crazy.

"Juniper," he says, reaching me, standing in front of me so I'm forced to stop. He's wearing his cricket whites and a little out of breath so his face is flushed, and for some reason I immediately imagine him in the shower.

I turn into a bright red ball of flame and look away, aware that everything between my skin and bones seems to be sizzling.

"Hey," he says, turning the grin up to full volume, every individual freckle on his face smiling at me. "How are you? You ran away from me yesterday, and then you weren't in English, so I didn't get the chance to say I'm sorry..." He swallows and looks nervous all of a sudden before continuing. "I'm sorry I told you I wanted to see the statues. I just thought... Well, I wanted to explain..."

"There's no need to explain," I say to the ground, breaking my resolve not to talk to him. "You can see the statues any time. The gate's open. Just go in."

I thought he'd be delighted, but when I manage to look up at him, I see his face has fallen. "Oh," he says.

It's his turn to look at the ground now, and it's strange- it makes me panic. I suddenly feel like I've said the worst thing in the world, and I'm desperate to make things better, to bring that smile back. I've upset him, and I don't know why, and every part of me wants to put it right.

Before I can say anything, Rory looks up at me again, the smile back on his face. *Phew.* He changes the subject. "Where are you off to, anyway? I was going to ask you if you wanted to come to the library with me after school today? So we could work on that project..."

I must look shocked because he starts to laugh.

"I thought I could just do the project myself," I mumble, my face burning. It's what I normally do with James anyway. I do the work for both of us. I can do it for Rory too; it's probably what he wanted in the first place.

"What's that?" he says, cupping his hand over his ear, grinning. "I didn't hear you. Could you repeat that, please?"

He's laughing at me again. He finds it funny. He thinks it's a joke that I struggle so much with talking to people, that my whole body goes rigid with fear every time I'm put into a situation where I might have to.

I must look like I'm about to cry because Rory takes a step forward, looking worried.

"Hey, I'm sorry," he says. "I was only joking..."

I shake my head at him. It's too late. I don't want his pity. I want to run. I want to melt into the ground and disappear. I want to spark something.

"Juniper," he says, gently this time, bringing me back before I can disappear inside my head. "The library? Come on... please say yes."

I frown. It's like he's desperate for me to go with him. He's not going to let me do this project on my own; it's not what he wants. He's not going to leave me alone.

"I can't today," I tell him, trying hard to look him in the eye. "I'm going to James's house now. He's back," I say, attempting a triumphant smile.

But as soon as I say the words, Rory's face falls again. This time it's worse than before. The smile is gone, and it's like the sunflowers in his eyes have lost their sun.

I feel bewildered again and stupidly guilty that I've made him look so hurt. I need to say something else to make it better. I don't know what comes over me, but I feel myself scrambling to find words.

"Err... tomorrow?" I say, not quite believing my own voice. "We could go to the library tomorrow, if you want. After school. To work on the project," I add.

"Really?" he says, raising his eyebrows. It looks like he can't believe it either. Anyone would think I'd given him a million-pound cheque or something. His smile is back with such a force it looks like it might fly off his face and soar into the sky.

Even though my brain is screaming at me, sending off all sorts of warning signals, I nod. I look away then, blushing, and annoyed with him, annoyed with myself. What am I doing? And then... *oh my God what is James going to think? What's he going to say when he finds out?*

Rory's teammates start shouting at him to return to practice. He looks over his shoulder and yells back at them, and he starts to run backwards, all the while smiling that insane grin at me. "I'll come and get you after your art lesson tomorrow, OK?" he says, and without waiting for me to respond, he turns and runs back to his game.

I stay still for a moment and take deep breaths. I wonder how he knows my last lesson is art, but it doesn't matter now. I've done it. And it doesn't matter what James says or what he's going to think. *James is the one who left me*, I remind myself. So what if James is angry? I don't care. It serves him right.

I start walking again, feeling braver, feeling more determined than ever. When I get to the Creed house, I stop at the little gate, hidden between the looming fir trees. There's music coming from inside the house, and it catches me off guard. Someone's playing the piano, and it's so mesmerising that it manages to make my brain stop thinking for a moment. It's the saddest melody I've ever heard, and it's beautiful.

I open the gate and walk down the path on autopilot, transfixed by the sound. Is that James, playing like that? I walk up the stairs to the front door and raise my hand to knock, not even thinking about what I'm doing. I just want to get to him. I haven't heard James play the piano in years and never like this, never so wonderfully, so woefully.

The music stops, and there's a loud bang that makes me jump. The sound of the piano being slammed shut with such massive force shocks me and wakes me out of my reverie. My hand is suspended in mid-air and I'm confused for a moment. Something's not right. Warning alarms start sounding off in my head, loud, urgent. *You need to leave. Right now. Turn around. Go*. But I'm frozen, feet pinned to the ground, my heart beating hard in my chest. It's not the nerves at seeing James or the anxiety over what he's going to say. It's a sudden gut instinct that something bad is about to happen. I'm in danger.

I should never have come. I start to turn, but the door opens and a hand grabs my arm, pulls me inside.

It's Trick, I realise, my breath coming out in gasps. I don't want to be in his grip. I don't want to be anywhere near him, ever. I try to pull away from him, but he's strong, and he's quick, and he's squeezing my arm so tightly it hurts, dragging me through the house.

"Don't you dare run away," he hisses at me, hauling me into the living room. He lets go of my arm and gives me a shove, and all I can feel is utter terror and total conviction that he's about to hurt me. He's going to do something terrible. He's bad. He's evil.

He slams the door behind us.

Lucy Creed is sitting on the sofa. Her whole body is trembling, and she looks up at me, wild, her eyes bulging, looking broken, her fingers clawing at her cheeks. I should have known. I should have recognised it in her voice when she called me last night. It was a trap, and we're caught in it.

The room starts to spin. I'm desperate to hold myself up, try to stop the dizzy feeling, my legs weak beneath me. I'm going to have a panic attack, right here, right now, I think, staring at Lucy, trying to take deep breaths.

Then a voice says, "Oh, hi, Juniper." The voice is calm. The voice is kind. It's a female voice. I turn to look at where it's coming from, and I see Becky, the police officer, the one who knows Kata, coming out of the kitchen.

I feel hot all of a sudden. Lucy turns away from me. For a split second I think I spot that look of grim determination on her face before she switches back to anguish again.

Trick stalks off to look out of the window.

Becky is carrying in a tray, balancing a pot of tea and several cups. She walks past me and places it on the coffee table in front of Lucy.

Where's James? I think, looking around. Then Becky turns to me, and I can see it in her face. She looks awkward, embarrassed. This isn't a trap. It's an ambush.

She sits next to Lucy and looks at me. "It's nice to see you, Juniper," she says, a fake note of surprise in her voice. "Would you like to sit down? Some tea?"

I stay glued to the spot. I couldn't move even if I tried.

Becky looks at Lucy, and something passes between them. As Becky pours tea, she says, "I'm not here on an official capacity; I'd just like to make sure you know that. I'm just visiting Lucy on my day off as she's going through a difficult time at the moment."

I look around me again for signs of James. *Where are you? Hurry up and come out already.* I rub at my arm where Trick was squeezing it. It hurts. It burns.

"I'm glad you're here though," Becky says, not looking at me. "You've been quite difficult to get hold of." She looks at Lucy again before continuing. "We were all wondering when was the last time you saw James? If there's anything you could tell us about his whereabouts?"

The words come out before I can even think them. "He's… he's not here?" I ask. It's so hot in here I feel myself start to sweat. I want to take off my coat, to get rid of layers, but I can't move, and I'm certainly not staying.

They all look at me. Even Trick turns away from the window to stare at me, a flash of confusion on his face.

"What do you mean??" says Becky, frowning. "James has been missing for twelve days, and no one's heard from him. Unless… have you?"

It feels like even the walls of the house are holding their breath, waiting for me to answer.

"Yesterday," I blurt out. "I saw him yesterday."

Their eyes snap towards me. I see Lucy draw in a deep breath. Even Trick looks at me in disbelief. And… is that a flicker of hope?

"I saw him at school," I continue, my voice speeding up, trying to get the words out as quickly as I can. I can make this better. I can make this go away. "He was in the art room while I was working, but he ran away before I could talk to him. And then… and then he followed me home."

Lucy lets out her breath, tears forming in her eyes as she looks at me. *That's hope,* I think to myself, relieved that I've been able to appease her.

Becky stands up. "Juniper, are you sure?" she says.

I nod. I want to leave. I want to get out of here. I want this to be over.

Becky starts to get her phone out, but Trick stops her. "It was me," he says, his voice thick, his face blank. He turns to face me, and I feel a chill run through my whole body. "I came to talk to you about James. I thought you'd know where he was. When I got there, you were asleep at your desk, and when you woke up and saw me, you ran away. I tried to catch up with you, but it was raining so hard and you started sprinting, so we called you and asked you to come here."

Trick turns back to look out of the window again. I can't believe my ears at what he's just said, so I stare at him, open-mouthed. *No.*

Lucy slumps on the sofa.

Becky sits back down and reaches across to her, puts a hand on her knee.

"OK," she says, looking up at me, still keeping her voice

calm. "Let's start again. Is there anything you can tell us about where James might be? Anything at all?"

I know this is the moment where I should tell them. I take a deep breath and go for it. "I saw James last Sunday night," I start. "He… he was leaving." I hear Lucy's sharp intake of breath. I feel Trick's eyes scowling at me.

"Can you tell us where he was going?" says Becky. There's a note of annoyance in her voice, and it makes me feel so stupid, so guilty.

"He went… he went to see his father," I whisper.

All their faces are still, wide-eyed and shocked.

I look at my feet. "He said his father was innocent, and he was going to see him to get some sort of proof. To clear his name."

After a split second of silence, the room comes alive. Becky is up, talking into her phone, rushed, strangled.

And then there's that horrible noise I heard in Mr. Brankin's office. It's coming from Lucy, that low, anguished wail, more animal than human, and it frightens me, makes me stop breathing. All of a sudden, she's up, off the couch, flying across the room to Trick, screaming at him. "This is your fault!" she cries. She's all over him, beating his face, attacking his body with her fists. She's half the size of him, but she looks so much bigger all of a sudden. "You've done this! You've done this to James!"

Trick doesn't fight back. He goes limp against the window, taking her blows, letting her pummel him, beat him with a force I would never have imagined someone so small and frail could be capable of.

As Becky rushes over to pull Lucy off Trick, I turn and run. I run all the way back to the gatehouse, back to the safety of Kata, of my home. I shut myself in my bedroom, in the dark, scramble onto the window seat and wrap my arms around my knees, in shock.

James isn't back. And the reaction I got when I said he went to see his father was terrifying, worse than Kata's. I can't get the picture of Trick's eyes out of my head. I caught a glimpse of them as he flinched away from his mum. And I had to go. Because I couldn't see anger anymore. All I could see were his tears.

CHAPTER TWENTY-FOUR

DECEMBER 22, 1991, Shackleston,

It's been a year and a half since I got this diary out, and it seems that our whole lives have changed since the invasion of our wonderful castle-dwellers.

Roger and I have become great friends, and his adopted family is enchanting. Since they moved back into the castle, they've turned it around. They put on weekly family dinners, and once a week, Lucy and I make our way up there to dine in the servant's quarters, simple meals that I feel so privileged to be a part of. These informal and noisy family meetings last for hours and leave me breathless and giddy, exhausted from the fabulous self-inflicted drama of the Panos girls and their father. And more than a little drunk on the ouzo that Papou pours so generously.

They are not what I would call private people. They're invasive and loud. They argue in public, in English and in Greek and in their strange mixture of both. They don't fit into this town, which I have come to believe is the most private town in the world.

Sofia is kind and soft, but wary of others and not afraid to speak her mind. She's a regular at town meetings, a voice in the crowd, standing up and asking the questions no one wants to answer. She hasn't been accepted here, but she doesn't care a damn, and I adore her for it.

The old man is a great laugh. He chases his daughters around, reprimanding, shouting, getting in the middle of their intense disagreements. They don't pay any attention to him, but he carries on, red in the face and shaking his fists. Everything he does, every movement, every word has a natural theatrical flair and he draws you in, especially when he starts on one of his Greek stories. Every day he works on the castle, rebuilding, fixing, a frown of concentration on his face. He's spent the past six months sitting on a huge lawnmower that Roger brought him, covering every inch of green. He's even employed some local kids to help him, and together they've trimmed and cut and brought daylight back into the estate.

Thirteen-year-old Kata is troublesome, both in and out of school. I don't know why, but she makes me feel uncomfortable. She looks at me with eyes that accuse me of something I haven't done. She goes to St. Augustine's, but I find myself thankful she's not in any of my classes this semester. She's made friends as easily as she's made enemies, and although she tries to act tough and grown up at school, she's very different at home. She sits in the gatehouse TV room and watches musicals on repeat, singing songs (terribly) about love and heartbreak that she couldn't possibly understand.

When they lived with us here, Kata was a real problem. I'd welcomed them into our home, but I'd also been firm. I was a little worried about Lucy. She'd been so fragile, and I was fearful of how she'd cope with these overwhelming, passionate and loud characters taking over our space. So I laid out some ground rules: no going into Lucy's mother's room. No trying to get into the locked and camouflaged basement door. Please try to keep the noise down after dark, a task I knew they'd find difficult. So, to lighten the mood, I'd added a final rule, tagged onto the end of my list: no cheese in the house.

It was intended as a bit of fun, an in-joke between Lucy and me, a reminder that it was a dislike we shared and had bonded over on our first date. I wanted one of those side-glances from her, a masked smile, one for my eyes only, like the kind she shares with Roger.

Instead, it was Roger she looked at, and they both turned pale, not daring to breathe. I couldn't understand it then; I still can't now. It was Roger who looked away first, down to the floor. It was a long moment before he looked up again.

And it was the cheese rule that proved to be the most problematic. I knew Lucy didn't like cheese, but I had no idea it was more than just a strong dislike- it's an actual phobia.

There were terrible scenes at our family dining table. Eruptions, the kind I'd never seen from Lucy before. Since the Panos's are a family who embrace everything in life, especially their food, they couldn't quite respect the no-cheese rule. And Kata would always find a way to slip it into meals and wait for the volatile effect it would have on Lucy when she realized it. Lucy's reactions were truly shocking. I watched her blow up, unable to control herself, unable to calm her anger. I saw Kata's cheeky smile replaced by fear every time Lucy reacted, and I watched the shock on Papou and Sofia's faces, the quiet sadness on Roger's. All this rage, all this animosity… over cheese? I didn't know what to do. Eventually, Roger had a quiet word in Kata's ear, and she listened to him. Everything stopped.

Roger explained to me that cheese was Lucy's father's favorite food. That her mother spent a lifetime working cheese into recipes, so much so that even the sight of it could turn Lucy's stomach. I'd never heard him talk about her father, or anyone related to her for that matter. I asked him for more, but he looked at me as though he hadn't even realised he'd said anything. Then he was quiet again, leaving me frustrated, needing more information that I don't think I'll ever get.

Last week, on one of our after-school walks around the gardens, I decided to ask Roger all the questions about Lucy that had been gnawing away at me. I asked him about her skin. I told him about the mottled scars, each one a film of transparent rubber, the same shape and size, covering her body. He turned pale. He was silent for a long time. He said that if Lucy hadn't told me, then he couldn't possibly.

It made me so angry. Not *at him, but at everything. I told him that I was fed up with this town, fed up with all the secrets. And Roger, gentle as he is, simply apologised. He wasn't annoyed at my outburst. He explained that this is what small towns do; they're full of secrets, and they always protect their own. Give them a child, he said. They'll warm to you then.*

He was joking, of course, trying to lighten my desolate mood. But I still want that so desperately. To have a child, to make us a family, to make us complete. All I ever wanted was to fix her, to make her better. I wish she'd let me try.

CHAPTER TWENTY-FIVE

TODAY is the last day of school before we break up for Easter. I haven't seen Kata yet, and I don't know what to tell her. I want to hide in my room, not have to face her this morning, not have to tell her about what happened yesterday, with Lucy, with the police officer, with Trick. I can't handle the worry on her face anymore, the fear.

I can't believe it wasn't James I saw. I can't believe he's not back. But still, despite the panic, despite the terrible fear on Lucy's face yesterday, the hurt in Trick's eyes, I can't help feeling a little relieved that I've told the truth now. I don't need to feel so guilty anymore. I've told Lucy and the police where James went, so it's up to them to find him now, and at least they know where to start looking.

As I'm trying to get a comb through my hair, I hear voices downstairs again. I panic, thinking the police have come back to question me or, even worse, arrest me for not telling them what I knew about James. *Can they do that?*

But then I realise Kata's not talking; she's singing. She sounds happy. Someone's singing with her. With a mixture of horror and some strange wild relief, I realise it's Rory Bryan. He's come back.

I'd almost forgotten about Rory. I was going to try and avoid him today, leave art early so he couldn't find me to go to the library with him. I was going to get his email address and send him a message over the holidays, tell him to just enjoy his break and forget about the project. I'd do it myself. I was going to tell him not to worry, that he'd be sure to get an A. But now he's back here, in my kitchen. He won't leave me alone.

It's weird. It's like my heart's sinking and fluttering at the same time. That fist that's been hanging out in my stomach is alternating between pulling me apart and turning into a million butterflies. I try to ignore it and rush to get ready, using serum on my hair to tame the curls. I put mascara on again, and it makes me feel stupid because I know I'm putting it on to look good. *For Rory,* says the evil voice in my head, and I blush hard, even though I'm alone.

"Hello," he yells at me when I walk into the kitchen. He's so loud I think all the pots and pans will fall off the wall.

They were mid-song, a duet from Les Miserables. It makes me smile, especially given Kata's less than perfect singing voice. She's clearly decided Rory's her new favourite person, and when I look over at her, she looks relaxed, happy. There are still dark circles of worry under her eyes, but she's shining again.

I make the decision right then and there. There's no need to tell her that James is still missing. There's no need to put that fear back on her face.

"I woke up early, so I thought I'd walk you to school again," says Rory. "I had something important to tell you, but… when I got here, I forgot it." He looks at me, grinning, his freckles radiating laughter on his face. *Yep, definitely butterflies.*

I don't know what to say. Kata laughs and hands me a cup of tea and a plate of toast. I try to avoid looking at her too much. I don't want her to start scrutinizing my face, looking for signs that there's something wrong.

I stay silent and sit, trying my best to smile, even at Rory.

He's handed his own plate of toast, his own cup of tea. For the second time, I'm struck by how weird it is to see someone else in James's place, doing what James does. They're so different. James always looks like he's got something to prove, and there's always such a hard look on his face. Rory seems so relaxed, so easy. Suddenly that thought makes me feel ill, like I'm betraying James somehow. I feel so sick that I have to look away, and my hands wrap themselves around my waist to make the panic in my stomach stop.

"What's wrong?" says Kata, her face switching from smile to concern.

Damn it.

"Nothing," I tell her, forcing myself to relax, loosening my arms. But I feel so hot and so trapped all of a sudden that I need to get out of here, fast.

Rory gets up as I do. Then he turns to Kata. "I'm sure Juniper already told you," he says, "but I just wanted to make sure it's OK. I'll be borrowing her after school today."

His eyes twinkle with mischief, and I see Kata's eyes do the same. *Oh no.*

"A date?" she says, gleaming at Rory.

I cringe in embarrassment.

Rory's smile widens even more. "Nothing as adventurous as that," he says. Then his smile turns wicked as he looks at me. "I thought I'd take it slow."

My heart races; my face burns. I must look horrified because they both laugh. I want to run and hide, not let anyone see how red I am. I grab my things and walk out while Rory stuffs a last piece of toast into his mouth and shouts goodbye to Kata. I need the cool air to calm my face. I hate them laughing and joking about me like this, like I'm not even here. I hate myself for not being able to join in.

Kata leans out of the doorway and calls out to us. "Rory, if you don't have any plans, perhaps you'd like to come round for lunch tomorrow? I know it's Good Friday, and you may be doing something with your family, but honestly, there's so much food in the house, it'll go to waste if we don't get help eating it."

I stand there, shocked. I can't believe my Aunt has just invited Rory round for lunch without even asking me first.

Rory stands next to me, beaming like an idiot.

Please say no, please say you're busy.

"I'd be delighted," he says, giving Kata a wave. He's made her day.

She nods, happy, and shuts us out in the cold.

"You don't have to, you know," I say to him, quietly, as we walk. I'm still bright red, but it's getting easier to talk to him.

"What do you mean?" he says, frowning. "And anyway, we have a project to work on, and I doubt we'll get it finished today."

I nod. The project. Of course. I haven't even looked at it yet.

As we walk out of the grounds, Rory stops and turns around, taking it all in behind us. He gives a low whistle.

I turn and look with him. From here, the castle in the distance is showing us its good side, the side that's not black and half crumbled to the ground. Even if all that's behind that façade is air, it still looks pretty impressive.

Rory clears his throat. "I'm sorry I told you I wanted to see the statues," he says. "It's not the only reason I've been… kind of following you around."

I glance over at him.

He's almost a little red in the face himself as he talks. "It's just… I always grew up wondering about that castle. I'm a sucker for fairy tales and I spent so much time daydreaming about it, and the real-life princess who lived inside…"

He smiles and turns away, starts walking again.

I can't help but blush at his words as I follow him. He doesn't care how cheesy he sounds. He talks with no thought or concern for what I'll think, and I get the feeling that's just the way he is with everyone. He seems so relaxed, so different from me. I wish I could be like that.

Rory clears his throat and starts talking again, nervous this time. "Now that James is back, I was kind of worried I wouldn't get to see you anymore. So I wanted to make sure you'd still come with me today, after school?"

"He's not back," I tell him, my voice only slightly shaking as I say the words.

Rory's face breaks into his widest smile as we walk. "Great!" he exclaims and then recovers himself, looking embarrassed. "I mean, it's not great. It's terrible, of course, that he's not back. I just..."

I watch Rory blush again as he tries to find words that aren't there. It's strange but almost comforting to know that other people go red too. I'm not upset at his words. I don't say anything, and after a while, Rory changes the subject.

While we walk, he doesn't stop talking. He talks so much, I find myself weaving in and out of consciousness, listening to some words, but losing others along the way. It's so different from walking to school with James, the two of us content in our silence, walking in step, breathing in unison. *James*, I think, letting the image of him wash over me. *Will you come back today? Tomorrow? Where are you? What have you done?* I breathe, reminding myself that at least I've told the truth. It's out of my hands. Finding James is not up to me anymore.

In school, Rory can't walk past anyone without shouting some sort of greeting. He smiles at every single person we come across, and everyone smiles back. And because I'm with him, the smiles filter down to me as well, turning me into a walking fireball all the way to English.

We're late to class, and everyone sees us walk in together, including Ms. Martin. She raises her eyebrows and mutters,

"Well, well, well," under her breath but loudly enough for everyone to hear.

What a bitch, I think to myself, feeling myself turn purple.

I want to turn around and walk out again, but Rory doesn't seem to notice. I take my cue from him. He sits next to me, of course.

"Moving on already, Juniper?" says Natasha's pinched voice from behind us. I'm not looking at her, but I can tell her face is twisted with cruelty. Everything about her is mean.

I look over at Rory, but again, his face is passive. He doesn't seem to notice. He doesn't seem to care.

He's waiting for me outside art, as promised. Mr. Stuart has been talking at Medusa for a good ten minutes now, and I've stopped listening. Rory comes into the room, shouts a "Hello" at the teacher, asks me how I am and, of course, smiles at everything.

I don't answer. I'm flustered at his loud entrance, and I'd managed to let the work absorb me again, so I hadn't been thinking about Rory at all. I hadn't been thinking about anything.

"It's going to be quite the piece," says Mr. Stuart, to no one in particular.

I blush, embarrassed and the tiniest bit proud at the same time.

"I agree," says Rory, staring at Medusa. "She's beautiful," he says, and then he smiles at me, and I get the feeling he's not talking about Medusa anymore.

I turn pink, which makes Rory laugh.

"Come on then. Let's go," he says, turning around and walking out.

I mumble a goodbye to Mr. Stuart and follow Rory out.

We walk out of school. The air is crisp this afternoon, everything green around us still shining from the recent rain. We walk up the hill towards the library, and after a while, I realise there's something strange going on. It's the silence. Rory isn't talking. He's been quiet since we left school, and I get the feeling that he's nervous about something.

It's unsettling. It wakes up the fist of nerves in my stomach, and with every step we take, I feel myself starting to unravel. *What am I doing? Why am I going somewhere with Rory Bryan?* There's suddenly something about him that I don't trust, and I have this awful feeling that I'm heading into another ambush. I start thinking I'm crazy for going anywhere with him, for not listening to my instincts. I'm going to have a panic attack, right here, on the way to the library. My breath gets caught in my throat, and for some stupid reason, I feel tears stinging the back of my eyes. The library building looms up ahead of us, and I know I can't go in there with him. I don't want to. I haven't been to the library in years. I used to love it, I remember, but then I stopped coming. And I can't remember why.

Rory doesn't seem to notice my anxiety. He keeps walking, his pace fast. His silence terrifies me, but I don't want to embarrass myself in front of him, so I keep up and try to swallow my panic. My brain keeps alternating between trusting him and knowing he's bad, he's out to hurt me. As we get to the door, he turns to face me.

"Don't be angry," he says, pushing the door open.

My eyes widen. *What does that mean?*

He steps to one side, and before I can turn around and run, I see it. In the middle of the library, surrounded by bookshelves, is a huge box made of glass. And in it is a miniature model of a castle. I stare at it. It's Shackleston Castle. My home.

I'm drawn to it straight away, walking in, forgetting myself and all my anxiety. It's beautiful. Everything is there. Every single statue my father ever built has been recreated, tiny and wonderful, right in front of my eyes. It's the castle as it used to be, in all its glory. Before the fire.

"They put it here a couple of months ago. I wondered if you'd seen it. But Mary over there told me you haven't checked a book out in a couple of years. So... I didn't think you knew it was here," says Rory, from behind me. And when I look back at him, my mouth open in amazement, he's blushing, looking at his feet.

I turn back to the castle, to my old home. I'm amazed. Rory's right: I had no idea this was here. I had no idea it even existed.

It feels right, somehow.

Rory comes and stands next to me. I can feel him twitching, wringing his hands at his sides.

"Who did this?" I ask. My voice surprises me. It sounds strong.

"It was made by St. Augustine's, by their Art Department. It was a few years ago, before I was even there," he says. "They changed the headmaster recently, and he decided to donate it to the library."

I turn back to the model, wondering how they could possibly have known where to put everything, how to make it so perfect. I look at my old home, how it used to be, its beauty, its light. I don't want to cry in front of Rory. I won't.

I feel him next to me. He's silent. He grabs hold of my hand and squeezes.

I squeeze it back.

CHAPTER TWENTY-SIX

JULY 6, 1992, Shackleston,

Last night, Lucy made me happy again, happier than I've been around her for a long time. I'm ashamed to admit how I've been feeling recently, how I've been behaving. I've been resentful and mean, short-tempered. The worst thing is, I knew I was doing it, and I couldn't help it.

But last night, we slept in the same bed for the first time in months. When she came to me in the living room, I was working away, marking exam papers. I heard her, but I didn't turn around. I was worried she'd want to start an argument again, but she didn't. She simply turned off the light.

I was immediately aroused, as I always am whenever she gives me her signal that she wants to be close to me. And I can't remember the last time we were close like that.

It was beautiful and special. It felt different, like we were really creating something. Something tells me we've made a life inside her, and this time it will work out for us. This is exactly what we need. When Lucy becomes a mother, all her problems will disappear I know it. Everything else will feel irrelevant.

Roger talks more and more about his life too, about himself. Today, he shared some of his own problems, the fact that he and Sofia are struggling to have a child. She has a medical condition that will make it difficult for them. Although he smiled when he spoke, he's clearly devastated, and it's hard not to notice Sofia's sadness. She seems to be losing her spirit, losing her shine. She doesn't deserve bad things to happen to her. She really doesn't.

So Roger's throwing himself into his art. Every yard will have a statue, everywhere you look will be a story. He's not doing it for the money or the fame. He doesn't even want to make it public, and God knows he doesn't need the cash. He's doing it for his unborn child, so that he or she would have a magical place to run around in. And even though they may find it difficult to conceive, he carries on. He tells me he doesn't want to be the last person in his family, the last to bear his name. He tells me they have other avenues to explore. He's quietly hopeful, I can tell.

Kata adds to Roger's stress. She's fourteen now, and this semester she's in my class, a great, wild, adolescent ball of trouble. She talks back, she's insolent, she argues and she despises any form of instruction. I get the feeling that most of the time she doesn't even know what she's rebelling against.

Maybe this boring, quiet town isn't enough for her. She's far too lively for it, and I can't help thinking she's going to get herself into trouble. I'd love to help her, but something's holding me back and I'm scared to try. I struggle to see where the line blurs between friend and teacher, so I've decided to stay firmly on the teacher side.

I pray for Roger and his family. They only deserve good things. And I pray for Lucy. I pray for us. I still love her so much. I hope that the closeness from last night was the beginning of a good spell. I hope it was a fresh start, the beginning of something new. The beginning of a new life.

CHAPTER TWENTY-SEVEN

I DON'T know how long I stay there, looking at the model of my old home. After a while, Rory lets go of my hand, and I feel him slip away. I get the feeling he knows I need to be alone for a while.

All my muscles relax as I stare, and my breathing slows right down. It hurts to see my old home looking so beautiful right here in front of me compared to how it looks in real life. But it's a good kind of hurt. It wakes up feelings inside me that I need to feel. I *want* to feel.

Memories rush at me, of all of us, the Slaides and the Creeds, each garden holding a story, an event, the sound of someone laughing. Our families were best friends. We were always together. The Creeds were always around us, and we were always stuck to them. Even *him,* Philip Creed. There are broken pictures of him blinking through my mind. I can't see his face, but I can tell he's smiling, laughing, reading… walking around the grounds with my father. They talked, often. They were friends. They were happy. I think back to the UK Crime Crypt entry. Was he really jealous of my father? Is that why he did it? Why he destroyed my home, my family?

I need to face things and stop pushing everything out. I need to know what James found out about his father. I need to be prepared for it, whatever it is, not just ignore it and run away. I need to be armed with information. *I need to know.*

I turn around, tearing myself away from the castle. I can't see Rory anywhere. There's hardly anyone left in the library at all. On top of my bag is a note, leaving me his number, telling me that he's gone to fetch his car and to call him when I'm done so he can take me home. The note makes me smile, makes me feel warm. Maybe he does care about me? Why else would he bring me here to see this?

I look back to the model, wondering if Kata knew about it, taking centre stage in the library, basking in all its pre-fire glory. Did James know? Did they both know and keep it a secret from me? *No, it's not possible.* The two closest people to me in the world would never have kept something like this from me. I suddenly can't wait to tell Kata about it, can't wait to show it to James. They'll be in awe of it, like I am. Even if we don't talk about the past, even if it hurts, it feels good to see it, like it's helped me. Maybe it would help them too.

I walk over to the computer section and sit, taking a deep breath. I type 'Philip Creed Trial' into the search engine and wait. When the list appears, it looks like everything I've seen before, a reiteration of the entry in the UK Crime Crypt, with no further details. But right at the bottom, an item catches my eye. It's an article in the Gilford Times written by a journalist called Jenny Mara in December 2006, a year and a half after the fire.

It feels so wrong to want to read it. I look around me, aware of the silence. It must be almost closing time. There's no one here apart from the clerk, over at the entrance. I turn back, take a deep breath, and click on the link.

Getting to know The Castle Killer: why the change of heart?
By Jenny Mara

He'd been a fireman for 12 years, but he'd never seen anything like this before. On the night of 5th August, 2002, Jeffrey Buck was struck by the blaze before him. When he arrived at the scene, he remembers a second of hesitation while he tried

to read the fire, tried to find its source. He remembers a moment of awe as he looked at the inferno lighting up the sky, the raging tornado reaching the stars, turning the moon orange. He remembers the smoke, twisting up the walls, the flames smashing through the windows. And the noise. He couldn't tell if it was the fire or the castle itself that was making that sound, that horrifying and animal-like roar of destruction.

He burst into action. But he remembers thinking that this was a fire that would never go out. It would burn forever in the hearts of the people of Shackleston who were beginning to gather at the scene. And he remembers hoping to God that this was an accident or a mistake, a natural cause. Because if someone, somewhere, had meant to start this fire, then they must have been, in his words, the cruellest, the most calculating, the most despicable, sick bastard in the world.

As it turns out there was no accident and no natural cause. The fire at Shackleston Castle was started by a man, a man who confessed in court and is now imprisoned for life. He didn't just start the fire that destroyed Shackleston's pride and joy, its showpiece monument. He started the fire that killed the family inside it, the well-known and well-loved artist, Roger Slaide, along with his wife and her father. They left behind an orphan, eight-year-old Juniper.

Like most of the country, I followed the trial of Philip Creed with some interest. And like most of the country, I was split in two. Up there in the dock, I saw a man with guilt written all over his face. But Jeffrey Buck's words rang alarm bells in my head. Philip Creed looked guilty, sure, but he was also shrouded by a sadness so deep I could feel it emanating from him inside the courtroom. Was he the 'cruellest, most calculating, most despicable man in the world'? Was he really a 'sick bastard'?

So I watched the prosecution present their evidence. It was

weak. They didn't have much, just some character statements from what I, for one, would certainly call unreliable witnesses.

First, there was Creed's wife, Lucy. It was from her that came the jealousy theory which eventually provided the prosecution's motive. She told the court that her husband was mean and spiteful. That he'd been wildly jealous of her best friend, Roger Creed, not just because of his success in the art world, but also because of her relationship with him. They'd been so close, she said. She wept at the loss of her childhood friend, and the whole world wept with her.

Then came the other witnesses. Prominent members of the Shackleston community. Mr. Ash, the local butcher, claimed that Creed had often spoken of feeling unwelcome in the town. Creed's boss, Headmaster Simon Cooke, alleged that Creed was constantly hanging around the Slaides 'like a bad smell, whining that Roger was taking all the limelight.'

I felt something lacking in all three testimonies. Truth.

There was no concrete evidence, nothing to place Creed at the scene of the crime. Yes, he'd run away and hadn't come forward willingly. But still, was it enough to convict him?

I didn't know, and the jury didn't seem to know either. But just when it looked like Creed was going to receive a not guilty verdict, something happened. He changed his plea. He pleaded guilty.

I looked at the man in the dock in front of me. I watched how he spoke, how he held himself. He wasn't the cruellest, most despicable man in the world. He was desperately miserable. The more I thought about it, the more I couldn't stop thinking about it. He was about to be acquitted. Why would he change his plea? Why would someone do that, be so insistent they were innocent and then change their mind? And once he'd changed his mind, he stopped talking entirely. He didn't say another word.

That was it. He looked dejected and shrugged his shoulders, even when questioned by his own, flabbergasted lawyer. He was held in contempt of court for refusing to speak. He said he was guilty, over and over again. And that was it.

I couldn't get his face out of my head, and I couldn't stop thinking about why he changed his plea. I couldn't for the life of me come up with a reason. But being the journalist I am, I had to find out.

Philip Creed refused to see me. It's unclear whether or not he's had any visitors in the year and a half that's elapsed since the fire, and I can't get this information from the prison. However, I do know that he hasn't requested visiting rights from either of his sons.

I took a little trip to Shackleston myself. I asked around. I went to the library, the school, the high street. I saw Mr. Ash, Mr. Cooke. Everyone spoke fondly of Lucy Creed and her boys, but no one, not one person would say his name out loud. No one would talk about Philip Creed.

I tried to talk to Lucy herself, but she slammed the door in my face.

I tried to talk to Kata Panos, the sister of the poor, deceased Sofia Slaide. She wouldn't take my calls, and she wouldn't even open the door. Her behaviour intrigued me, so I decided to start with her and dig a little deeper into Ms Panos.

She'd been living with her father in the castle's gatehouse at the time of the fire. A regular socialite, the twenty-six-year-old had been out when the fire started. She'd returned late that night, only to discover that her family was dead, and she had inherited guardianship of her niece.

Incidentally, the castle and its grounds, along with all of

Roger Slaide's fortune, were also inherited by Ms. Panos. It's strange to think of a twenty-six-year-old inheriting an eight-year-old girl, along with the fortune that goes with her. And perhaps she had more in common with Philip Creed than anyone can know.

Because Shackleston is a strange town. It's unwelcoming to people from outside its community. It protects its own. It's a town that feels vindicated by the outcome of the trial, happy that the American, the foreigner, has been put away. The townsfolk are fiercely protective of Lucy Creed and her sons, but not of her outsider-husband. They're fiercely protective of Juniper Slaide, being the daughter of the local prominent artist. Understandably, Juniper suffers from a severe anxiety disorder since the fire, and the town does its best to cosset her and to make exceptions. But her guardian, Kata, being originally from Greece, is outcast.

And this strange town protected all of them from me, a nasty stranger, who was told to go back to where I'd come from.

My curiosity was piqued. And I wondered, why did they stay? Why did Lucy Creed continue to stay in Shackleston and raise her sons in the house of a convicted murderer?

Why did Kata Panos choose to stay in the castle's gatehouse, force herself and her niece to walk past the wreckage of their lives every day?

There is something bizarre about the whole case. Did Philip Creed do it? Or is his confession a lie? I can't get over the feeling that something isn't quite right about this story. And I plan to uncover what it is.

As I read Jenny Mara's article, I feel myself go cold. Her words spark a fear in me. They make me want to run, to hide, to go back to not knowing, not thinking, not talking about the past. But at the same time, I can't help this morbid curiosity. I need to know what she found out. *Is this what James found? Is it possible that Philip Creed didn't do it?* The hairs on the back of my neck start to prickle. *If Philip Creed didn't do it, it would mean that someone else did...* No, it's not possible. *It can't be.*

I'm about to click away from the page and look for follow-up articles by Jenny Mara, but all of a sudden I sense there's someone behind me, and I freeze. I have this awful feeling I'm doing something wrong. I need to cover up my screen, not let anyone see what I'm looking at. I fumble as I try to shut it down, get rid of it, before whoever it is can see it.

But I don't have time to do anything because I'm yanked out of my chair, away from the computer. Trick Creed is in my face, grabbing my arm, his nostrils flaring as he pulls me up towards him.

"What are you doing?" he hisses at me, his eyes blazing into mine.

I feel myself shrinking in fear, trying to wrestle out of his grip but he holds on tight to my arm. I don't want him to see the screen behind me, so I try to block it with my body, but he wrenches me back. It's too late. He's seen it. His eyes flicker over the article, quickly, briefly, and I can tell it's not the first time he's seen it.

"Why are you looking at that? Where's James?" he says, his voice sharp, angry.

I squirm under his gaze. He looks like James, but there's more of him. The dark blue eyes are darker, the coarse blonde hair is thicker. Everything about him is bigger, wilder, more intense.

"Look, I've told you everything I know," I say, trying to

meet his eyes. "James went to see your dad. He… he said he was going to find proof that your dad was innocent."

"That's a lie," Trick roars in my face. I see the vein bulging in his neck, and I'm terrified he's going to hurt me or worse. "James would never go and see my father," Trick says. "He despises him. We all do."

"Haven't the police checked it out?" I say, panicking. "Didn't they call the prison and find out where James went afterwards? They can find him. They can find out when he went there, when he left…"

Trick lets go of my arm and takes a step back. He deflates right in front of me. All his anger, all his strength disappears. "They *are* checking," he says, quietly this time. "We haven't heard back from them yet." He looks right into my eyes, searching for something. "I don't understand it. James tells me everything. Why would he not tell me about this?"

I frown, confused. What does he mean, James tells him everything? James hates him.

"We have to find him," Trick continues, his voice breaking, unaware of my confusion. "Something's happened to him, Joo. Something bad." To my surprise, his eyes start filling with tears as he says the words.

I don't get it. I don't understand the pain in Trick's voice. I can't reconcile his words with everything I know about him. This evil, cruel twin, who hates James more than anything in the world, is standing in front of me, worrying about where James is? It doesn't make sense.

"Why?" I whisper. "Why do you care? You hate James. You can't stand each other…"

My voice trails off when I see his face crumple. I see the pain so clearly in him now that I can feel it. I've hurt him, and it's genuine.

"What are you talking about?" he says, perplexed. "I don't hate James. I could never hate James." His voice is quiet, less violent now, the tears still there in his eyes although he's doing his best not to let them fall. All the anger, all the fight in him has gone.

I shake my head. What he's saying doesn't make sense. Has he forgotten everything he's done to hurt James? He just doesn't sound like the Trick I know. He doesn't sound like the Trick who had to be sent away for fear that he'd hurt his brother. Or worse.

He looks back at the screen. "I had no idea James even thought about our dad," he says. "James and I… we're so close, I don't understand why he wouldn't tell me what he's up to."

Close? His words make me reel, make me question everything I've ever known. But Trick is oblivious to my confusion. He has no idea the effect his words are having on me.

"We're linked," he says, looking at me again. "I only have to look at him to know what he's thinking. I can always feel him, no matter what. I can feel what he's feeling. I know when he's hurt, I know when he's confused, I know when he's happy. It's not even weird; it's just always been this way. It's the same for him. It's like he already knows what I'm going to do, even before I do. So him looking into all this stuff," he says, "pointing at the screen behind me, "is just weird. I don't believe it."

"But it's true," I tell him, trying to push past how crazy this is. "He told me he found something, something that proved your dad was innocent…"

Trick shakes his head. "But what?" he says. "What did he find?"

I turn around to look at the article. Could it be this? Is this what James found? When I look back at Trick, he's shaking his head. "It's not that," he says, reading my mind. "James and I read that one years ago. We laughed at it at the time. I remember."

None of this feels right. It can't be. Trick and James hate each other. This must be a joke. An idea forms in my head. "If you're linked, then can't you feel where he is now?"

"That's the thing," says Trick, his voice breaking again. He looks away. He's trying so hard to stop the tears from falling that it brings tears to my own eyes. "I can't feel anything anymore."

The weight of his words falls heavily in the air around, and I swallow, not sure if I can trust myself to speak.

"You have to help me, Joo. I know James would probably hate to know that we're talking, that I've even seen you. I have no idea what he's told you about me, but I don't care. I just can't think of anyone else who can help me. Something's happened to him. We have to find him, please..."

The terror and desperation in his voice are frightening me. He can't be right. *Of course nothing's happened to James. Of course James is coming back.* The police will call the prison. They'll find out where James went, and they'll bring him back.

But I nod, because I don't know what else to do and because I don't want to be here anymore, looking at him, making my heart ache and my brain spin. For a moment, his wild eyes seem to be satisfied at my response. Then he turns around and walks out, desperate to not let me see the tears falling down his face.

James is coming back, I tell myself. He'll come back and I need to be prepared for whatever it is he's found out. I look back at the screen, back at Philip Creed's name staring at me. So much feels wrong, like I'm missing so much information. I never wanted to know before, but now, all of a sudden, I need answers. I need to talk to someone who was there. There's only one thing for it. Regardless of how much it hurts her to think about the past, I need to talk to Kata.

CHAPTER TWENTY-EIGHT

DECEMBER 23, 1992, Shackleston,

I think I must be in shock. I know I'm angry, disgusted- I don't know how else to be. All I know is that I have to write it down, put it on paper, try to make sense of what's just happened.

The dinner party at the castle tonight was a special one, not in the servant's quarters but in the main dining hall. Roger had some interest from an important gallery, and all the buyers were coming. It was a big deal for him and his family, and he wanted us to be there. Having me there, with my 'American charm,' would reassure him, he said, would help him to say the things that he's often too shy to say. All month the family had been nervous, excited, the anticipation of success just around the corner. I was excited for them. I thought Lucy was too.

We got ready at home. Lucy had been in one of her low phases recently, more quiet than usual, spending more time in that room. I wasn't dealing with it well, I'll admit. I think I've just lost my patience. Honestly, I'm bored of it.

Tonight, I was ready before Lucy, and I was excited. I'd bought a tuxedo since the dinner would be a formal affair, and festive too, so close to Christmas. When she appeared at the top of the stairs, I could see the bottom of her long black dress, shiny and swaying around her heels as she stepped down. I could see her face, glowing and gorgeous, her blonde hair piled up on her head. She took my breath away, and I couldn't believe the transformation, the effort she'd made for her friend. I actually felt proud.

But her body was obscured by the shadow of the chandelier in the staircase. It was only as she came down the stairs that I noticed the rest of her dress. I noticed the tiny bulge of her belly, invisible to everyone but us, containing our secret pregnancy, a secret I hadn't even told Roger. I saw the top of the dress, the plunging neckline, the barely-there straps loosely hanging over her shoulders. Her arms were naked, her neck was exposed; the ugly red gashes on her body glared at me under the harsh light.

It was the first time since I've known her that she's dared to show any part of her skin. Why would she decide to show off her body tonight of all nights? She reached the bottom of the stairs and twirled for me, asked me if I liked it.

Did I like it? Of course I didn't like it. It would have been great for me to think that she was coming to terms with her past, uncovering herself, little by little, gaining the confidence she needs to forget, to deal with it head on. But not like this. Not on a night so important to Roger and his family.

I didn't answer her. I couldn't.

Her face fell, and she hated me for not saying the words I was supposed to say. And I knew then that because of my failure to tell her she looked beautiful, she'd be in a terrible mood, one that would set the tone for the whole evening. My heart sank as we got in the car and drove off in silence.

When we arrived, I was embarrassed for her. I couldn't help it. I saw a tiny flicker of shock on Roger's face as he saw her, but then he took it in his stride. He composed himself and embraced her.

I watched Sofia take a step back before rushing to greet her. I saw Kata turn around and gag when she entered the drawing room. I saw Papou look lost and not know where to look. I saw the guests, who stared and stared.

And I watched Lucy smile. I saw her relish the attention. She walked straight in and sat down.

But this isn't what ruined the night for everyone, for Roger, for his family. This isn't what ruined the night for me and, quite frankly, ruined what little opinion I have left of her. Tonight, she did the unthinkable. She got drunk, drank everything that came her way. She's pregnant with my child, and she looked me right in the eyes and downed champagne, then wine, then more champagne. After dinner, she could barely stand, and when Papou brought out the ouzo, she held out her glass. She smiled at me as she drank, defying me to say something, challenging me to make a scene in front of Roger's buyers. Inside, I was breaking. But how could I cause a scene when Roger was trying so hard to impress?

I took Lucy to one side and hissed at her to stop this awful game. What she said turned my heart to ice. I'm doing what I do best, she said. I'm killing it. Then she smiled and walked away. Stunned, I followed her back into the room, and that's where I saw her smoking one of Roger's cigarettes, the smoke curling around her pregnant body like a snake. I exploded, I couldn't help it. I saw red. I forgot who and where I was. I actually wanted to hit her. I wanted to knock that smile off her face. I wanted her to take back those words. I lost it.

Sofia, protective as always, came flying to Lucy's defence. Let her loosen up for a bit, she said. It's so nice to see her enjoying herself.

I looked around the room then and realised what I must sound like. Papou averted his eyes. Roger looked at me, embarrassed. His clients must have thought I was some kind of controlling husband, upset with his wife for drinking, for smoking. Hell, they probably thought I'd *done that to her skin.*

I couldn't take the looks, the glares in my direction. So I blurted it out. I told the whole room Lucy was pregnant.

There was a shocked silence. Everyone tore their eyes away from me and looked at her. Everyone watched her pick up the bottle of ouzo and fill up her glass. The smile never left her face.

I walked out.

Roger followed me and guess what? He started trying to explain. He defended her. I tried to listen to him, to let his words calm me, but it was impossible. She's damaging my child, the only thing I've ever wanted, and there's nothing I can do about it. Roger told me to be patient, to not hate her, that I'm good for her, I'm making her better.

But am I? Right now, I don't feel like protecting Lucy anymore. Not this version of her anyway, this twisted, horrible monster. She's nothing like the woman I married. I have to keep reminding myself about our wedding day, the vows we took. Reluctantly, I need to remind myself of one line, in particular.

Yours, for better, for worse.

CHAPTER TWENTY-NINE

"HOW was your date?" Kata asks me as I walk into the warmth of the gatehouse. She gets up from the kitchen table, her eyes shining with smiles and excitement, ready to hear about Rory.

I swallow and shake my head. I watch the smile slide from her face. She tries to give me a hug, but I feel stiff in her arms and I can't quite return it.

"What's wrong?" she says.

I sit, and she sits opposite me. I take a deep breath. She's watching me, waiting, fiddling with her thumbs.

"Nothing's wrong, Kata," I tell her. "Not really. It's just that Rory took me to the library today, and you won't believe what's there..."

But I stop. Kata's gone pale, her grey eyes bulge. She tries to recover, but it's too late. I saw it in her face. She knew about the model.

I feel so deceived in that moment that tears spring to my eyes. "Why didn't you tell me it was there?" I whisper, not quite believing she could keep something like that from me.

My aunt sighs and leans back in her chair. "I'm sorry, Joo," she says. "I... I didn't think you'd want to see it. You've tried so hard to forget about the past. You won't even look at the castle, and you never visit the statues... I didn't think you'd want to have it thrust in your face like that."

I take another deep breath, taking in her words. It makes sense, I suppose. She was just trying to protect me. And she's right. I have tried hard to forget about the past. But not anymore. I swallow.

"Maybe it's time I remembered," I say, my voice quiet.

Kata's eyebrows fly up in shock. She starts to shake her head, but I press on. "Maybe it's time we talked about it, Kata. Maybe it's time *we* remembered. Together."

"We don't talk about the past," she whispers, paler than I've ever seen her. And then something dawns on me. Maybe it was never me that didn't want to remember. Maybe it was Kata all along. All those times she'd say those words, '*we don't talk about the past,*' all those times she taught me how to focus my mind on other things. It was she who couldn't take the pain of remembering. Not me.

I don't want to hurt her like this, but I need to carry on. I need to know. "Kata, while I was at the library I did a bit of research... about the fire, about Philip Creed..."

The look on her face stops me again. In an instant, she switches from pale to flushed, from raw pain to blazing anger.

"That boy!" she says, hitting the table with her fist as she pushes herself up from her chair, almost sending it flying.

I flinch.

"Putting ideas in your head like this! What's he been saying now? What's all this rubbish about his father?"

I stop her. "Kata, James hasn't said anything because he isn't back yet."

Her lips part in shock. She puts both hands on the back of the chair to steady herself. Her voice turns into a whisper again, and I can see fear in her eyes. "What do you mean?"

"I haven't seen James. It wasn't him I saw- it was Trick," I tell her.

Kata is silent. All her irritation at James seems to have disappeared. She looks like she's been hit hard, like my words have slapped her.

"That's why we need to talk about the past, Kata," I tell her, as gently as I can. "Because James found something out, something that made him think his dad's innocent. What if he's found something out that changes everything?" I hate the effect that my words are having on Kata, but I have to continue, I need to make her understand. "What if Philip Creed really is innocent?" I say "I've been reading about the trial today, and there are all these questions, all these things that don't seem right. Did you know that he changed his plea? He started off by saying he didn't do it… I'm sorry, Kata," I say, looking at her, how white she is, the tears in her eyes, how much my words are hurting her. I look down. "I think the past is about to be dragged up whether we want it to or not, and I think we need to be prepared for it, that's all. So we need to talk about it. We need to talk about it now…"

"Juniper, stop," says Kata, her voice quiet, but urgent. She's using my full name, and there's an undercurrent to her words, a tone I've never heard from her before. It makes me look up at her again, those grey eyes bearing down into mine. "You need to leave this alone," she says. Her voice is soft, but she's clenching her jaw, and she looks hard, unforgiving. "Nothing good can ever come from digging up the past. So you give this up, right now, do you understand me? What's done, is done. And that's final."

"But Kata," I say, not understanding why she sounds so cold, why she looks so rigid all of a sudden. "We need to talk about it because James is coming back, and when he does…"

She slams her hands on the table again, making me jump. "You listen to me now. You'll give this up if you know what's good for you. Is that clear?"

She doesn't wait for me to respond. She turns around and walks outside, slamming the door of the gatehouse behind her.

I stay still, not daring to breathe. Her words scaring me,

scarring me, leaving me with only questions burning through my brain. It's more than the fact that she doesn't want to talk about the past because it's too painful. She's covering something up. She's hiding something.

It's all wrong. She knew about the model of the castle. And her tone, the hint of threat in her words as she spoke to me just now... And how she lied to the police, easy, like it was nothing. The hand in my stomach lurches, making me gag. I can't shake the feeling that something's very wrong, and Kata's right in the middle of it.

CHAPTER THIRTY

MAY 6, 1993, Shackleston,

We lost the baby, as I knew we would. Lucy cried for days. I could hear her upstairs, and I couldn't understand why she was so upset. I still don't get it. I didn't care about her tears then, and I don't care about them now.

She did everything she could to lose that baby. There's no way now that I could reassure her that the other two miscarriages weren't her fault. Somehow, and it pains me to even think it, but maybe the other miscarriages were on purpose too. She's too broken for me to fix. I give up. I've stopped trying.

I feel myself becoming more and more hateful, more and more bitter.

And now there's something else happening in my life, something I can't seem to control, something that Lucy would despise. Kata, fifteen years old, has decided she's in love with me. The poor girl came to me last Christmas, on the night of the dreadful dinner party, and tried to console me, tried to make me feel better. She put her arms around me and not in a child-like way. Something about her gestures were suggestive, wrong. At the time, I was upset, and I didn't deal with her advances well. I sent her away, telling her she was just a stupid child.

She sulked for months. But she's convinced she's in love with me, and she's persistent. She lingers after class, tries to tease me, blushing when she asks me questions and letting her arm brush against mine whenever she can. She's growing up, losing that air of innocence that goes hand-in-hand with childhood. And, while Lucy gives me nothing but scorn, I find it harder and harder to resist Kata, who's turning into a woman before my very eyes.

I can't think about these things; I mustn't. I'm Kata's teacher, and Roger's best friend. But this is what Lucy's done to me, what she's reduced me to. I'm the loneliest, most pathetic human being in the world. Everything she does pushes me further away, and while I try to ignore Kata and walk away from her whenever I can, I find myself thinking about her, late at night when I'm on my own. Sometimes I imagine myself with her. Sometimes I imagine how much pain that would cause Lucy. And the thought of causing her pain makes me feel better.

CHAPTER THIRTY-ONE

I DON'T hear Kata come back, and she's not there when I wake up in the morning. I walk into the kitchen feeling disorientated by the bright sun shining through the window and groggy because I'm not even sure if I slept at all. I spent a good part of the night tossing and turning, stinging from Kata's words. The picture of my aunt in my mind from last night, her face twisted with that quiet fury, is so far away from the Kata I know and love that I can barely remember it. It doesn't even feel real anymore. I've been trying to persuade myself that I imagined it. It wasn't my Kata at all.

But it *was* her. And she's been lying to me. I get the feeling she's been lying to me for a long time.

I keep hearing that threat in her voice. *You'll leave this alone if you know what's good for you.* I've never disobeyed my aunt before, but there's no way I can leave this alone now. Still, the guilt is ingrained in me, like it's automatic, as I use my phone to run the search online. It's not just because Kata told me to leave it alone, but it's because I'm using the Internet on my phone again, something we don't do because it costs money we don't have. Then I remember the article by Jenny Mara, saying Kata had inherited my father's fortune. *Fortune? What fortune?*

I've never once asked Kata about money. I've never even thought about it; I just always knew we didn't have any. We had money back when people were visiting the statues, but that stopped after the fire, and Kata's always been so careful about money. But then… she's never worked, I realise. It feels like there's another secret, yet another thing my Aunt has kept from me.

As the memory of her anger makes me flinch again, I don't feel so guilty anymore. I type 'Philip Creed Trial' into the search bar and wait.

It takes ages to load, but when the words finally appear, they don't give me any more information than they did yesterday. So I start again, this time typing 'Jenny Mara Articles' into the search bar.

Nothing happens. It's so slow! I curse my phone. I think about going outside, walking up to the bridge, seeing if I can pick up a signal there. But then there's a knock at the window and I look up to see Rory's face beaming into the kitchen.

Damn it. I'd forgotten about Rory Bryan.

He breezes through the door, shouting his hello and disturbing the silence, upsetting my concentration. I try to smile back at him, but I wish he wasn't here, no matter how hot he looks. He's wearing a dark purple t-shirt that clings ever so slightly to his body, and all of a sudden my stomach decides to go on the roller coaster ride of its life. I feel ridiculous, like any self-control I have just evaporates around him.

"What's for lunch?" he says, clapping his hands and walking over to the fridge. I'm about to tell him that I'm sorry, I can't do this today, but he looks so happy and so eager I can't bring myself to say it. And now I'm panicking. Because Rory Bryan is in my kitchen, and Kata invited him to lunch, and she's not even around to help me deal with it.

"Err, Juniper, there's nothing in here..." he says, ignoring my silence and opening the fridge door, sticking his head inside. "Except this," he exclaims, putting an envelope in front of me. "It was taped to the middle shelf."

I feel my heart race as I look at the envelope. It's got my name on it, so I open it, puzzled, worrying about what Kata's done now.

Dear Joo,

I'm so sorry about yesterday, and you're right. We do need to talk. We can talk tonight, if you want.

In the meantime, try to enjoy yourself and your lunch with Rory. There's a picnic basket in the pantry.

Love Kata xxx

PS. Hi Rory

Guilt hits me instantly. I may have forgotten that Rory was coming but my aunt didn't. And she's obviously gone to the trouble of preparing a picnic for us... The weight lifts off my shoulders with her apology, and relief shoots through me from head to toe.

Rory's jumping about from foot to foot next to me, like an excited puppy. "What is it? Is it a treasure hunt? An Easter egg hunt?"

His enthusiasm is infectious. I roll my eyes and walk over to the pantry, pulling out a huge, heavy picnic basket. Knowing my aunt, it'll be filled with odd things and only some of them edible.

Rory is smiling with glee as he takes the picnic basket from me and tries to shake it, impressed by its weight.

My appreciation for Kata shoots sky-high, and I want to hug her. She may have lied to me, but she's done it for my own good, I know it. She would never hurt me. She's sorry, and she accepts that we need to talk. The relief almost makes me feel light-headed.

I look up at Rory, excitement radiating from his whole body. All of a sudden I feel like I actually want to spend time with him. In fact, I can't think of anything better than spending the afternoon with someone who has no idea about anything that's going on in my life. He's never once asked me if I know where James is; he's never tried to talk about it. It's like he exists on his own planet, and I want to live there with him, away from everything, just for one day. What harm can it do to take my mind off everything for the afternoon? I lead Rory out of the gatehouse and towards the woods. I know exactly where we're going for our picnic.

As usual, he chit-chats the whole way. I try to focus on what he's saying, to listen to him and not float off in my head. When we enter the woods, I almost want to tell him about the statues that are surrounding us as we walk. They're hard to see through the trees, but they're there, their colourless eyes following us as we move. I know he'd probably jump for joy, but he'll want to stop and look at them all, and I don't think I'm ready for that yet.

"So, you didn't call me yesterday to come and get you at the library. I came back, by the way, but you'd already gone." says Rory, stepping over a fallen branch.

"I'm sorry," I tell him, not wanting to admit I was so shaken by Trick and the article I'd read about Philip Creed. "I did want to say thanks though. For taking me there." My voice sounds just about all right. It's getting easier to talk to him, and I'm not glowing a horrible shade of red.

He nods, smiling.

I want to ask him why he did it, but before I can, we're at the clearing, and the lake is right in front of us. It silences even Rory.

Its beauty stuns me every time, even though I know it off by heart. The huge stretch of water is hidden away out of sight from the castle, out of sight from the gatehouse. And it's dazzling, especially with the water so still and glistening in this sun. Rory and I are motionless, like time has stopped around us, and all I can hear is him breathing it all in. I lead him through the overgrown grass to the bank of sand, my very own private beach.

My thoughts try to turn to James because I've never been here with anyone except him, but I don't let them. I'll think about James later. *Try to enjoy yourself*, said Kata's note, and maybe I should, especially if she's prepared to talk to me later. Whatever James has found out, Kata and I can face it together.

Rory starts to unpack the basket, laying out the cloth on the sand. Out comes the food, and it makes my eyes and mouth water. Kata's Greek specialities: pita wraps, black olives, fresh feta cheese and a beautiful-looking filo pie, oozing with creamy spinach. Inside my head, I thank Kata again. She must have spent hours fixing all this up last night. I can tell by the look of delight on Rory's face that he's happy too. But when is he ever not happy? I think, watching him.

After the food comes the weirdness. Rory practically squeals with delight as he starts pulling things out of a basket that could have been packed by Mary Poppins. An umbrella (in case it rains). Two books (in case we get bored of each other or, in Kata's warped mind, decide to read to each other). A broken clay pot and some glue (OK, message received). A tin of beige wall paint which flabbergasts me... No idea what she was thinking with that one, especially as there's no paintbrush to be seen. A torch (in case we stay out late, and it gets dark...). Then Rory pulls out two towels and smiles mischievously at me.

"I guess she wants us to go swimming," he says, his eyes twinkling at me as he looks over at the lake. He's on his knees, making a big show of emptying out the rest of the basket, and then he winks at me.

"Nope, no swimming costumes in here," he says, turning

the basket over and shaking it out to make sure.

I turn bright red at his words. *Thanks a lot, Kata.*

She's messing with us, of course, because it's still far too cold for swimming. But Kata's basket is making me feel so much better. It's like she's packed her sense of humour in it with all the food and weirdness, and that means she's fine. There's nothing wrong. She's just being Kata. She's being herself; she's being normal. *Phew.*

For the next hour or so, I surprise myself by enjoying Rory's company. We eat Kata's amazing food, and Rory talks and talks. More about his family, sometimes about the castle, asking questions that he answers himself. I try to talk about the English project that I haven't even looked at yet, but he waves it away and simply says, "Later." I begin to feel at ease with him, focusing on his voice and his stories, even laughing at his jokes.

When he announces that he's full, he lies down on the blanket, closes his eyes and goes completely silent. *Is he asleep?* He starts snoring softly, and I'm astounded at his ability to be two opposite things in such a short space of time. It's almost like he lives each moment in time to its maximum point, with no regard for the previous moment or the next.

I'm impressed. I wish I was like that. I want to be like him. I lie down too and close my eyes, the sun hot on my face. I try to focus on relaxing, focus on my breathing. And surprisingly, my body seems to listen. I drift off.

But I can't stop the dreams. I dream about before, when the castle was alive. I dream about Papou, pretending to be the monster in the lake and chasing us around, making James and me laugh so much it hurt.

I dream of Kata, of how she was back then. She was so much fun, so pretty, so wild. She was my mother's younger sister, my naughty aunt who told stories that shouldn't be told to children and did things we weren't supposed to know about. She stayed out late and often made Papou swear at her in Greek while my father looked on in amusement.

I dream about my mother, Sofia, ethereal and floating around, like she was on a different planet. James and I would be told to be quiet, to not wake her while she slept all day. And when she'd get up, sometimes late at night, she'd stay in her nightdress and glide around outside for a while, pale and almost ghostly, before going back to bed again.

The sound of a twig snapping startles me out of my dreams. I'm wide awake in an instant, desperate to get away from the images that are invading my head. I haven't dreamt about my mother in a long time. I sit up, rubbing my face, and then look behind me at where the noise was coming from.

My heart skips a beat as I make out the outline of James, and just as quickly realise it's Trick. I can tell from the way he's standing, from the tension that seems to be filling up the air around me. He's hovering at the edge of the trees, staring at me, scowling.

The fist in my stomach starts swirling around at the sight of him standing there, waiting for me in the woods. I look over at Rory, who's on his back, sleeping peacefully. Lying there in the sun, his brown curls framing his still half-smiling face, he looks like one of my father's statues. I don't want to see Trick now. I want to stay here, with Rory, where there's only fun and enthusiasm, where people smile even when they're asleep.

I get up, stumbling a little, careful not to wake him. Whatever Trick's doing here, Rory's not a part of it. I'm going to tell Trick he's not welcome. That he's delusional if he thinks something's happened to James. That James will come back when he's finished doing whatever it is he's doing.

I feel myself shaking as I walk towards him. At first I think he's standing still, but as I get closer, I notice his fists clenching at his sides, the angry twitch in his jaw. His eyes are feverish, like he's been awake for too long, and the fear bubbles up inside me again. My heart is pumping hard and fast in my head.

"What do you want?" I ask, my voice shrill. I'm careful not to get too close to him. He looks so angry I worry he's going to grab me again.

Trick looks over at Rory, and when he looks back at me, there's an accusation in his eyes that I don't understand. I find myself feeling ashamed even though I don't know why.

"We need to talk," Trick says, his voice simmering with rage. He takes a step towards me, and I automatically step back, my heart racing.

I shake my head. "Not now," I tell him. "Not today."

He looks like he might be about to explode. "Yes, now. My brother disappears, and you're with Rory Bryan? Don't you even care about James at all?"

I frown and feel myself getting hot. I realise the two boys know each other. Of course they do. They both went to St. Augustine's before Rory left and came to Shackleston School. But Trick has no right to judge me. And I'm desperate for Rory to be kept out of this, whatever it is.

"Of course I care about James," I tell him, surprised at my own voice, at how angry I sound. "But James has left me here alone. He's gone off doing God-knows-what to try and hurt my family. So yes, I'm here with Rory, and I'm having fun, and I don't want to think about you or your brother right now. OK?"

I'm shocked at my outburst, shocked at how easy it is to say the words. And by the looks of things, Trick is shocked too. He is open-mouthed for a second, and before he can reply, I carry on, feeling empowered. "James hasn't disappeared, you know. He hasn't gone missing. He's coming back." I try to look at him as though he's stupid for even thinking it. If he's as close to his brother as he says he is, then he should know this about James. *James is coming back.*

But Trick shakes his head. "Do you really believe that, Joo?" he says, quietly now, looking at me, his eyes searching mine for signs that I'm lying. I don't see anger anymore. Only that horrible sadness that I caught a glimpse of in the library. "Stop and think about it for a minute, please," he says. "James would never leave you for this long. He would have come back by now. You know he would. He's been gone for two weeks, and have you heard from him?"

I shake my head, feeling a little sick. I start to repeat what James is up to, that he's gone looking for answers about his father, but Trick interrupts me.

"He never went to the prison," says Trick. "The police called us yesterday. He made an appointment to see my dad, but he never turned up."

My eyes widen. *James never went there? Then where did he go?*

Trick carries on. "I guess you were right. He was looking into the past. I didn't think he cared about Dad, but the fact that he made an appointment to see him says it all..." Trick looks so crestfallen at his words that it almost makes me want to reach out to him. Then his face turns hard again. "Do you really think James could go for two weeks without seeing you?" he says. "You've seen each other every day for the past- how long?"

I look back at Rory, wanting to remind myself that he's there. I don't want to hear these words. Trick looks at Rory too, his face darkening.

"Look," he says again, forcing me to face him, trying to

control himself. "James has disappeared, whether you want to believe it or not. He never went to see my father. And I need to talk to you, OK? I found out some stuff… about James. About your family. You need to listen to me, Joo, please," he begs.

I want to turn around. I want him to leave. I don't want to listen to what he has to say. But my feet are glued to the ground, and I can't move. Something about the desperation in his voice makes me stay.

"After that article you read yesterday, I looked up that journalist, Jenny Mara. I wanted to see what else she found out."

My voice is a whisper. "And?" I say, because I'd been curious about that too.

"There was nothing," he says. "Jenny Mara never wrote another article. She disappeared, Joo," he says, searching my eyes again. "She went missing after that first article she wrote about my dad. Don't you think that's weird?"

I freeze, shock coursing through me. *That doesn't mean anything.*

"There's more," he says. "I found this in James's room." He thrusts an envelope at me. It's got my name on it, in James's handwriting. I don't want it, but it ends up in my hands anyway. I look down. It's been opened.

When I look back up at Trick, he looks guilty. "Yeah, I opened it. Sorry. But Joo, I don't understand it. It's got something to do with you, and it's got something to do with James disappearing. And you need to help me figure it out. Because when I looked through his room, there was nothing there. It was like someone had been through it and taken out everything personal. Everything except this, cello-taped to the underneath of his sock drawer."

Hands shaking, I pull the paper out. It's a single page, a

letter from Dr Banner's office. A medical record from 1992, belonging to my mother. I blink. I've seen this before.

"This has got nothing to do with anything," I tell him, as firmly as I can. I want him gone. I want to get rid of him. I want to be alone, to disappear inside my head.

"Then why was it hidden under his sock drawer? Why did he put it an envelope for you if it doesn't mean anything? Please think about this, Joo. What if Jenny Mara was made to disappear because she found something out?" His voice breaks as he picks up speed, trying to get the words out. "What if James was made to disappear because he found out the same thing? What if my dad didn't start the fire? What if the person who did it is still out there? Joo, please..."

I close my eyes and try to block out his words. I don't want to hear him anymore. I turn away.

"I'm not going anywhere, you know. I'll find out what happened," he says to my back, his voice rising.

I turn back to him. "Nothing has happened," I tell him, as firmly as I can. "James is coming back."

But as I say the words, they sound hollow and empty in my mouth.

Trick shakes his head, his eyes forming into slits. "OK, well you carry on believing that if you want. Go back to *him*," he says, looking over at Rory in disgust. "But ask yourself this. Don't you think it's weird that Rory Bryan is all over you like a rash since the day James disappeared? You can't trust him, Joo."

I walk away. That's it. I don't want to hear him say anything about Rory. *Don't bring him into this. Please.*

But Trick continues, calling after me. "Don't you think it's a bit suspicious? Has he mentioned James at all? Has he mentioned me? Has he even told you about us?"

What?! I turn around, shocked at his words. *What does that mean?*

"I didn't think so," says Trick. And he turns around and walks away.

CHAPTER THIRTY-TWO

4th OCTOBER, 1993, Shackleston,

I can only imagine saying these words to Lucy's face and seeing the pain they'd cause. Sometimes I actually close my eyes and watch myself telling her everything that's been going on behind her back, all the things that would hurt her, make her feel as I've felt these past few years.

But I can't. I'm not like her. I'm not vicious and twisted and cruel.

I feel no guilt. I thought I'd feel terrible at what I've done, or at least feel ashamed of myself, ashamed at breaking my promises. But there's nothing there. All of this, everything that's happening now- it serves her right.

I do feel guilty about Roger. I feel guilty about his beautiful wife and his remarkable father-in-law. I know what I'm doing is wrong, and it would hurt them, but I can't help it. Lucy has reduced me to this.

I tried to ignore Kata for a long time. I exhausted myself trying to avoid her, trying to prevent this from happening, but she was so persistent. And she's so different from Lucy. So sweet and loving, affectionate in a way Lucy could never be.

There's no doubt in my mind that what I'm doing is wrong. I know that Roger, Sofia, and Papou would be horrified at my actions, and they'd never forgive me. But the truth is that Kata caught me at a time when I was at my lowest. I should have been stronger and tried to resist her, but instead, I was weak. I caved in to her advances. I was drunk.

The castle dinner parties continue. They're endless, these evenings that I used to love so much, that now fill me with dread. It seems that only Lucy and Roger still pretend to enjoy them.

The two quiet ones are the ones who try to keep the conversations flowing, try to force everyone to be how we used to be. The truth is no one enjoys anything anymore.

Kata is no longer wild. She's no longer outspoken. She doesn't flirt with me openly anymore, and there are no more advances in public. She stays silent at dinner and barely even looks at me. I wonder if Lucy has noticed the difference. I wonder if she thinks anything's strange, anything's weird in how Kata behaves around me now, like I don't even exist. I wonder if Lucy suspects anything at all. If she does, she doesn't show it. And if she does, I just don't care.

Kata is seventeen now, almost grown up. I'm a little more than ten years older than her, which makes me feel sick with shame, but I can't help it.

She hides her feelings well in public, but as soon as we're alone together, she turns those grey eyes on me, and I see the softest, most genuine love in them. I see trust and warmth and everything I never found in Lucy. I find myself thinking this is the real deal. It's no longer an adolescent crush.

I know I shouldn't be doing this, but Lucy has driven me to despair, and Kata is bringing me back. Now that it's started, I can't seem to stop it, whatever it is. I'm under no illusions here; I know it's wrong. Kata may look way beyond her years, but she's still a minor, and I'm still her teacher. I'm still in a position of trust.

So we hide. We have secret signals, secret places. I keep this diary hidden behind the books in Roger's library, somewhere no one will ever find it.

I'll find a way to leave Lucy, and with time, Kata and I will find a way to be together. I'm not sorry for breaking my promises to Lucy. I can't fix her. No one can.

CHAPTER THIRTY-THREE

AS I walk back towards the sleeping Rory, the urge to light something is so strong that if I had matches on me now, I'd set fire to the first thing I could get my hands on, not caring who can see. I need to get rid of Rory and go back to the gatehouse, do the only thing that can help me clear my mind right now.

I start packing up the plates, putting everything back in the basket. Rory sits up at the noise, rubbing his eyes. "What's happening?" he says, still sounding sleepy. His smile is slow and lazy, but it's still there. It doesn't matter. I don't trust him anymore.

I don't respond. I feel like I've taken ten steps backwards. I was doing so well at talking to Rory without freaking out, and now I can't even look him in the eye. Trick's words spin around in my head. *Don't you think it's weird that he's all over you like a rash since James disappeared?*

"Joo, what's wrong?" says Rory, concern on his face.

I don't answer, but I feel the tears stinging my eyes. I don't want to cry in front of him. Trick's right. Of course it's suspicious. Of course I shouldn't have trusted him. Of course it's weird that he's never asked me about James. He knows James is gone. And clearly there's a history between him and Trick, and even James. *Has he even told you about us?*

The worst thing about all of this, I think, as I look up to try to keep the tears from falling out, is that I feel like James is slipping away from me. My best friend in the world- I thought I knew everything about him, and yet I keep learning things that I didn't know, that I never thought were possible.

Rory is silent. He frowns and starts helping me pack up, sensing that I want to get back to the gatehouse as quickly as possible.

I start walking, and he matches my pace.

When we're almost home, Rory stops. "Joo," he says, quietly. "I don't know what happened while I was asleep. I don't know what I did wrong, but we were having such a good time..."

I keep walking.

He tries to grab my arm, but I pull it back with such force it shocks him. When we get to the door, he waits for me, blinking, biting his lips.

I don't care. I want him gone. I want to be alone.

"I meant to ask you before," he says, looking nervous. "You're invited for Easter roast on Sunday. With my family."

I raise my eyebrows. Go to lunch, at his house? With his family? Even before Trick made me doubt him, I could never do that sort of thing...

Rory takes my silence for anxiety and grabs my hands.

The touch sends heat through me despite my best efforts at hating him. I try to pull my hands back, but he holds on.

"Don't worry," he says, smiling, like he knows the effect his touch has on me. "I've explained that you probably won't talk, and they're fine with that."

I need to get rid of him, and I can't take an argument, so I nod. I just won't turn up. He squeezes my hands, and for a moment I worry that he's going to hug me or even try to kiss me or something. I turn bright red and try to squirm out of his grip, but he just grins and lets go of my hands. He turns around. I can practically hear him smiling as he walks away.

I get inside, desperate to be away from him and relieved that Kata's not here. I run upstairs, grab my matches and the newspapers stashed away in my room, and then I lock myself in the bathroom.

I haven't lit anything for a couple of days. I thought I was getting better at coping without it, but now I'm desperate for it; I need it. I draw the blinds so I can shut the sun out, get the full glow from my flames. Then I hold the newspapers over the bath and light them, carefully, page by page. The heat covers me all over, like it's giving me a layer of protection. My eyes fix on the flames, and I let the fire take my mind away with it as it burns, reaching high, almost hypnotising me. I don't know how long I stay like that, lighting paper after paper over the bath, using each sheet to light the next. After a while I start to feel the room darken as night falls outside, and it makes my flames even more stunning. Calming. Breathtaking.

The door slams shut downstairs. It bangs so hard it shakes the walls of the bathroom. *Kata.*

I freeze. If she finds out what I'm doing in here, she'll go crazy. How have I let time go on so much? I start to panic as I realise I got lost in what I was doing. I open the windows, flush away the remnants of burnt paper in the toilet. I dash around, wafting the smoke out, spraying perfume all over the bathroom. I run a bath, so the steam can help get rid of the smell.

I open the door a little. I can hear Kata downstairs, the usual clanging of pots and pans. She leans her head out of the kitchen door. "Joo?" she shouts.

"Just in the bath," I call down to her. My voice sounds weak and empty, and I hate it. I grab my loofah and scrub hard at my legs, making them red and raw, making the pain force my mind to go where I want it to go. I stay there, scrubbing every inch of my skin until it burns, and my mind can only focus on the pain. I stay so long that I'm sure there's no more smell, no signs of what I was doing in here.

Then I go into my room and crawl into bed. When Kata knocks on my bedroom door, I tell her I'm tired and we'll talk tomorrow. I hear her sigh, but I'm not sure if she's annoyed or relieved. I can't deal with her now. I hear her pad on to her room.

When everything's quiet, and I'm breathing normally, I feel like I can sort through everything in my head.

I'm stung by Trick's words about Rory. But it doesn't matter. I should have listened to my instincts. I knew he was hiding something. I knew there had to be a reason he was following me around like that. I was stupid to think he might actually like me. In my head, I kick myself. I don't care what it is; I can just avoid him from now on and that's that. I put Rory away, lock him in the box in my mind that's reserved for things that are over.

On to James. *Where are you?* The thought that Jenny Mara disappeared makes my breathing speed up. I don't want to dwell on it too much, but I force myself to look it up anyway. I need to see for myself. I switch on my phone and open the search engine.

It takes too long to load. As it does, I close my eyes and take deep breaths, trying not to panic. When I open them again, the words aren't all there, but I can make out what the articles are saying. Jenny Mara was a journalist who was apparently heavily into drugs. She went on holiday to the Caribbean and never came back. My breathing starts to slow down, return to normal. There's no link to James here. It's not the same thing at all.

I think about Trick. Pieces of the past don't seem to fit together in my mind. The idea of Trick and James being close, closer even than James and me is so alien to me it feels weird... wrong. I search my mind, wrack my brain to remember what happened, to remember the fire, remember how things were before and after. I try to picture us, Trick, James and I, together, as friends. But I can't remember. It's too far gone. The memories have been rinsed from my brain.

Is it possible that James could have lied to me about Trick?

Is it possible that everything I ever thought about James was wrong? Is it really possible that James and Trick were as close as Trick says? But why would James lie about that?

I take out the envelope Trick gave me, the letter from Dr Banner, my mother's medical report. It's from way before I was born, almost twenty years ago, and James found it amongst some of my father's things on one of his missions to sift through junk that was collected from the castle remains. Why would James still have this? Why would he stick it in an envelope with my name on it and leave it hidden in his room?

We must have been about twelve years old when James first showed me this note. I remember he tumbled through my bedroom window early one morning and started jumping up and down on my bed in excitement, trying to wake me up. I was trying to get him to shut up, paranoid that he'd wake Kata, but he told me he knew a secret about me, and I was intrigued.

He'd handed me the envelope with the naughtiest of smiles. "It looks like you were right," he said. "You're adopted."

I looked down at the piece of paper with my mother's name on it.

Sofia Slaide: Clinical depression, infertility due to severe damage to fallopian tubes.

I remember being shocked at the words, not entirely understanding them. And then James announced, with huge delight, that it meant my mother couldn't be my mother.

The theory that I was adopted had started long before we found the letter. It was a stupid theory, based on the fact that I'd never felt very connected to my mum. I loved my parents, and I knew they loved me, but my father was always so busy and so quiet. And my mother was beautiful, but distant and unavailable. Early on we were told to leave her alone, to just let her sleep. Papou explained to me that sometimes people just need time in their own heads. I never felt unloved... just disconnected.

After they died, I clung on to the fact that perhaps I was adopted. I think I tried to persuade myself that I still had parents, somewhere out there. And when James found the note, it was the proof that we needed; it was right there in front of us in black and white. I couldn't have been the daughter of Sofia Slaide if her insides were damaged, *right*?

At the time, even though I was glad that I'd been right all along, I was still totally miserable. And I was scared. It threw my whole world into question, and so I waited until James had left, and I cried.

Kata heard me crying and came into my bedroom. She picked up the paper James had left on my bed, and I watched her face change from concern to fury as she read it. But when she looked up, she laughed my tears away and hugged me. Her laughter made me feel better, like it always did.

She'd been so cross with James that she almost called his mum, but I persuaded her not to. Then she sat down and looked at me with her most serious look. She told me that my parents did have problems trying to have me but they'd managed. That my mother loved me very much, and my parents were one hundred percent who I thought they were. And then she hugged me again and said that all kids go through this. Everyone thinks they're adopted at some point.

I believed her. And after that, I was fine. Kata had stern words with James, and he never mentioned it again. But she took that paper and got rid of it. So why has it turned up again now, years later, stuck to the underneath of James's sock drawer?

I'm not twelve years old anymore. And remembering Kata's face last night. There's something in her words that I don't trust.

I get my phone out again and search for 'severe fallopian damage.' As expected, my phone takes ages to load, and even when it does, not all the words appear on the screen again. But I make out the gist of it.

It would have been practically impossible for my mother to have had me. Sofia Slaide couldn't have been my mother.

I pull the covers up over my head. *Is this another thing that Kata's lied to me about? And what's it got to do with James?*

It's all too much. My mind switches from Trick, to James, to Rory, to Kata, to the half-hidden face of Philip Creed, until they all merge into one, and I fall into a restless sleep.

CHAPTER THIRTY-FOUR

JANUARY 2, 1994, Shackleston,

Kata thought Lucy knew. She said Lucy had been different these days, the way she smiled at Kata in a strange way, a way that made her shiver. The way Lucy seemed to be following her around, suddenly appearing behind her in the drugstore or the grocery store, and being too close without Kata realising. Apparently, Lucy was saying hello in a different way, almost being nice, nothing like she normally was. Kata was frightened of Lucy, which was strange to me because she's usually so fearless. It amused me, Kata's paranoia. I put it down to her flair for drama, her need for excitement.

But I shouldn't have found it so funny. I should have listened. I should have seen it coming. I'd spent so much time convincing Lucy that she was the only one that by the time those words became a lie, they came out of my mouth so easily, so practised, with no hint of betrayal at all.

I'd been feeling strong, empowered. Kata was giving me life, giving me the strength to go up against Lucy whenever I could. I was in love with Kata, I still am, but that's ruined now.

I've been wracking my brain to remember when, how... Lucy and I were barely even acknowledging each other then, let alone close. She stayed locked in that room every day, and in the evenings, when I came home, I'd shower Kata's scent off me and relish my secret in private.

But it's there, a vague, curdled memory of one night a few months ago when Lucy surprised me. I'd been drinking alone downstairs, drinking too much, I know that now. All of a sudden there she was, in a blur of ice-cold splendour. She sat on the chair opposite me and looked at me, really looked at me for the first time in a long time. She poured herself a whisky and leaned back in the chair, relaxed. She was wearing the same black dress she'd been wearing that day at Tally's when we first met, almost nine years ago. I remember thinking I didn't know she still had that dress, and I tried to say as much, but my words were slurring, and Lucy poured me another drink. She smiled, and we drank in silence for some time. I felt uncomfortable, but I was so hazy I could do nothing but wait to see what she wanted. Then, she reached across to the coffee table between us and turned the light off.

I woke up the next day feeling like I'd made a terrible mistake. I felt guilty, like I'd been unfaithful to Kata, even though Lucy's the one I'm married to. When I think about that now, it's twisted. It's wrong. But the truth is, what I felt for Kata was real. What I felt for Lucy was never real.

It doesn't matter. None of it matters now.

Kata's gone, and I'm not surprised. Lucy decided to deliver her blow at dinner two nights ago, on New Year's Eve, choosing her moment just before midnight. She rose from the table and cleared her throat, commanding silence with a glorious smile, a smile so bright that I remember being shocked by it. I felt a cold fear slice right through me. I remember thinking that smile doesn't belong there. It looks like it wants to run away to someone kind and warm, not sit there, uncomfortable on that callous face.

She was shy when she told us she had an announcement to make. She looked down and paused in the right places before telling everyone her news. I'm pregnant, she said, overcome with fake joy. There was silence at first, and then it was midnight, and everyone was up, caught between surprised congratulations and shambled best wishes.

Lucy looked me in the eye and raised her glass. I realised then that she'd been drinking water all night. She'd been refusing wine for months. My heart sank.

Kata gave her a tight hug and wished her well before walking out of the room. She didn't look at me once.

I sat back in my chair and raised my glass to Lucy in return. I don't know why, but I wasn't even shocked. Well played, Lucy. Well played.

Kata left yesterday, for good. She didn't say goodbye. Roger told me she's gone back to Greece, a spur of the moment departure. You know what she's like, he said.

So there we have it. Lucy has ruined my one chance of happiness by forcing me into another. I wanted a baby so badly. I spent years longing to have a family with her, coveting her, loving her, trying to fix her, help her, make her happy. And just when I gave up, just when she'd driven me to the end of my will to live, just when I was about to leave her, she pulled me back in with a child that I no longer want.

And I see it in her face. We're going to have a baby this time because this time she won't do anything to harm it. This is her way of keeping me with her, unwillingly, forever.

CHAPTER THIRTY-FIVE

WHEN I walk into the kitchen, I'm momentarily blinded, and I have to shield my eyes. The morning sun is streaming through the open door, shining a beacon across the table, illuminating the whole room. When my eyes adjust, I see Kata, sitting with her back to the door, stirring sugar into her tea. She doesn't look up at me. She looks sullen, as sombre as I feel despite all this brightness. The air around us is fresh from the open door, but it feels heavy, thick with unspoken words.

I shut the front door, shutting out the light. I sit opposite Kata, and she pushes a mug towards me across the table. One of us needs to say something, to start off this conversation, a conversation that I'm dreading. But Kata has answers, and I need them.

I rub my eyes. I slept fitfully, dreams from the past attacking me as soon as I felt myself drifting away. Images twisted around my mind, just outside the edge of my memory. Every time I got close to remembering something, something that felt important, I'd wake up, and the pictures were gone, leaving me with the sense that I'd almost grasped the truth, but not quite.

I look at Kata and feel my shoulders tightening, my neck aching. I'm ready to hear it. No more lies.

Just as I'm about to talk, she looks up and tries to give me a smile. "How was the picnic with Rory?" she asks. But there's no cheer to her voice, and her face falls when she sees mine. Her words float away into the air.

I don't want to talk about Rory. I can't even bring myself to thank her for the picnic basket now. Rory is a different problem, one that I want to forget about. Right now, I just want to get to the bottom of all the other questions coursing through my brain.

Kata frowns "OK, Joo," she sighs. "I'm sorry. I shouldn't have shouted at you like that. It was wrong." She lays her hands flat on the table and looks me right in the eyes. "You know how much I hate thinking about the past, and you caught me off guard. But it's no excuse for the way I spoke to you, and I'm sorry. I guess I've always known that you'd have questions one day, so come on, let's get this over with. Ask away. If I can answer your questions, I will."

I swallow. I don't trust myself to talk. She's expecting me to ask about Philip Creed, about the trial. Instead, I slide over my mother's note from Dr Banner. She reaches over and picks it up, a puzzled look on her face. As soon as she realises what it is, I see the anger flash in her eyes. She flicks the paper back to me and leans into her chair, folding her arms across her body.

"That boy!" she says, annoyed. "He'll be the bane of my life, I swear." She's shaking her head at me, at the paper, at an audience that doesn't exist. "Not this again, Joo. I explained this to you, years ago. I can't believe James would bring this up again. He's such a..."

I cut her off. "I looked it up, Kata. She couldn't have been my mum," I say, my voice breaking. *Come on, Joo*. Now is not the time to cry.

Her eyes soften. She shakes her head, gently this time. "Juniper, don't ever say that," she says, letting her words drift off. But she's stalling. She's going to lie.

When she talks, her voice is firm. She looks me right in the eyes again. "This," she says, eyeing the paper, "is rubbish. You are your mother's daughter, Joo. Yes, it's true that your mother struggled to have you. Yes, it's true that she had some damage inside, which made it difficult for her to get pregnant. And yes, it made her depressed for some time. But you already know this. What did it say when you looked it up? It said that it was difficult, but not impossible, right?"

I frown. Did it say that? I guess it did...

Kata lets out an exaggerated sigh, as if this is stupid, as if it's just a small misunderstanding. As if I'm an idiot for even thinking it. "You were Sofia's little miracle baby, and she loved you very much," she says. At the mention of her sister's name, I see tears spring to her eyes, and I feel them prickling the back of my own.

I want to believe her. I really do. But then I remember how easily she lies, so I hold my head up and stick to my guns.

"Where's my birth certificate?" I ask.

I watch her swallow. I watch how difficult it is for her to say the words. "It's gone, Joo. It burnt... in the fire."

She looks at her hands and takes a deep breath. When she looks up at me again, she purses her lips. "You were born at St. Mary's hospital, in Gilford. If my word is not enough for you, then you can go there and check the medical records yourself. They'll have a copy of your birth certificate there."

I swallow. For a moment, I almost feel guilty for testing her like this, for not taking her word for it. But what she's saying sounds true. I nod. I can check the birth certificate later.

She puffs out her cheeks and exhales loudly. "Shall we move on? What else? Hit me."

I hate the way she's making this out to be trivial, like all my questions are unnecessary. Stupid ideas from a silly little girl.

"Why did Philip Creed change his plea?" I ask her, the fist in my stomach grabbing at me as I say the words. I watch Kata carefully for signs of a lie, but now she just looks sad.

"I don't know the answer to that question," she says. "I'm sorry."

"Is there a chance that he could be innocent? I read an article that said there was no evidence..."

She interrupts me, but gently this time. "He *confessed.* Philip Creed confessed to the fire, to the murders..." There are tears in her eyes again, and she looks up at the ceiling, blinking. When she looks at me again, she tries to smile. "The reason I don't like to talk about the past is because it hurts too much. All I know about the fire is that the man who confessed to it is in prison, serving a life sentence. I don't know any more than that, Joo, and that's the truth."

I think I believe her. But I can't keep the panic out of my voice. "But what if he didn't do it, Kata? What if James comes back here with some sort of proof? What if someone else did it, someone who's still out there?" I hear my voice rising as I say the words out loud.

Kata reaches across for my hand to calm me down before the panic can escalate. "Philip Creed *confessed.* Do you really think that anyone would do that if they weren't guilty? What reason could he possibly have to say he did it if he didn't? Think about it..." she says, softly, tilting her head to the side. "Would anyone actually go to prison for life, for something they didn't do?"

I breathe. She's right. But there are still holes, things that don't feel right. Why would James say his father was innocent? What did he find?

Kata pre-empts my thoughts. "James may want to think that his dad is innocent. He may *need* to think it. But honestly, Joo, he has no right to go saying that to you, putting all these ideas into your head and then disappearing like that. You know what he's like. I'm sorry, but I've been glad he hasn't been around. I just... you've seemed so much better without him. With Rory..."

She trails off as she looks at me. I feel my face harden, my jaw setting at the mention of Rory.

Kata clears her throat. "Now, can I ask you a question?" she says.

I nod. *As long as it's not about Rory Bryan.*

"Do you honestly not know where James is?"

I sigh and push back the tears. "I honestly don't," I tell her. "He said he was going to see his father, and that he'd be back when he found what he was looking for."

"Well then, I think he'll be gone a long time, Joo," she says. "Because there's nothing to find."

And that's that. It's Kata's final word. She gets up and goes to her handbag. "I got you this," she says, placing a gold-wrapped chocolate egg in front of me. "Happy Easter."

I feel guilty for not getting her one and even more guilty because I'm not quite finished with my questions. "Do we have money?" I ask her, quietly.

I find myself holding my breath. I'm terrified of her answer, terrified that my aunt has been lying to me since my parents died.

She walks across to the sink so I can't see her face. When she turns around again, she takes a deep breath before answering.

"I guess the article you read was by that reporter, Jenny Mara, right?"

I nod.

"She was a drug addict, Joo, did you know that?"

I nod again. But there's more; I can feel it. I watch her wrestle with her thoughts. She seems to change her mind each time she starts to say something and then think better of it. Finally, she walks back to the table and sits.

"I was going to wait until you were older, your eighteenth birthday's coming up..." She trails off before starting again. "*We* don't have money," she continues, "but *you* do. Your parents left behind a lot of money. I've kept it safe for you, of course. I've hardly touched anything at all, just small amounts from time to time, for things that you needed or wanted. It's your money, it's in your name, and you have access to it whenever you want. I thought… I thought I was doing for the best," she says. "You were so young. I just wanted to keep it safe for you, until you knew what you wanted to do with your life…"

I believe her. And I feel the relief wash over me. She may not have told me about the money. But it wasn't a lie, exactly. It was for my own good.

Asking how much feels wrong, but I want to know. Kata passes over a slip of paper, and my eyes widen. Wow. So we *are* rich.

There's a thought pressing into my brain, and I say the words out loud before I can stop myself. "Is this enough money to rebuild the castle?" I whisper. I didn't know how much I wanted it until I said it out loud. Seeing that model in the library, seeing the Castle how it used to be, has awakened something inside me. I feel like I owe it to my parents. I owe it to my family to get it back, to turn it back into something beautiful, something to be proud of.

Kata's eyes are shining with joy now, not pain. She looks like she might cry for real. "Yes, of course," she says. "If that's what you want. Nothing would make me happier."

I smile back, holding my own tears down. This is my aunt. This is Kata. Who loves me and has always looked after me and would never do anything to hurt me. *Damn you James for ever making me doubt that.*

She gets up. "I'm glad we've sorted everything out," she says. "No more silly ideas, OK?"

I nod.

Then she asks me if I want to take a walk around the castle

grounds, look at the statues, and perhaps start to think about what needs to be done. I'm apprehensive, but maybe it's the right thing to do. Maybe it's time I face things physically, as well as emotionally. So I nod, surprising both of us. Maybe this is exactly what I need.

Kata claps her hands together in excitement and sends me upstairs to fetch our coats and scarves while she quickly washes up.

As I run upstairs, I feel better, lighter, happier. There are still questions in my head, and my heart still sinks whenever I think about Rory, but at least everything with Kata is clear. I grab my scarf from my bedroom first and then race into Kata's. I fling open her wardrobe door, a gorgeous walk-in wardrobe that Papou made in the eaves of the gatehouse. I look around for her scarf, but I can't find it anywhere. I look on the hangers, on the floor. I reach around on the top shelf, pushing around some shoe boxes, some handbags.

I grab hold of something soft and pull it towards me. As I stand on my toes to look, I see what I'm holding, stuffed away in the top corner of the eaves. Confused, I reach further, to try and pull it towards me. I feel cold all of a sudden, terrified at what I'm looking at, terrified of what I think it is.

"What are you doing?" says Kata, her voice shrill and sharp, nothing like I've ever heard before.

I shove the thing back again, push it away. *It can't be.*

"Nothing," I stammer, "I… I was looking for your scarf." Suddenly, I'm scared of her, scared of how she's looking right now. She walks towards me, her face hard, cold. As she reaches me, she walks past me into the wardrobe, pulling her scarf out with her. It was there, on the floor right in front of me.

"Well, come on," she says, smiling, but she's white as snow, and her face is pinched. "Let's go."

I have no choice but to follow her out of the room and down the stairs.

I can't be sure of what I saw. It looked like a red strap. It looked like it was attached to a red rucksack. James's rucksack, the one he had when he was here, the last time he was here. And it's stuffed away, hidden in the top of my aunt's wardrobe.

CHAPTER THIRTY-SIX

AUGUST 14, 1994, Shackleston,

Today, Lucy gave birth to not one, but two, beautiful baby boys. They're my pride and joy, my only reason for living since Kata left.

I didn't even know we were expecting twins. Lucy's been so surreal these last few months, almost floating around the house, floating around Shackleston. She's asked me for help, smiled at me in public and even reached for my hand, pretending we're still in love.

I was never able to fix her, but I can't help wondering if perhaps our sons will. I see the love in her eyes when she looks at them, especially our second-born, who she's decided to call James. She's given me free reign over the choice of name for our oldest twin, and I've chosen to call him Trick, because it was the first word that came into my head, and I like it. And so, here we have it, Trick and James. Born today, on August 14, 1994. I make a promise to you, my boys, and I will keep this one: I will love and protect you both forever.

There is another piece of quite wonderful news. By some miraculous intervention of modern medicine, Roger and Sofia have also had a baby. It seems that Sofia got her wish after all, although she still seems distant and a little bewildered by it all. Their daughter, Juniper, was born a few days before our boys, and she's delightful, tiny and beautiful. She looks like Sofia, of course, but she has Kata's eyes, and there's something about her that screams Kata at me every time I look at her. I long for those grey eyes, that girl that I lost, that Lucy drove away. I can't help but wonder if she'll come back to meet the new addition to her family. And I don't know how I'll feel when she does.

CHAPTER THIRTY-SEVEN

KATA always leaves early for church on Sundays, so she's gone by the time I wake up. We never did go for a walk around the gardens yesterday. I ended up having a panic attack as we were about to leave, and I couldn't make myself step outside. I couldn't see through the onslaught of tears, and I felt as though something inside me was breaking into a million pieces, clogging up my whole body, obstructing my airways, stopping me from breathing.

Kata sat me down in the kitchen and stroked my back in silence as we waited for it to pass, for the calm to come back. We both pretended my anxiety had gotten the better of me because I was nervous about going to see the Castle and the statues. We both pretended that I would need a bit of time to work up to it, and that impulse decisions like that are bound to have some kind of undesired and negative effect on me.

But really, we both knew it was because of what I saw in Kata's room.

Now, I'm lying on my bed fully dressed with the curtains still drawn, daylight trying to force its way in around the edges of my window. I need the darkness to help me think, to help me focus. Is there a chance I could have imagined it? Maybe it wasn't James's rucksack. Maybe it was just a bag that looked like James's. Maybe it was something else entirely, not even a rucksack at all.

I need to check. I need to see if my mind is playing tricks on me, if I really saw what I think I saw. Kata won't be back for ages. Sometimes I don't even see her on Sundays she gets back so late. I get up and march into her room before I can talk myself out of it and throw open her wardrobe door.

It's not there, of course. Whatever it was, it's gone.

I don't know what to do. And then, a horn beeps outside, and I walk over to the window, puzzled, then panicking that she's come back for some reason or another. But it's a car I don't recognise. My heart sinks and flutters at the same time as I watch Rory Bryan step out and make his way to the front door.

I think about staying up here and hiding. I don't want to see him. But then he looks up and sees my face at the window before I can move away. *Damn.* He smiles his brightest smile and waves. I freeze. I watch him disappear inside the door underneath me. My reflection in the window wavers a little as the door bangs shut downstairs.

I hear him cluttering around. I'm going to have to face him. I try not to panic as I make my way down and walk into the kitchen, where he's busy putting on the kettle, making himself at home.

"Where's Kata?" he says, turning around and beaming at me.

I stay standing near the door. I want him gone. Annoyingly, tears sting the back of my eyes as I think about Trick's words. *Has he even told you about us?* Told me what? I feel like an idiot.

"Joo, what's wrong?" he asks, walking over to me. His face is a picture of fake concern.

I back away from him as he approaches and he stops, holds his hands up. "What's the matter?" he says again, alarmed.

I swallow. "What do you want from me?" I ask him, trying to convey strength, but my voice sounds strangled, and I can't keep the tears from showing up in my eyes.

He frowns. "I came to pick you up. For lunch?" He stares at me, his eyebrows knotting together. He looks genuinely perplexed. "I guess I just fancied a drive and... honestly, I was worried you wouldn't come if I didn't pick you up," he says, smiling.

When he sees I'm not returning his smile, his face falls again. "Joo, please tell me what's wrong? I don't know what happened on Friday at the picnic. Did I say something in my sleep? You were so happy, and then... everything changed. What did I do?"

The way he's looking at me, the kindness and concern in his eyes, it's as though he really does care. I look away from him. "Trick Creed turned up while you were asleep," I say.

When I look back at him, his face has darkened. The smile is gone, and his eyes have lost their sparkle, narrowing into slits. It makes me go cold. I never imagined the happiest person in the world could look so angry.

But then it's gone. He's back to normal. He sits at the table and put his hands down flat, face down. He takes a deep breath and looks up at me. He looks exactly like Kata did yesterday, I think, and that thought makes me nervous.

"What did Trick want?" he says.

I stay standing by the door. "He told me not to trust you. He said it was suspicious that you were hanging out with me since James disappeared."

Rory sighs deeply. "Is it that hard to believe that I like you?" His voice is quiet, and he looks away from me.

Yes. It is that hard to believe. "So why did you only talk to me once James had left?" I whisper.

"Are you kidding?" he says, his eyes wide. "James Creed would never let anyone get near you. Even when he wasn't talking to you for a couple of weeks, every time I tried to approach you, he was there, snarling at me like he's your guard dog or something. He was always around you, always next to you. It was just weird. And you didn't seem to have any other friends. All I wanted was to talk to you. To get to know you."

"But why?" I ask him. I need a reason. I need the real reason.

"Is it that hard to understand?" he says, flushing. "I like you. I think you're… I don't know…special. Yes, I've always wanted to see the statues… but that was kind of an excuse. I just like you, that's all."

I gulp. I've never seen Rory lost for words before. I've never seen him flush this deep red colour before. I don't know what to say. I walk across to the table and sit opposite him.

He looks at me. "I know I haven't asked you about James. But I wanted to be the guy who didn't talk to you about it. Everyone was asking you questions all the time…I thought maybe if I didn't talk about it with you, I'd stand out, and you'd want to spend time with me."

I blink. He looks embarrassed, but he's right. "If you do want to talk about it, we can. I was just hoping I was helping you to forget about him a bit. I didn't want to be like everyone else. And everyone knows James just does this, just goes off without telling anyone… so… I mean, if you want to talk about it we can?"

He looks so uncomfortable I actually feel myself softening towards him a little. *He likes me.* Can I really let myself believe that? I want to, I realise. But then Trick's words force themselves into my head. *You can't trust him.*

"Why did Trick tell me not to trust you?" I ask.

He clears his throat, looks away from me. "That's a whole other story." He doesn't look angry anymore; he just looks unhappy, like the story, whatever it is, will be painful for him to talk about. I don't care. I need to hear it. I wait for him to carry on.

He looks back at me and takes a deep breath. "I guess I

haven't been entirely honest with you. About James," he says.

Here we go, I think. I brace myself.

"Trick and I used to be friends when I was at St. Augustine's. I guess you could say that we kind of grew up together. We were never that close because, well, you know what James is like. He hated anyone even talking to his brother..."

He trails off when he sees my face. I know I've gone pale. I shake my head at him. "What do you mean?" I ask, my voice wavering.

"I mean, you know how James doesn't like to share. He's the same way with Trick as he is with you." He stops again, looking at me, a frown on his face.

I don't know what he's talking about. I don't know how it's even possible.

"How can you not know that?" Rory says, astonished. "You know how possessive James is, surely."

When he sees that I'm not going to answer, Rory continues. "OK, well, James was always turning up at school, in the afternoons or on weekends... He was always coming to see Trick. Sometimes he'd even sneak into the dorm at night and sleep there, with his brother. And Trick was only ever friends with me when James wasn't around. As soon as James turned up, Trick would ignore me. It was just the way it was. It didn't matter to me; it was just what happened. Even if it was strange, I guess we just grew up like that."

I try to keep a straight face, but it feels like everything I know about James is a lie. He doesn't hate his brother. I thought they hadn't seen or spoken to each other in years, but I was wrong. It explains why Trick's so upset that he's gone, but still, it's hard for me to take in.

Rory's looking at me carefully, watching me. He carries on. "One day, I don't know what happened, but James went crazy.

I went to the dorm in the afternoon to get something, and he was there on his own, waiting for me. And then he started… I don't know, he started hitting himself. Beating himself up, throwing himself around. It was so weird, so… crazy. I never wanted to tell you this because, well, I didn't know if you'd believe me. No one else did. I was trying to stop him from hurting himself, but then Trick came in, and James told him I'd been beating him up."

Rory looks so upset then I can't help but feel sorry for him. What he's saying, his words, they sound so wrong and yet so real at the same time. It leaves me with a sour taste in my mouth.

"It was ridiculous, really," Rory, carries on, looking down. "I just stood there, not knowing what to do. And Trick just went mental. He exploded. Everything just blew up, and we had this fight. And then… then I was expelled. I hadn't actually done anything wrong, but Trick and James, they… they're so tight. And the school was never going to expel Trick, were they? He's the piano genius. So… I ended up coming to Shackleston School."

Rory looks up at me again, and I see how much he wants me to believe him. I feel like I've been smacked with this information, hit hard in the face. The image of James playing the piano when we were little is replaced with Trick. And then I'm assaulted by the images, coming thick and fast. Of James, furious, smashing Trick's piano to pieces. *Not the other way around.*

Rory's unaware of the effect his words have on me. Like a door is closing, and a million other doors are opening in its place. When he talks again, he looks me in the eyes. "I swear, Juniper, me liking you had nothing to do with James or Trick or anything like that. I'm just… I'm not like that. I just wanted to forget about the whole thing and move on. It wasn't like I wanted to get my own back or anything. And I didn't tell you because… well I was embarrassed. I thought if you knew, you'd believe James anyway."

He looks so downcast, so upset. I want to believe him, but it's so hard. I spent so many years convinced that James hated his brother, and it turns out it was all a great big lie. *Did I really know James at all?*

Could Rory he be right? I thought that James was always protecting me, by speaking for me, covering for me, helping me work through my anxiety. But maybe… maybe he was making it all worse. Maybe Rory's right. Maybe James *was* possessive. Maybe he just wanted me for himself. Maybe he was the same with Trick.

I try hard to think about James, to really think about what he was like. But he feels so far away from me now that I can hardly even picture his face. It's like he's slipping away from me. He's somewhere I can't see him in my mind. Then I think about Kata. The two closest people to me in the world have been lying to me. And it makes me feel so lost, so totally alone.

I look up at Rory. I need to get out of here. I need to clear my head. And I believe him, I realise. He looks so nervous as he waits for me to say something.

I try to give him a smile. When he smiles back at me, it lifts the whole room. Suddenly the air isn't so heavy anymore. "Shall we go?" I ask him.

"Really?" he says, and before I can I roll my eyes at him, he's up, pulling me up with him. "OK, OK, so I need to warn you…"

He starts telling me about his family as I grab my coat and we get into his car. He talks the whole way to his house, not about James and Trick but about his family and what I might expect when we get there. I'm overcome by this feeling that Rory's just normal. He's a normal guy, albeit a very good-looking one. He doesn't have a sordid past. He doesn't have any issues; he's just… normal. And nice. There's nothing twisted or dark about him. And maybe, just maybe, he actually does like me.

CHAPTER THIRTY-EIGHT

MAY 2, 1995, Shackleston,

Our sons are nine months old now, and there are some things I need to put down on paper, to organise myself in my head somehow. Perhaps seeing the words in front of me will help me to understand, help me to make sense of what's happening.

When they were born, Dr Banner explained to me that Lucy may need some help getting over the trauma of birth. Some mothers go through so much pain during childbirth that they can't help but associate the child with the pain, and they have a hard time forgiving them for it. When I heard him say those words, my heart sank. Of course that would be Lucy.

After watching her behaviour for months, I'm now convinced of it. Giving birth to Trick hurt her so much that after him, James was easy. And I know her; I know how her mind works. Once she's been hurt, once she's been wronged, she doesn't forget it.

But I wasn't prepared for this. She loves James like he's the only thing that exists in this world; they're glued to each other twenty-four hours a day. He's the light that shines in her eyes, he makes her calm, he's everything she ever dreamed of. He's fixing her, bit by bit. I can see it; I can feel it.

But... I'm shaking as I write this. I feel the fear, the dread rising in me and I have to put the pen down, close my eyes and take a breath before I can go on.

It's how she behaves with Trick that frightens me. She leaves him alone, leaves him out, pushes him to one side. He's just a baby. How can she blame him for hurting her? How can she do this to him? How can she stand the piercing sound of his tears when she refuses to feed him? I've become so used to hearing Trick's screams from across the green when I'm running back from work. They slice right through my heart as I try to get to him as quickly as possible, to pick him up and check him over, hold him in my arms. Lucy sits in her rocking chair with James at her breast and looks me right in the eye. She smiles sweetly and tells me that she thought she'd fed Trick before, but since they're so alike perhaps she fed James twice instead. Then she laughs, like it's normal, like it's the most natural thing in the world. I could understand it happening once, maybe even twice. But not like this, not every day.

James sleeps in that bed with her every night. She locks him away with her in that room, leaving Trick alone in his crib in the hall. She's separating them. She's driving a wedge between our boys while they're only babies. She's creating this horror story, this hole in our family that I had such high hopes for. And I just don't know what to do.

Dr Banner tells me to give it time. That she'll come around. But there's no way he'd ever say a bad word about Lucy. He blames me, the outsider. I can see it in his eyes. It's my responsibility to make sure she's OK and provide for her, provide for our sons.

Then, yesterday happened.

When I got back from work, I heard the cries as I walked through the gate. It wasn't the usual piercing, hungry screams but a more muffled, hollow cry, filling me with dread. As I ran towards the house, the cries got louder, more insistent. I followed the sound, searching frantically for our boy, but I couldn't find him anywhere. And Lucy was nowhere to be seen.

Then I saw it. The painted-over door to the basement, the lock broken, the paper around the edges torn. I yanked it open and ran down those stairs as fast as I could. There in that dark, dank basement of our home was our baby, naked and on the floor, alone, and screaming.

He could have died.

Lucy returned at seven with James safely nestled in her arms. She said Trick had been making James cry, that he'd been wailing so loudly that neither of them could take their naps. So she left him in the basement because he seemed too hot, and he needed cooling down. He needed to learn a lesson.

Words stuck in my throat, tears blinded my eyes. I know, with all my heart, with every ounce of my being, that I must take my boys, both of them, as far away from her as I possibly can. Roger tells me to stay strong. He's offered sanctuary for Trick at the castle, and from now on, I'll drop Trick there on my way to work and pick him up on my way back. Just for a while, until Lucy gets used to having two babies to look after.

I know Roger feels sorry for me because he started to tell me Lucy's secret. He started to tell me about her father, that he'd left her as a little girl and started a new family in this very town. Lucy and her mother were forced to watch him be a father to someone else, right in front of their eyes. He told me that Lucy's mother was devastated and blamed her for her father's betrayal. He led me to believe that Lucy was punished for it, that she may have been locked down in that basement herself from time to time.

He looked as though he might tell me more, but I didn't want to listen, and I cut him off. I'm not sure I care about Lucy's Story anymore. There's no excuse for the monster that she is. She needs help but not from me.

Yesterday, when I heard the screaming from the house, and I couldn't find her anywhere, the first thought in my mind was that she was dead. And the only I thing I felt, for one second, one moment of clarity in my mind, was relief.

CHAPTER THIRTY-NINE

WHEN we get to Rory's, a huge one-level house just outside of town, he suddenly gets nervous and goes quiet. I've been in a mild state of panic since we left the castle grounds, terrified about meeting his family. Rory's been trying to reassure me, trying to convince me that they want to meet me, they don't bite. Now he's standing next to me looking at the house, wringing his hands.

I take deep breaths so as not to freak out. He grabs my hand and pulls me down the alleyway to the left of the house, towards the back garden. As we get closer, I hear laughter, the sound of glasses clinking together.

We round the corner, and his family are all there, standing around a garden table, smiling at each other, sharing silly insults, telling jokes.

I freeze. Amidst all the talking, there's one thing Rory forgot to tell me. Standing in the middle of them all is his mother, and I recognise her instantly. *Of course*, I think to myself, as I remember her card in my bag. Becky Bryan. Sergeant Becky Bryan, the one in charge of the investigation into James's disappearance, is Rory's mum.

I feel sick. This is another ambush. I pull my hand out of Rory's grasp. I want to turn around and run away. But before I have time to freak out, she walks right up to me and pulls me into a hug.

"I'm glad you're here, Juniper," she says, taking my arm and dragging me along to the table. She begins introducing me to the rest of the family, Rory's dad, his brother, his brother's girlfriend, the dogs... Before I know it, I've been pushed into a chair, and there's a glass of white wine in my hand.

Rory looks at me from the other end of the table. He shrugs and gives me a smile of encouragement. Perhaps this wasn't an ambush after all. I'm not sure Rory has any idea I've met his mum before. He walks around and sits next to me, grabbing himself a glass of wine too. "Are you OK?" he whispers.

I nod. *I'm OK,* I think. I really am.

Lunch is a success. Rory's family is kind to me and kind to each other. They talk and laugh often, and they ask me questions from time to time that they never leave hanging in the air for too long. No one seems to notice or care that I don't talk, and I begin to forget about it myself. I feel myself relaxing, and I even start to enjoy myself. Every so often, Rory squeezes my hand under the table, and it makes me feel warm, reminds me that I'm OK.

Rory's mum is in plain clothes, a long loose skirt and a t-shirt. She explains that she's on call, so she can't drink, but not on duty, so she can still relax. She seems happy and so like Rory I can't believe I didn't get the resemblance before. Not once does she look at me for too long or try to ask me anything about James. Not once does she make me feel guilty, like I shouldn't be there, like I should be at home, worrying about where James is. I start to let myself forget, to not think about James, or Trick, or Kata.

At one point Rory's dad clears his throat, and everyone miraculously shuts up. Seated at the head of the table, he lets his warm eyes take in each person briefly before settling on me. "It's lovely to have you all here," he says, his voice calm and deep.

I'm holding my breath because he's still looking at me, and everything around me is too quiet.

"Especially you, Miss Slaide," he says, smiling.

I swallow. I'm the centre of attention. I feel Rory holding

his breath next to me as everyone is silent. "It's lovely to be here," I say, managing to smile back.

The chatter picks up again instantly, and everyone ignores the fact that I spoke. Except Rory, who's squeezing my hand under the table like he's never going to let it go. He looks at me like he wants to kiss me, and then I panic because I realise I want him to.

When he walks me home, we're both a little tipsy from the wine, and Rory makes me giggle, telling anecdotes about his family. It feels like there's something in the air around us, some pressure, and I can't help wondering what's going to happen when we get back to the gatehouse. When we arrive at the front door, Rory turns to me, and my heart speeds up as he leans towards me.

"Thank you for coming to meet my crazy family," he says.

I'm aware of my hand in Rory's as he looks at me. I'm bright red, but I tilt my head up towards him anyway, the wine making me feel brave.

He doesn't need any more encouragement than that. His lips are soft on mine at once. The kiss doesn't last long, but it's warm and it's fuzzy and it makes my head spin.

"I'll come and see you tomorrow," he says, pulling away from me. He's flushed too, and I can't help but smile. "Bye Juniper," he says, and he turns around and walks back up the path.

I stay like that, on the gatehouse doorstep, staring after him, trying to stop the spinning and relive the kiss at the same time.

As I unlock the door and go straight up to my room, I let myself think about James. About how much he would hate this. He'd be furious to know that Rory Bryan kissed me. And it makes me smile. I feel myself breaking free from the Creeds a little, and right in that moment, I realise it's all I've ever wanted.

During the night I get hot, so hot I think I'm on fire. I'm asleep. I know I'm asleep, but for some reason my brain is awake before my body, and I think I've done something terrible. I've lit something up, and I can't control it; it's gotten out of hand, it's all over me, I'm burning, I'm alight with flames. There are flashing lights and police sirens in my dream, screeching in the distance, but it's too late, I'm on fire, and I can't stop the heat, the burning, the flames licking at me, smoke in my hair, in my eyes, in my lungs. I know I'm dreaming, but I can't breathe. These flames are not my friends; they're not here to calm me down. They've turned on me, again.

I'm shaken awake. "Juniper!" says a voice I can't quite place. "Juniper!"

I'm hot. I'm too hot. *It's OK. I'm OK. It was a dream.* I'm fully clothed, on my bed. I must have fallen asleep, and I have no idea what time it is, or what's going on. Something's weird, something's not right. I can still hear the sirens wailing even though I'm awake now. I can still see the flashing lights outside my window. And there's the faint but unmistakable smell of burning.

I start to scream. I can't help it. The lights are on all around me, and someone pulls my hands away from my face. "Juniper," says the voice again, and I try to focus. There are people in my room. Someone's shaking me, pulling me up, pulling me into her arms.

The voice doesn't belong to Kata. It belongs to Becky, and she's in her uniform. She's telling people to leave, pushing them out the door. "Juniper, it's OK. Juniper, listen to me. Calm down."

She says my name over and over again, and I try to focus on it, to hear her, to let her voice bring me back. I breathe. I shut up. I look at her.

There's someone else in the room. It's old Dr Banner, and he's checking me over, looking at my face, pointing a light at my eyes that makes me flinch. Becky asks me if I'm OK, but I can't answer her because I don't know if I'm OK or not. I can taste it, the burning, the smell of it in my hair.

"You're OK, Juniper," says Dr Banner. "You're OK. Just breathe."

They lead me downstairs. There are people in my kitchen, and the front door is wide open. Men run in and out, men in uniforms. *Firemen,* I realise. There's a fire somewhere, but it's not here, it's not at the gatehouse.

I want to run outside. I need to see it, to see what's going on. I can see people standing around in front of the gatehouse, and there are more people at the edge of the woods, shouting. I can see the butcher, Mr. Ash, as well as Detective Pastelle. There are lights everywhere, and the sirens are so loud it's piercing my brain, stopping me from thinking properly. Someone is screaming over the noise, and it's a sound I need to get away from. I need to disappear inside my head, shut it out.

Becky sits me down. She puts her hands on my shoulders. "Juniper, there's been a fire. I don't want you to panic. The firemen are working on putting it out," she says.

Where's Kata? I look around for my aunt, but she's not here.

I look back at Rory's mum, staring at me with concern. *A fire?* I want to go to it; I need to see it. I jump up and push past her and run outside. She tries to grab me, but it's too late, I can see it there in the distance, something deep in the woods is on fire. Glimpses of flame are in my eyes. The fire's raging, fighting back, fighting for its life.

"Juniper, it's going to be OK. Can you hear me?" Rory's mum is shouting at me above the sirens, holding me back. But all I can feel is the heat. The fire's getting closer.

"There's nothing to worry about," she shouts. "The woods are still wet from all the rain. It can't spread too far. Juniper, listen to me." She turns me away from the fire, makes me face her. But I can still see the flames. I can't tell if I'm seeing them in her eyes, or they're still stuck in mine.

"Juniper, we need to go back inside," she says. "I need to ask you a question, and I need you to think about it and answer me, OK?"

I nod.

"Do you know where Kata is?" she says.

I look around me outside again. Kata's not here. I shake my head, feeling the dread prickle all over me. *Oh, my God, Kata. Where are you?* She went to church today, and she's not back. Something's happened to her.

Rory's mum turns away from me and talks into the microphone in her breast pocket. I can't hear what she's saying because there's that awful screaming again. I turn around. It's Lucy Creed. She's screaming and crying and Detective Pastelle is holding her back, stopping her from running into the woods.

Trick is there. He looks at me, his face white.

Then I see the stretcher being carried out of the woods, the badly burnt body lying on top of it. I can't make out who it is. It all feels like a blur, like I'm still in my nightmare, like this isn't happening.

The fire has been put out. The roaring has stopped, but my ears are ringing with the sound of Lucy's anguished screams, penetrating my soul, getting louder and wilder.

A fire. A body. Too badly burnt to be identified. Kata's missing. James is missing. Everything's wrong. And I'm scared. I'm so, so scared.

CHAPTER FORTY

AUGUST 1, 1996, Shackleston,

Our twins are almost two years old, and Lucy is still obsessed with James and uninterested in Trick. I'm forced to take Trick everywhere I go, so that she can't hurt him or damage him in some way. He spends his days at the castle while I'm at work, where Roger, Sofia and Papou are more of a family to him than Lucy could ever be. They treat him like they treat Juniper, and I'm so grateful, so relieved that I don't have to leave him alone with her anymore.

I'm not sure she even notices Trick is gone. She's never asked where he is, and she doesn't care. Her obsession with James rules her life.

When I pick Trick up after work, he doesn't want to come back to this house. I watch his little eyes blink a goodbye to the people who care for him, and I hate myself for ripping him away from them. I wish he could stay with them forever, but he's my responsibility. This whole mess is my responsibility.

Our boys and Juniper were christened six months ago at the castle. I will never forget the day, not just because I felt so proud of them, but it was also the day Kata came back. She's godmother to Juniper, of course, and I think she's needed here since Sofia is still bordering on the edge of depression.

When I saw Kata, my heart stopped. I couldn't stop staring at her, back here in Shackleston after all this time, her dark hair in a long plait down her back, her white dress complementing her olive-skin, her perfect curves... The past couple of years have changed her, have made her even more beautiful than she was before. I'd forgotten what it felt like to want to be with someone so badly, to trust and adore someone so much, to feel nothing but joy at seeing them.

She didn't look at me once.

But Lucy did. Her eyes radiated with white hot jealousy, pure undiluted hatred. I'm not sure if it was the sight of Kata herself, so young and fresh next to Lucy's cold hardness, or if it was the sight of me, of my face, when I saw her. I don't care that Kata refuses to speak to me, doesn't look me in the eye when she hands Trick back at the end of the day. I'm just happy that she's back, that she's here. Life will be better with her in it; I know it. I'll get her back. I'll make her love me again, and with her by my side, I'll find the strength to leave Lucy. I need to take my boys and start a new life, as far away as possible, where Kata and I can be happy, and my boys will be safe, far away from their mother, this monster who's desperately trying to destroy their young lives.

CHAPTER FORTY-ONE

A LONG time ago, my father built a wooden horse. I remember it was huge and hollow, with a hidden trap door underneath it, designed for us to hide in, to play in. James loved it. It was his favourite of my father's statues because it was different, made of wood not stone, and it felt more like a toy than a piece of art. Even Papou had been involved in its creation, and James had been so excited when it first appeared in the middle of the woods.

It became James's horse. He wouldn't just play and hide in it. He'd trawl the castle grounds for interesting things to put inside it. Rocks, stones, branches. Once he found a dead rabbit and that went into the horse. It smelt foul for days until James agreed to get rid of it. But then there were other dead creatures. Birds, mice, shrivelled-up house spiders that he'd cello-tape to the insides.

I stopped going with James when he'd spend time there. I felt uncomfortable around that horse even before James started using it as his own personal catacomb. In the stories my grandfather told, that horse was used to hide an army, an army that destroyed a whole city. In my mind it became the death-horse, and I stayed away from it.

The black and burnt body that was pulled out of the burning wooden horse was the body of James Creed. He had to be identified by his dental records, but since the police knew what they were looking for, it didn't take long.

It wasn't the fire that killed him, and he didn't die of smoke inhalation. The coroner put his time of death at around two weeks before the fire. There were dents in his bones where he had been beaten, and it was likely a blow to the skull that caused his death. He'd been lying dead in that horse for two weeks, just like the carcasses he used to stash there.

The police said James had been killed somewhere nearby and then dragged into the wooden horse. Whoever did it had waited until the rain dried up before they could start the fire.

Apart from whoever killed him, I was the last person to see James alive. Well, myself, and Kata.

She appeared a few moments after the ambulance left with James's charred body, although no one knew at the time it was him. She'd had to leave her car over the bridge, unable to get through to the gatehouse because of all the people gathering at the castle grounds. She rushed into the gatehouse, tears streaming down her face, grabbed me, hauled me up out of my chair and held me so tightly I couldn't breathe. I was relieved to see her at first, but I couldn't return her embrace. I couldn't even look at her.

Both Kata and I were taken to the police station for statements, and the police questioned me for what seemed like hours. It wasn't Becky Bryan, although she was in the room, sitting next to me. It was Detective Pastelle and another officer whose name I can't remember. Detective Pastelle seemed less hostile than he'd been that day in our kitchen. He just looked tired.

I refused a lawyer. I refused to have a nominated adult present, since the only person that could be was Kata, and I didn't want to be near her. I don't remember much about the questions, just that I told the truth, or as much of it as I could remember.

I told them about seeing James two weeks ago. I told them about how he'd appeared in my bedroom and everything he'd said about his father being innocent. I told them he'd had two bags with him, a sports bag and a rucksack, and that he said he was going away to see his father, to try to prove his innocence.

I told them that I'd been angry with him, so angry that I'd hit him, I'd hit him really hard and that it was my fault that he hadn't come back. I told them that Kata had pulled me off him and that she'd heard me tell James to leave me alone, to never come back. I told them that Kata had gone out that night after James had left. And I told them that I'd seen James's rucksack in her room.

But Kata, questioned separately, carried on with the lie. She said she couldn't remember the last time she'd seen James. She didn't tell them she'd seen him the night he disappeared, and she denied leaving the house that night. She denied having his rucksack. After that, because she'd lied, she was detained at the police station for further questioning. I was escorted home.

I stopped talking, to anyone. I heard Dr Banner tell the police that I'd been suffering from something called social anxiety disorder since I was little, and that given my condition, I shouldn't be forced to stay anywhere other than in my own home. And they let me, providing an officer stayed with me until Kata came back.

In my mind, I didn't know if Kata would ever come back at all.

The officer left in charge of me was Becky. She tried to talk to me, tried to smile, even tried to hold my hand at one point. But I wasn't interested in her, and I didn't want her in my house. I didn't want to be reminded of Rory, of the kiss, right there on my front doorstep while my best friend lay dead, less than a hundred metres away.

The castle grounds were searched. The gatehouse was searched. I was never alone, I couldn't even light anything because my stash of matches had been removed. I didn't know if I even wanted to light anything. I felt numb, like my body was there, but my soul, my *self*, my insides, had been burned away with James.

A few times, I heard Becky talking downstairs on the phone. I heard her say that there'd been no confession from Kata, and that there was no motive, as far as she could see.

But I knew. Even though it was hard to believe that Kata had a motive to kill James. He'd gotten too close to the truth. If James had been right and his father was innocent, it would mean that someone else had started the fire that killed my parents.

And Kata had a motive for that too. She'd inherited all the money. And Kata had left the gatehouse the night James had been here. I remember hearing her creep downstairs, the front door clicking shut behind her. I'd seen his rucksack in her wardrobe.

But was Kata capable of murdering someone? Of beating James to death? Of killing her own sister, her own father? And mine? And why would Philip Creed cover for her? Why would he confess?

My mind wouldn't stop swimming with pictures, with images, with sickness and fear.

So, I stopped talking. I just gave up. I stayed inside my head and waited for everything to become clear. I waited for Kata to be arrested. I waited for the truth to come out.

In the end, Kata came back. Detective Pastelle accompanied her into the gatehouse, and she just walked straight past me and went upstairs to her room. She looked drawn and tired, and she didn't even glance at me.

The Detective explained that they'd had no reason to hold her. She had an alibi for the burning horse and no motive to kill James, nothing that would suggest Kata had anything against James at all. There was no trace of James's rucksack anywhere. The police had found the sports bag filled with James's clothes buried in the woods, but no rucksack

And Lucy Creed told the police that James never owned a red rucksack.

But there was no doubt in my mind. That rucksack existed even though no one believed me anymore. Kata was lying. Lucy was lying. And I was going to find out why.

CHAPTER FORTY-TWO

AUGUST 7, 1999, Shackleston,

It's been three years since I last wrote in this diary, three years since I took it out of its hiding place and brushed off the dust. In a week, the boys will be five years old. They'll start school in September, with little Juniper, at St. Augustine's College.

What a relief that they'll be in school and out from underneath Lucy's claws, at least during the day. At school, they'll be under my care. I can watch them, try to repair the relationship between my boys that Lucy has so badly damaged. I'll be better able to sleep at night, knowing that I'm not going to have to leave James at home alone with her all day.

I can't bear the thought of what she's doing to our sons, but it's not just her, is it? It's me. It's what we're *doing to them, since I'm to blame. I'm weak. I can't call myself a man. I hope they'll know that I tried my best. But even I'm not sure that's entirely true.*

It's still hard to write. I find myself drinking, gulping down wine while I write, so that it eases the edges of the memories, tempers down the horror of it all. It's been torturous to watch my children grow up under her influence. They've been taught to hate each other, yet they struggle with a bond that even she can't break.

Trick is independent. He doesn't trust anyone. He looks up at his mother from eyes clouded with scepticism- and he's only five. He adores his brother, who does nothing but belittle or ignore him, as Lucy has taught him to do.

James is a menace. He may be my son, but even I know that he's mean and hard-hearted. He detests the friendship that Trick and Juniper share, and he'll go out of his way to come between them whenever he can.

And yet, there are moments, these strange, frightful moments, where Lucy turns on James. She accuses a five-year old of not loving her enough. I've witnessed her hurt herself in front of him. I've seen her make him think he's the one who's hurting her, even though he's standing two metres away, rigid and terrified of what she's doing to herself. She screams and screams and screams while James looks on, frozen and distraught. And who steps up to comfort him? His brother.

I can only stand there and look on in shock. I can't say anything or do anything because Lucy holds my secret to my head like a loaded gun. I was getting ready to leave her, to take my boys and go. Kata is back by my side again, and although she knows nothing of the horrors Lucy's putting us through, she was ready. She was going to help me. But I can't leave, not anymore. Lucy holds me here in this town like a prisoner. If I try to leave her, I'll never get custody of my sons; she's made sure of it. I know your dirty little secret, she said. What court would hand the boys over to a man like me? A man who sleeps with a sixteen-year-old girl, a teacher who takes advantage of one of his students? And of course, the whole town would stand by Lucy.

She's always known about Kata. When I told Lucy that we were planning on leaving together, she flew off the handle. She did to me what she does to James, hurting herself, pulling at her hair, throwing herself across the living room, hitting her head against the wall and slamming her body into the furniture.

Roger was outside when it happened because I'd asked him to accompany me, even though he didn't know why. He came in and told Lucy to calm down while I watched on, pathetic and idiotic in the background of my life. But she listened to him. She respects him. She admires what he's done to his castle, what he's created for his daughter. She looks at his success, and then she looks at me, to remind me of everything I've failed to do. But I heard her whisper to him then, under her breath. I heard her say words I never thought I'd hear from her, to her best friend in the world.

I know your dirty little secret too.

And he just nodded at her. He looked so sad, so beaten. He turned around and walked away. I have no idea what it is Lucy holds over him, and I don't wish to know. She's evil. Pure evil.

I dream of accidents. Of Lucy dead, gone, a car crash, a bus running her over, a motorbike, a truck. I imagine the police turning up here to announce her death and how sorry I'd have to act. How I'd try to pretend I was upset, horrified, angry. I imagine her funeral, her eulogy, which Roger would give, of course. There's no way I could stand and talk about how wonderful she is because the truth is she's so far from the woman I thought I loved that I feel sick at myself for ever imagining it.

CHAPTER FORTY-THREE

TODAY is James's funeral. I know it's today because Kata pushed a card underneath my bedroom door. I had no idea that people send cards out for funerals, like it's an invitation to a birthday party or a wedding. A get-together with friends and family. A celebration. *James's deathday.* I haven't spoken for five days.

Rory's called the gatehouse every day. I've heard Kata talking to him. I've heard her pause and ask me if I'd like to speak to him, and I've watched her sigh and turn back to the phone, tell him I'm not ready.

He's turned up a couple of times, but I've barricaded myself in the bathroom upstairs and closed my eyes, closed him out. I can't speak to him. When I forget to stop my mind from wandering back to that kiss, I fall apart inside, all over again.

Kata walks around with red eyes, and she's not talking either. She looks at me with a face full of accusation. Her face is a mirror image of mine.

Every day, Becky comes to the gatehouse to check up on us. She tries to engage us in conversation, but I don't respond, and I'm not sure Kata manages to give her more than one or two words.

James's deathday. It's Saturday 19th April, and I'm walking alone to the church. I can hear Kata scurrying along behind me, but she keeps her distance, and I don't turn around.

As I get closer to St. Augustine's College, I take my usual detour, avoiding looking directly at the school. The whole place makes me shudder. This is Trick's school, and Rory's. This is where James was coming, every day, apparently, to see his brother, something I knew nothing about. I feel like I have memories buried in these old buildings, but I can't access them. I don't think I want to. It's a place of lies.

Past the school, I walk alone down the road to the old church, the bright sun on my face. It shouldn't be like this; it shouldn't be warm and peaceful outside, not today.

I stride straight into the church and walk right up to the front. I don't care that it's already half full of people and that everyone's watching me, their beady eyes devouring me, covering every inch of me like slime. I keep my head up. I won't cry. I won't fall apart. I won't give them the satisfaction of watching me break.

I walk past Natasha Shelby and her swarm of bees, their eyes full of fake tears. I walk past the butcher and old Dr Banner. I walk past my teachers, Ms. Martin, Mr. Stuart. The headmaster is there, looking awkward. I walk past Rory, feeling his eyes burning into me, willing me to look at him. I don't return any of their stares. I take a seat right at the front on the right hand side. I'm not hiding away at the back today. Not for James.

Father Daniel nods at me as I sit, but I don't look at him. I clench my jaw and look straight ahead, straight at the box that contains James's burnt body.

Kata slides in next to me. She reaches for my hand, but I pull it back and move an inch away from her.

No one else sits next to us.

The atmosphere is stuffy, the muffled noises and whispers behind me getting louder as the church fills up. Father Daniel walks towards Kata and me, a sad fake smile on his face.

I stare straight ahead, blocking out his condolences. But something he says makes me snap towards my aunt and look at her, really look at her for the first time in days.

"It's good to see you, Kata," says Father Daniel with a warm, sad smile. "I wish it was under better circumstances that you came back to us."

I feel her bristling. She loses her composure for a moment, and she makes a noise that doesn't quite answer him. She can feel me looking at her, but she doesn't face me and I watch her ears get redder and redder.

I'm confused. The way he's talking, it's like he hasn't seen Kata in a long time. But she's here every Sunday. She's been coming here every Sunday for years. *Right?*

"It's been so long since I saw you," he says, his words leaving me cold. "I'm sure you could use a good dose of prayer in your life right now. And you, Juniper," he says, but his voice trails off when he sees the look of horror on my face. He clears his throat and shuffles away.

It's another lie. I don't know where Kata's been going every Sunday since I can remember, but it's not here, not if Father Daniel hasn't seen her in a long time and not judging by her reaction to being caught out.

When Kata looks back at me, there's shame all over her face. My aunt, the person who's always loved me, always cared for me, always looked after me, is not who I thought she was. She's been lying to me about a lot of things, and this is the last straw.

I feel disgusted at her. I turn to the front, back to James. As I do, I spot Trick and Lucy, sitting across the aisle from us.

Lucy's dressed in black but looking unkempt, her body crumpled in on itself. She can't control her tears. Father Daniel walks over to her and reaches for her hand. The sobbing stops momentarily as she looks up at him with eyes full of heartbreak. I don't hear what he says to her, but she starts crying again, louder, long moans which make me want to rip my skin off. I feel so sorry for her, so sick at the thought of what she's lost.

I've lost my best friend, but she's lost her son. She's going through something no mother should ever have to go through.

Trick is next to her. He's wearing a black suit that's too small for him, and he looks uncomfortable, awkward. *It's James's suit,* I realise, feeling sick. I feel sorry for Trick right now, and I can't help wondering why he's wearing his brother's suit. Doesn't he have one of his own? His eyes are like Lucy's, red and savage. He doesn't comfort his mother, in fact leans away from her slightly, recoiling at the sound of her tears. Like me, he stares straight ahead at the box in front of us.

A silence descends upon the church as Father Daniel walks back to his altar and begins his sermon. Lucy's muffled sobs become part of the background as I try to focus on his words. He talks about death and the sorrow that it brings. He talks about the powerful community of Shackleston and how we will rally together to help the Creeds cope with their terrible loss. He talks about the comfort they find in knowing that we're there for them and that we should all seek out this comfort, knowing that we're there for each other. He says we should hold on to the thought that we will, all of us, meet again.

He talks about James. A boy with a good soul, taken from us too soon, for reasons we can't explain. A boy who was loyal and kind, a charming personality, full of love and laughter. He tells anecdotes about how funny James was, about how his only goal in life was to make people laugh. He talks about James like he was a model citizen, the kind of guy who helped old ladies cross roads and picked up other people's litter.

Not the kind of guy who collected dead animals. Not the kind of guy who told lies to keep his friends and family separate. Not the kind of boy who was wildly jealous of anyone stealing attention away from him, who couldn't share his friends, his clothes, his possessions.

I hear the crying all around me, the sniffing, the sobs. It's everywhere. Even Kata is wiping a tear from her eye.

But I can't cry. I look over at Trick, and he turns, grabs hold of my eyes with his, a look that says exactly what I'm feeling.

Let's get out of here.

We both stand, our eyes still locked onto each other. Father Daniel pauses in his mindless sermon and frowns at us. I can feel everyone staring, looking from me to Trick, wondering what on earth we're doing. How dare we interrupt the funeral of Shackleston's wonderful, model teenage boy?

I don't care. I push past Kata and watch Trick scramble over his mother, without even flinching at her gasp of horror. We meet in the middle of the aisle, eyes never leaving each other, then we turn, and we walk right out of the church, past the gaping faces, and into the blazing sunlight. As we leave, I hear Father Daniel start up his words again, words about James that aren't true.

CHAPTER FORTY-FOUR

MAY 15, 2000, Shackleston,

As soon as I can, I'll put the twins into full-time boarding at St. Augustine's. They're too young to be accepted now, but I have to get them away from her. I'm desperate. Lucy's behaviour is more and more alarming; it leaves me cold, open-mouthed, unable to talk. I have to get out, get the boys away, but how? She's got me completely stuck, strangled within her grip. There's nothing I can do.

I want to leave. I could take the boys and run, disappear in the middle of the night and drive away with Kata by my side. It's the only way to do it now, to leave and hide and stay hidden, go where no one will find us, and no one can take the boys away from me and hand them back to their mother. But Kata won't go. She won't leave Shackleston; she won't leave Juniper, and she won't leave her sister.

I understand. Sofia is depressed, and no one can snap her out of it. When I see her around the castle, which is rare these days, she looks gaunt. There are dark circles under those eyes that blink all the time.

Kata is distraught, as are Papou and Roger. They try everything to help Sofia, but she can't seem to find her way out of the darkness she's in. Kata keeps the family together, looking after Juniper, looking after everyone. She keeps Roger organised. She's even opened up the castle to the public, taking visitors, letting the world see the incredible statues that Roger's created.

She doesn't know about everything Lucy does. She has enough on her plate; I can't burden her with the horror story that is my life. I can't tell her. I'm too ashamed, ashamed at the man I've become. I don't try hard enough to get in between Lucy and the boys. I tell myself I'll get them into boarding school, and then they'll be safe. But deep down, I know I'm a weak, pathetic man. And I don't want Kata to know that. She's the only thing good in my life. She's all I have left.

Sometimes I think that perhaps the bond my boys have will save them. James doesn't want to hurt his brother. It's all Lucy, pushing him, pressuring him, forcing him to do it. And James is afraid of her; I can see it in his eyes.

Yesterday I was caught off guard. I could hear them all in the bathroom as I walked up the stairs, and they were laughing. They sounded so happy. I moved up to see what they were doing, and what I saw made my heart melt. Trick was playing in the bath, with Lucy and James on the floor, watching him, making him splash and twirl for them. It shocked me to see James and Lucy pouring attention onto Trick, behaving like a real family. I stayed frozen to the spot, not daring to breathe, not wanting to disturb the moment. I heard Trick's laughter. I felt how happy he was to be getting attention from his mother and brother who so often leave him out.

Then I saw the flash of worry on James's face. He was holding a kettle, and he looked at his mother with questioning eyes. I knew instinctively that that kettle had just been boiled and was filled with burning water. I shouted and moved as quickly as I could, but I didn't get there in time. Lucy nodded at James, and I watched him pour the boiling water over his brother. I saw James wrestle with his emotions as he watched his brother scream in pain. I saw James's tears for his brother, tears at what he'd done. I watched him hide his tears from his mother.

But they're twins. They're linked. Even she can't break that.

That night, I caught James sneaking into Trick's room. I

heard the apology coming out of his little mouth, and I wept with sadness for them both. They're close despite everything she does to keep them apart. I hope to God they'll love each other and be there for each other, despite everything she puts them through.

CHAPTER FORTY-FIVE

WE step outside, and Trick grabs my arm. I'm not sure if he's as blinded by the sun as I am or if he's holding on to me for support. Either way, it helps. We walk. I breathe.

We get to the little wall that surrounds the church. Trick pulls himself up and then reaches for me. We sit, dangling our legs, in silence. There's no need to talk. We both know that what Father Daniel was saying wasn't true. James wasn't a nice person. He wasn't kind or pleasant or charming. But he was ours. He was my best friend, and he was Trick's brother. And there's no way either of us could sit a moment longer in that church listening to people cry fake tears about a boy who wasn't James.

After a while, Trick starts talking. He goes straight into it, and I feel like he needs to get the words out, bitter as they are, about who James really was. He tells me about the time James stubbed a cigarette out on his scalp while he was sleeping. He tells me about how James smashed his piano to pieces because he was so jealous of Trick's talent. About how even his mother couldn't attend his recitals because everyone was always so afraid that James would find out Trick was getting attention. He tells me about a time when James wanted him to play an underwater game that ended with Trick in hospital because James held him down for so long he lost consciousness. Another time, on a rare occasion that Trick was allowed home, James locked him in their horrible, dark basement. He was nine years old, and his mother had gone out for the evening. He spent two whole days and one night down there, and the memory still haunts him, wakes him up at night in a cold sweat.

It pains me to think of all these stories that I'd heard upside down, where James was the wronged brother, and Trick was the evil one. I think, deep down, I knew. But it's only now that James is gone that I can let myself believe it.

Trick talks about all the times that James screamed in the night when they were little. How the only person who could comfort him was Trick. How James cried in his arms the day his father was found guilty. How James was wildly protective, the most loyal person in the world. How he'd never let anyone hurt Trick, unless, of course, he was the one doing the hurting.

He tells me how much he loved his brother despite everything.

I stay silent. I understand everything Trick's saying. I knew it, of course I did. But I loved James so much I ignored all his faults. I made excuses for him. I pretended that he was protecting me every time he stopped me from talking. Every time he told me that no one would ever want to be friends with me apart from him. I loved him.

"And he loved us, Joo. You and me," says Trick.

The door opens, and people start spilling out of the church, blinking in the sunlight when they step outside. Father Daniel frowns at us. Kata looks like she wants to have a go at me, tell me off for being so rude and leaving in the middle of the eulogy. But she knows she's in no position to tell me off about anything, so she stalks off past us and walks home.

A man walks out who I've seen before but can't quite place. He stares right at me as he walks past us, flanked by two men on either side of him. They walk straight out of the churchyard and into a car that drives away immediately. I'm confused by the man's face; it's like I've seen him before, but I don't know where. I look over at Trick to see if he knows who it was, but Trick just stares straight ahead, rigid and stiff next to me, a blank look on his face.

Before I have time to ask, I see Lucy Creed marching up to us. Her nostrils are flaring with anger, and all of a sudden I feel terrible, so guilty at what we did. All that anger mixed with all that pain, she looks almost murderous, like she wants to rip us apart. But Trick is calm. Trick is quiet. He sits on the wall and stares at her, coolly, as she approaches us, while I can't help but wince at her face, masked with hatred.

When she gets to us, she doesn't even acknowledge me, doesn't even look my way.

"How dare you," she spits at Trick. Her whole body is trembling with rage, her eyes are narrowed slits of fury. "Your own brother's funeral. You could have at least pretended for once in your life to have some sort of feeling for him. You're despicable," she hisses at him.

I'm cowering; I can't help it. The force of her anger is overwhelming. But Trick jumps down from the wall and squares up to her. He's taller than her by several inches.

Her eyes widen ever so slightly, and I see fear in them, for just one second. I can tell Trick's never stood up to his mother before.

"Fuck you," he says, his voice full of meaning, his words making me cringe.

The shock flickers on her face. Then she says words that leave me breathless.

"I wish it was you," she hisses at him, and even Trick is taken aback, the air around us filled with the force of her words. And then, she loses it. She breaks. Crumples on the floor in a heap and starts wailing, pulling at her hair, her eyes, so distraught I can't watch, and I don't know what to do.

People run up to her. They stare daggers at Trick and me, and they try to comfort Lucy as she howls and kicks and bats people away.

Trick turns around to me, his face white. He holds out his hand, and I take it, jumping down from the wall. We walk, hand in hand, away from the mess, away from the scene of a mother having lost her only son, or at least, the only one who mattered.

He grips my hand as we walk. When we're outside the churchyard, I turn around. I see Rory staring at us, seeing me hand in hand with Trick. He's hurt, I realise, but it doesn't matter. I'm not ready to forgive him for making me forget about James. I'm not ready to forgive him for making me like him, for letting me get caught up in feelings I've never felt before while my best friend was lying dead in my own garden.

We walk into the fields towards Trick's house and sit under the old oak tree in the far corner of the rec. "Sorry," Trick says, taking off the too-small jacket and undoing the top button of his shirt. "My mother's a psycho."

I nod. It's clear she's a mess, and she's suffered a terrible loss. But no mother should ever tell her son she wishes he were dead. I cringe at the memory of her words, her face as she spat them out.

"She'll put on a show for the whole town. That's what she does," says Trick, pulling the grass out in chunks with his fist, like he's angry with it, like it doesn't deserve to be growing.

Then he stops and faces me. "We have to find out what happened to James. We need to find out who killed him," Trick says, brushing tears away with his hand.

I think about telling him about Kata. About the rucksack. About all the lies. But I just can't bring myself to do it. I can't bring myself to admit to anyone out loud that I think my aunt could have something to do with it, that she could have killed James. That she could have started the fire that killed my family. *There has to be another explanation.*

Trick goes back to ripping out grass. "Did you ever find out about that medical note of your mother's?" He asks me. "I don't know why he left it for you, but it must have something to do with what happened to him."

I shake my head. "I don't think it does," I say. "My mother was depressed because it took her a really long time to get pregnant. She had problems, but they managed eventually. I just can't see what that's got to do with James..."

Trick frowns. "OK," he says and then pauses before looking at me again. "You know I have to go and see my father." The words are visibly difficult for him to say, the thought of visiting his Dad is terrifying for him, making his hands sweat so he has to wipe them on the grass. "I need to know what James found. I just... I need answers," he says. "Could you... would you come with me?"

My breath catches in my throat. Visiting Philip Creed in prison is the last thing I want to do. I don't want to come face to face with the man who killed my parents. *But what if he didn't?* I need to know, too. I nod and watch Trick breathe a sigh of relief. We'll find out the truth together.

"There's only one visiting day a week," says Trick, "and that's tomorrow. So I'll pick you up?"

I nod again, swallowing. Tomorrow is Sunday. There are alarm bells ringing in my head, but I don't know why and I push them away. Trick needs me. *James needs me.*

Later, when Trick is gone, and I'm back at home, alone in the darkness of my room, I hear my phone vibrating from somewhere around me. It's a number I don't recognise, and when I answer it, all I can hear is sobbing. It's Trick, I realise, tears coming to my own eyes straight away. He doesn't say anything; he just sobs. It makes me cry, the first tears I've had since the fire in the horse. We cry together like that for what feels like ages, and after a while, the line clicks off. He's gone.

But I can still hear the crying. I run over to the window and look outside.

Trick is there, on the path in front of the gatehouse, holding onto his phone, tears streaming down his face.

I fly downstairs to let him in.

In my room, we fall apart in each other's arms, holding on to each other as if our lives depend on it. We cry so hard I can't tell if it's his tears or mine that are covering my face, forming sheets of pain over my eyes. He couldn't go home, he sobs, not to his mother, not today. I help him out of James's suit and we get into bed, wrapping ourselves around each other. We're so close and so broken that we just hold on, crying, until we fall asleep against each other, the first night's sleep either of us have had in days.

CHAPTER FORTY-SIX

DECEMBER 13, 2001, Shackleston,

There's been another fire, and this time James took the blame. He admitted setting fire to some paper in the school bin last week, and he's been expelled. Juniper followed him, as everyone knew she would.

They'll both go to Shackleston School now while Trick will stay at St. Augustine's alone. The boys are separated, much to Lucy's delight. She seems happy that James was expelled. She's happy I can't keep an eye on him anymore and that he has no hope of boarding now. He'll have to stay here, with her, and come home to her every day. And there's nothing I can do about it.

Kata came to see me at school a few days after it happened. She came into my office and broke down, told me it wasn't James who started the fire- it was Juniper. The poor sweet girl admitted it to Kata in floods of tears, not sure what to do because James had taken the blame for her. I was surprised. Not that Juniper had done it. I've seen the way her eyes light up at barbecues, how she fixes on the flames, how she can't seem to look away when there's a fire going in the library or the great hall at the castle. But I was surprised that James had taken the blame. It may be the first and only selfless act he's ever done.

Kata asked me what we should do. I knew I could get James back into St. Augustine's if Juniper told the truth, but I couldn't hurt Kata like that. And there's no way James would go back without Juniper anyway. He'd have a tantrum, a major one, and Lucy would punish him for it, him and his brother. So I told Kata to leave it, to say nothing. She looked so relieved I knew I'd done the right thing.

But she does need to be careful with Juniper. The Slaides will need to nip this fire obsession in the bud before it gets out of hand. I have a strong feeling it was Juniper who started the fire in the rosebush at the castle a few months ago, even though Trick got the blame. I saw her face, the guilt and anxiety in her eyes as James blamed his brother, said it was Trick who found the matches, Trick who set fire to the first rose. But she said nothing and neither did Trick. He took the blame and was punished for it.

It's awful to see how inseparable James and Juniper are these days, and how they leave Trick out in the cold. It started before the two of them were expelled from school; I watched it happen. James became possessive, started leaving his brother out. He took Juniper away from him.

It's strange. I can see how much James loves Juniper. I can see how much he loves his brother. But he can't stand the thought of them being friends. He can't bear the thought that they might do something without him, that they might exclude him or prefer each other to him. So he's separated them. He's managed to manipulate them into being wary of each other. He's learnt it from his mother. Juniper belongs to him now. She's one of his toys, and there's no way he'll let Trick anywhere near her.

The only saving grace to this is that it upsets Lucy. It angers her how much James dotes on Juniper. It annoys her that someone other than her can make James's eyes shine. She hates how much time James spends with Juniper, and there's nothing she can do about it because they're at school together all day.

Kata is the only thing that keeps me going. She's my love, my heart. Her passion, her care, her affection are what's keeping me from going insane. I need to find a way to take my boys and run, with Kata by my side. But she won't leave Shackleston; she won't leave her family. I'm just so stuck. I have no idea what to do.

CHAPTER FORTY-SEVEN

NOTHING can prepare me for Rory's face when he bursts into my bedroom. I know it's morning because when I can focus, the light hurts and I have to squint. My eyes are still stuck together with overdue sleep and too many tears, and I'm still entangled in Trick's arms. Trick who isn't wearing a top, I realise, as he sits up, naked from the waist up. I sit up too, registering the look of total shock, pain and confusion on Rory's face.

He doesn't say anything; he just turns around and walks right out again, bright red and clenching his jaw. It startles me when I hear the door slam shut downstairs.

Trick shrugs his shoulders, brushes it off. He doesn't care about Rory; that much is clear. But there's a part of me that doesn't want to hurt Rory. I don't want him to think anything is happening here. *I don't want him to stop liking me,* I realise.

The door bursts open again, and this time it's Kata. Rory's shock at seeing Trick in my bed is nothing compared to what happens when Kata barges into the room.

"I saw Rory. He was so upset…" she says, but she stops when she sees us. And then I see my aunt as I've never seen her before. She loses her cool. She starts pulling at Trick, screaming at him to get up, get out, leave us alone. She's bright red; she looks like she's about to start throwing things, like she wants to hit Trick she's so mad.

We scramble out of bed. Trick's telling Kata to relax, that nothing happened. I'm saying it too, but Kata's so upset. Her anger only lasts a few seconds, and then it's replaced by a sadness so great I can feel it all over us. She goes and sits on the window seat and puts her head in her hands. Horrified, I think she's about to start crying.

"Kata, please," I say, troubled by the sight of her. "Trick didn't have anywhere else to go." It's the first thing I've said to her in days.

She looks out of the window, taking deep breaths, trying to regain her composure. She almost looks like herself again, but her face is wet with tears, and her eyes look sore. She looks at Trick. "Don't you think your mother's going through enough at the moment?"

Trick's face darkens. "I'm not going back to her," he says. And everyone can tell he means it.

I try to plead with my aunt. "Kata, nothing happened. It's not what you think, I promise. We just... we fell asleep," I tell her. "But Trick needs a place to stay." I'm begging her inside, willing her to understand.

She looks at me for a long moment. Then she gets up and brushes herself off. She rubs at her eyes. She looks everywhere but at us. "You can stay here," she says, staring at her feet. "But not in the bed. You can stay on the sofa. Downstairs. Not here, not in this room. OK?" She doesn't wait for a response. She sniffs and walks out, without looking at us.

I look over at Trick, appalled at Kata's outburst. I don't know why she got so mad. It isn't like her to lose it like that. She's caught James in my room a million times before, and she's always cross, but it's almost funny, not this kind of wild panic I just witnessed from her.

"I'll go and get some clothes and come back to pick you up," Trick says, and I remember that today is Sunday and that we're going to visit his father.

I nod, but the thought fills me with dread. There's no backing out now. I need answers too.

Kata is downstairs at the kitchen table when I walk in,

dressed and ready for Trick to come back. There's something strange about seeing her here, moping into her tea. All my embarrassment at her outburst is gone, and I'm angry with her again.

"Not going to church today, then?" I ask her, bitterness in my voice as I remember Father Daniel asking her when she'll be back. I wonder where on earth she's been going all these years, and how many other secrets she has. I shake my head at her, feeling the disgust rising up inside me like bile.

I feel brave. I want to confront her. I want to hurt her. "And where's James's rucksack, Kata?" I say, looking down at her. "I know you've got it. What have you done with it?"

Kata looks up at me, tears in her eyes again. Then a horn beeps outside, and I walk past her and out of the kitchen before she can lie to me again.

Trick drives us to the prison in James's car. I cry when I see it, and he shakes his head at me, holding his own tears in. It takes us two hours and seven minutes to get to Gilford, and we're silent the whole way. Trick grips the steering wheel, his knuckles white, and his whole body rigid. I feel like I'm sitting next to a bomb that's about to explode. We haven't spoken about what's going to happen when we get there. We haven't discussed what we're going to say, or how this is going to work.

When we arrive, we register our names with security and hand over our identification. It surprises me how quickly we get inside, how easy it seems, like we're visiting a patient in a hospital, not a murderer in jail.

Trick signs us into a logbook. He's taking a long time to do it, and when he finally turns away from it, he seems to be getting more and more nervous, more and more upset. His breathing is fast, like he's almost hyperventilating, and his eyes are darting around everywhere. I recognise the signs of a panic attack and put my hand on his arm, force him to look at me, force him to take deep breaths. In his eyes, I see fear. He's terrified of seeing his father.

We're led into a small bright room filled with tables and chairs. I don't know what I was expecting, but it's not this. There's nothing prison-like about this room, aside from the guard at the door, but even he seems kind and relaxed. After a while, another door opens, and in walks Philip Creed.

He's small, with grey hair. He looks old and tired, with the kind of face that's been through a lot of darkness but has finally arrived at some peace. He's the man I saw at the funeral yesterday, I realise, feeling myself start to spin.

As he approaches, Trick stands up, and so do I.

Philip Creed walks right up to the table, and we stare at each other across it. He doesn't look at Trick, not once. He just stares at me, deep into my eyes, a look of fascination on his face.

I start to feel myself sweat. I look around me, uncomfortable. Something's not right about this man; it was a mistake to come. *I'm looking at the man who killed my parents*, I realise. The way his eyes are on me, it's freaking me out, making my legs weak. It's me that's going to have the panic attack. I don't want to fall apart, I need to get out of here. Right now.

Trick, standing still next to me and staring at his father, starts to cry. He sobs, into his hands, in front of this man, who doesn't even look at him, doesn't even acknowledge that he's here. When he manages to compose himself a little, Trick turns around and walks out.

I run out after him, and we leave the prison as quickly as we can. We walk back to the car, Trick sobbing so much that it has the same effect on me as yesterday, and I start to cry too.

We get into his car, and he puts his head in his hands on the steering wheel and pours all his pain and suffering out with his tears.

I don't know what to say to comfort him, to make it better. When he manages to get himself together, he says, "I could hardly look at him, Joo. It's not because of what he did, whether he killed your family or not. I'm sorry, I mean, I care about that... I just don't care, you know? I'm sorry if that sounds heartless. It's what he did to *my* family. It's how he just left us there, me and James. I thought he'd be suffering in there, but he's not. He's... he's fine there. He's locked away from it all. He's fine."

I'm shocked at his words, but what Trick is saying makes sense somewhere inside me. Philip Creed didn't look like a man who was suffering for his sins. And why was he staring at me like that? It makes me shiver just thinking about it.

As we drive back, I can't help but feel disappointed. I feel like we didn't accomplish anything by coming here. We're no closer to finding anything out than we were yesterday or this morning.

When I say as much to Trick, he shakes his head. "We are though, Joo. Didn't you see the logbook?"

I shake my head, confused. I hadn't even looked at it. I'd signed our names on the way out, but I hadn't looked at anything other than the time and date.

Trick takes a deep breath. The tears have stopped, and I'm glad. "Look, let's just get back, OK?" he sighs.

On the drive back, I don't press Trick for answers because I know he'll talk when he's ready. I can't get the image of Philip Creed out of my head, just staring at me, refusing to even look at his son. When I start wondering what Trick meant about the prison log book, I start to sweat. I feel it, rivulets of cold beading down my back.

At the gatehouse, Trick parks in front of the door and leaves the engine running. I look at him, puzzled, but he gets out of the car and walks up to the gatehouse door. I follow him into the kitchen.

"You're not staying?" I say to his back as we walk in.

I see Kata, sitting at the table, looking solemn. She stands up as we enter and looks at Trick. They stare at each other for a few moments, and I frown. I don't know what's going on. Kata looks restless, frightened of something. She's wringing her hands, looking from me to Trick and back again, not saying a word.

Trick turns away from her and looks at me. "No, I'm not staying," he says. "Too many lies." He glances back at Kata, a look of disgust on his face. "Too many liars."

"What do you mean?" I ask him. But I already know. I knew in the car when he asked me about the logbook. I knew when I realised Kata wasn't going to church this morning, when I found out she was never at church on Sundays. When Trick told me that Sunday was the only day of the week you could visit inmates at Gilford Prison.

"James didn't visit my Dad, Joo," says Trick. "But someone else did. Your aunt's been going there for years." He throws Kata a look of pure disgust. Then he turns around and walks out. I hear the car tires crunch on the gravel as he drives off.

I look at Kata. She's red in the face and looking so ashamed, so guilty.

I feel tears stinging my eyes. It's just another horrible discovery that points fingers at Kata. *Were they in it together? Her and Philip? But why?* I need the truth from her now. No more lies. There are too many questions. I start with the obvious one.

"Why have you been visiting him?" I whisper. "Why have you been visiting the man who killed my parents?"

She stands there staring at me, paler then I've ever seen her. "He didn't kill them, Joo," she says, her voice quiet, but firm.

I don't know what I'm expecting her to say next. *That she did it? That she killed my parents? My grandfather? James?* But looking at her, I get so confused. I can't get my head around it. If I was looking at a murderer, surely I'd feel afraid right now? Instead, I'm looking at my aunt, my beloved Kata, who's only ever loved me and protected me and done whatever she could for me.

"So, who did it?" I ask her, my voice rising. "Who killed my parents and Papou? Who killed James?" I whisper.

Kata rubs the back of her neck and takes a deep breath. Then she gets up and turns around, walks out of the kitchen and up the stairs.

I sit down, confused, listening to her rummaging around in her room, trying to stop myself from trembling. When she comes back, I feel the cold slice right through me. In her hands is James's rucksack.

She puts the bag on the table in front of me and opens it up, pulls out a big old book and pushes it over to me. "This is what James found, Joo. This diary. It should explain some things," she says, sitting opposite me.

I look at the diary in front of me. I knew all along she had the rucksack, and I can't help feeling stung yet again by her betrayal, her lies. But she pushes the diary over to me and leans back in her chair.

With shaking hands, I open it up, and I begin to read.

CHAPTER FORTY-EIGHT

AUGUST 5, 2002, Shackleston,

I went to see Lucy's father. I had to do it because she was changing again, and it was troubling me. Something about her was different, and I couldn't put my finger on it. There was an odd atmosphere in the house, like we were all waiting for something to happen.

It started with all the cooking. Until now, I'd always been the chef of the house. I made the meals, and Lucy either ate with us, or she helped herself to leftovers. But she's never cooked, and she's never shown the slightest bit of interest in it.

Two weeks ago, she started baking. I came home from work and found her, busy in the kitchen, playing at being a wife, playing at being a mother. And since then, it's been constant, every day, all bizarre dishes, things she would never normally eat. There's been pasta, lasagne, macaroni. Homemade pizzas, laid out on the table for James I when I pick him up from school.

Trick is boarding full-time these days since I managed to get him accepted early by Simon Cooke. I didn't think Lucy had even noticed. Then, when the school year finished, I put him in summer camp for the whole of July. I thought he'd be better off there, better off away from Lucy, away from us. He seems happy there. He still looks at people with suspicion, and he hasn't made many friends, but he seems more at peace there than here.

For some reason, Lucy insisted that Trick come home in August. She wanted him back next week, and all this cooking, she said, is for him. She looked at me with a sad, strange smile on her face and told me she missed him.

I was shocked. I almost allowed myself to be hopeful. Was this it? Was she finally changing? Was she finally going to love our sons equally? Going to stop this torture on their relationship?

It was when James asked for a snack, and Lucy brought out cheese on toast that I realised what was weird about all the cooking. I'd known it for a while, but it hit me just then, when I saw the crazed smile on her face as she handed him his plate, the cheese sizzling, oozing over the sides of the bread. All these dishes she'd been cooking. All these meals, full of cheese. I went to the fridge, and there were bags of it, shredded, all different kinds, all different colors.

I was speechless. Her hatred for anything containing cheese has always been so strong. I remember Roger telling me that it was a symbol of her father, of how he gave up on her, left her with a mother who blamed her for his departure. I thought that perhaps she was finally getting over it. I thought that maybe all this cooking was therapeutic, that she was finally coming to terms with her past.

But somewhere deep inside me, I couldn't let myself believe it. And I was so bewildered by it all, so freaked out by her behaviour that I did something crazy. I had to know. I looked her father up and found him, still alive, living in Gilford, no less, only two hours away. Before I could change my mind, I got in the car and drove right up to his house and rang the bell. He invited me in straight away. I recognised her in him, in the shape of his eyes, probably their color too, although his are watery with age, less piercing than Lucy's. He's frail but fully capable of looking after himself even though he lives alone. We sat in his small kitchen, where there are photos of his second wife covering an entire wall. I feel like she's looking out for me, he said with a forlorn smile.

He asked about Lucy. He asked how she was. But just like the locals in Shackleston, his eyes glazed over when I started talking, telling him about our lives, our sons. He wasn't interested. He'd disowned her long ago, and it was clear he had no interest in her now, no interest in knowing anything about his grandsons. He started to fidget when I told him that we were still in his old home. He changed the subject and talked about his second wife, the sons she bore him, how proud of them he was. It seems Lucy has two half-brothers. Twins, just like ours.

I asked him about Lucy's mother, about what she was like, about how she'd treated Lucy after he left, and I watched his eyes go dark. He said that the woman was incapable of love, and that was why he left her. Then he steered the conversation back to his sons, his pride and joy. He's forgotten Lucy. He's forgotten all about the past.

But it's more than that. He's ashamed. I see guilt all over his face. He didn't want to know. He couldn't bear the fact that he'd abandoned her, left her with a mother who wasn't capable of loving her.

I felt like I had to leave then, so I stood up to go. I stopped seeing Lucy in him, and I was starting to see myself. A weak, pathetic man. Too weak to take responsibility for his children. Too pathetic to acknowledge his role in their lives.

I was walking away when he offered me a bread roll. Cheese, as it happens, freshly baked. Perhaps I could take some home with me, he said. He looked so hopeful then, and I looked at him, really looked at him properly. I told him that perhaps I would take a few. That Lucy had always hated cheese, but recently she'd started enjoying it again.

He froze right in front of me; he turned pale. I thought he was going to die, have a stroke right there in his house with me watching. His eyes went wide and wild and then he lost his focus; he didn't seem to know where he was. And when, finally, his eyes met mine again, he whispered words that chilled me inside.

You get your boys out of that house. You get them out right now.

Later, back at home, I had a moment. One of those life-changing moments that slaps you in the face and pushes everything into focus. It was while I was looking at Lucy in the kitchen, mystified again because she was busy, focused on her task of grating cheese for some new dish or another. I watched her as she rubbed the block of cheese over the metal grater in complete focus, totally concentrated on what she was doing. She was making mountains of it, all over the kitchen. There were plates piled high with shredded cheese all around me. She was moving her hand so vigorously that she was sweating. She was angry. She was furious. She was punishing something.

I looked over at the basement door, which she'd managed to unearth from its hiding place again, the wallpaper torn around the edges of the door, the padlock broken on the floor.

And I thought about Trick, who'd be home in just a few days.

And it hit me, hard. Those marks all over her body. What her mother did to her. Every time her mother bumped into her father while he was still living in Shackleston, right under their noses, she took it out on Lucy. She took it out on her down there in that basement, using that metal grater on her body, all over her, scraping out the bad, punishing her for her sins, for the sins of her father.

I don't know how to describe that feeling, that utter dread, this breath-taking fear for my sons. She won't hurt James, I know; she adores him too much. But Trick…Trick can't come back here. Not until he's old enough to look after himself, to protect himself against her.

I called the school. I booked him into summer camp for all of August, right up until the start of the semester.

And you know what? Right now, Lucy wins. It's the best I can do for him. I'm no match for her, for Lucy, for her twisted darkness. I'm going to leave, just like her father. And he's fine. He lived a happy, loving life after he left. He pushed Lucy away, he got rid of his memories, and he was fine. I need to leave all this behind, start again. This is what she's driven me to.

I've booked myself into that little inn in Bramsley for the weekend to collect my thoughts. I'll call Kata from there, and she'll come and meet me. I know she will. I'll tell her everything. I'll tell her all about Lucy, and everything she's done. We can start afresh, Kata and I. We can start a new life, somewhere else, together. She'll understand. She'll know why I have to go; why I have to leave the boys. Trick will be looked after at school, and Lucy will never hurt James. So I can just go. We can leave. I've done everything I can for them.

This will be my last entry in this diary, and I'll leave it buried where it can never be found. I'm not taking the past with me. I'm leaving it where it belongs, these dreadful words in this dreadful town. I'm going to do what her father did. I'm going to forget about her.

CHAPTER FORTY-NINE

WITH Kata sitting across from me, I read the diary of Philip Creed, chronicling fifteen years of his life. I read about how he fell in love with the mysterious Lucy Creed, about his desperate curiosity to know her secrets, to fix her, to be her saviour. I read about how excited he was to start a new life in England, right here in Shackleston.

I read about Lucy. About how she suffered at the hands of a mother who didn't love her. About how she went through several miscarriages before she had her boys. How she was broken by the darkness of her past, and that ultimately, although he tried, Philip failed her.

He found comfort in the arms of someone else, and that someone was Kata. He fell in love with her when she was just sixteen years old. I look up at her when I get to that part. She's looking at the table, lost in her own blackness, her own memories of the past and of everything she's been through. She's still in love with him now. I can see it in her face full of shameful determination. She's been visiting him in prison for years because he's the only man she's ever loved.

I read about James and Trick, about how Lucy treated them. About how she struggled to love Trick, and how much it hurt her to have him. I read about my own friendship with the twins, about the role I played in Trick's isolation. It breaks my heart to read it, but as I do, I begin to remember. I remember my friendship with Trick, how we played in the castle every day. I remember how angry James got. I remember his threats, his emotional blackmail. I remember Trick's pain at being left out, at being abandoned by his best friend and his brother at any given opportunity. I remember it being funny when Trick cried.

I remember laughing at him because James was laughing at him, and I always wanted to do whatever James was doing. James manipulated the people around him, just as his mother taught him.

I read about the terrifying atrocities that Trick suffered at the hands of his family. I read about the terrifying atrocities that Lucy suffered at the hands of hers. My heart bleeds for Trick, but it also bleeds for her, for Lucy Creed. I can't help but feel sorry for her, for everything she went through. I can't help but feel the loss of James through her own eyes, her own heart. She loved him; he was the only person she's ever truly been capable of loving. And now he's gone.

Most of all, I read about a man who couldn't have started the fire at my home nine years ago. I read about a man who loved my father, who loved my Greek family. A man who didn't have a jealous bone in his body, who was proud of my dad, proud of his success and everything he accomplished. Philip Creed may have been weak, he may have been pathetic, but he wasn't capable of murder; I know it. The last entry, the 5th August, 2002, is the night of the fire. If his diary is correct, he wasn't even in Shackleston when it happened. He was a man who was running away from his life and leaving his boys behind.

There's something else, something cold and sickening that comes over me when I get to the last few entries in his diary. It's the parts about me, the parts that make me flinch, make me feel nauseous, like I want to get out of myself, I don't want to be me. I don't want to be that girl, Juniper, in these pages. *I can't be.*

I'd always thought that my obsession with fire had started after the one that destroyed us. My Stockholm Syndrome theory had gotten me through my grief; it had helped me to justify why

I am the way I am, why I always turn to flames to calm me down, to help me get through my anxiety.

But it was a lie, and Philip's diary confirms it. My fascination with burning things started long before the fire at the castle. It started when I was a little girl.

I remember the fire in the rose bush. I remember lighting that first match and watching the flames take hold with James egging me on. I remember how James blamed Trick. And I just let it happen.

I remember St. Augustine's, being a student there, along with James and Trick, the three of us together. I remember dropping those burning pages into the bin full of paper. I remember the alarm going off and how scared I was when the fire pushed itself out of the bin and rose too high. I even remember the day James was expelled for it and how I cried until Dad told me I could go with him. And I know now why I avoid St. Augustine's, why I never allow myself to look at it. Because I'd erased the memory of ever being there. I'd pushed it so far out of my mind that any images of the school weren't welcome; they didn't belong there.

I remember it, losing control of the fire, each time it happened.

It was me.

I look up at Kata, aghast. The cold, sickening feeling spreads over me, turns me to ice. *Did I set fire to the library while everyone was asleep? Could I have done that? Started the fire that killed my parents, killed Papou?* I remember starting the fire in the rosebush and the bin at school. I remember them vividly, how it felt, watching those fires take hold, the thrill of it, the excitement, the heat. But I don't remember setting fire to the castle. That memory is too far buried. *Was it really me?*

The way Kata's looking at me now confirms it. She never

wanted me to know. She never wanted me to remember. That's why she forced the memories out of me. And she made Philip Creed take the blame for me. He was in love with her, so he did what she asked him to do. He confessed to my crime, for Kata.

I'm too shocked to cry. The hand in my stomach has turned into a thick dead weight, heavy inside me.

Kata is quiet, her chin down, shoulders hunched. She can't look at me, but she can feel my eyes on her, staring, wondering who she really is. I'm not sure if I even know her at all. I'm not sure I even want to.

"I only ever tried to protect you, Joo," she says, still avoiding my eyes, her voice quiet. "I only ever wanted what was right for you. I only ever wanted you to be happy. I tried so hard... But James was such a bad influence. At first, when Roger and Sofia died, I was happy that James was still there for you. He was so protective, so determined to help you, to make you forget and move on.

"But he was so controlling. So possessive. He hated you having any other friends. He never accepted that his father had started the fire. And when he found that blasted diary, God knows where, he started this whole ball rolling. He was asking questions. He was going to visit Philip. He was close to the truth."

"So you killed him?" I whisper, not wanting it to be true but knowing it, knowing it deep within me.

Her face snaps up then; her eyes finally lock onto mine. "No!" she exclaims. "How could you think that?" She's blinking back tears as she looks at me, the confusion plain to see on her face.

But I know she's lying. She does it so well. I've seen her; I've been at the centre of her lies for years. She killed James because he got too close to the truth, and he threatened to expose her. She may think she did it for me, to protect me, to not let me take the blame. But she did it.

I stand, grabbing the diary, my chair crashing to the floor. My pulse is racing; I can hear my heartbeat thrashing around in my head. I need to get out of here. I need to get away from Kata, from her lies. I need to tell the truth, the truth about what I did. *I started the fire that killed my family. A man is in jail for life because of something I did. And Kata killed James because he got too close to the truth.*

My father, my mother, Papou and James are all dead, because of me.

I walk out of the gatehouse, clutching the diary and leaving Kata behind. I don't know what to do or where to go, but I need to get away from her. Should I go to the police? To Rory's house, talk to his mum and tell her everything? As I walk out into the night, my phone rings in my pocket.

"Joo," says Trick's voice, strangled, hurt. I swallow. I know where I need to go.

"You need to come here," he says, just as I say, "I'm on my way."

The line clicks off. I can hear Kata calling out behind me, shouting at me to stop, to wait. But I don't want to be anywhere near her. I run over the bridge and all the way up the hill, past St. Augustine's and through the rec, straight to James's house. The Creeds, Trick and Lucy- they're the ones who deserve to know the truth. They need to know that Philip didn't do it, that it's my fault he's in prison. I can't bring James back, but I can give Trick his father back. I can tell the truth.

And they need to know what happened to James. They need to know why he died. They need to know that I'm sorry. I'm so, desperately, sorry.

When I get to the Creed house, I'm out of breath. I can't see Kata behind me. I don't think she's followed me. I stop at the gate and pause to get my breath back. *I have to do this.*

I walk up the stairs and ring the bell. There's no answer, so I try the door, and it opens. I walk in.

It's dark inside. I hold the diary tight against me, knowing that reading this is going to hurt Lucy and Trick, but perhaps it will give them a sense of peace. Perhaps it can change things for them. They'll finally get the truth. They have a right to know.

There's a small sliver of light coming out from underneath the kitchen door. "Hello?" I call out, still breathless, walking towards it.

There's no answer, so I push it open, not sure what to expect on the other side. I feel the resolve deep within me; it's time to tell the truth. But still, there's that ice-cold fear, snaking around my gut again. It's rising to my throat, making me feel sick.

There's no one in the kitchen. My eyes immediately go to that horrible basement door, the one in the corner of the kitchen that's usually always locked and covered up. Right now, it's wide open. A deep black hole in a bright room.

I walk towards it, feeling the tension everywhere in my body. "Hello?" I call again.

"We're down here," calls a voice. It sounds like a song, full of light, full of joy. It doesn't belong in that dark basement where bad things happen. It's Lucy Creed. She doesn't sound upset or hurt or full of pain. She sounds nothing like the woman in the church yesterday, broken and desperate, screaming from the pain of losing her son.

I'm confused. Every inch of my body is screeching at me, *don't go down there, don't set foot in that basement.*

"Trick?" I call out.

"I'm here," he says, his voice muffled. He sounds weird. "Joo, can you come down here? Please?"

Every bone in my body is screaming at me not to go down there, but I owe it to him. I owe it to them, to Trick, and to Lucy and to James. Gripping the diary close to my chest, I take the first step down into the darkness.

CHAPTER FIFTY

LUCY and Trick are sitting around a small wooden table in the centre of the room. A gas lamp sits between them, playing shadows on their faces. It's cold, and I can feel the damp air clawing at my skin as I walk down the stairs towards them. There's a bottle of whisky in the middle of the table and two glasses.

"Juniper," says Lucy. "Come. Join us."

I pause, unsure of what to do. Something feels wrong. Her voice is bright and welcoming. She looks like the Lucy I know again, her face perfectly made up, hair scraped back into an immaculate bun. She's smiling up at me as I hover at the bottom of the stairs. In the shadow of that small gas light, her smile looks strange, too full of teeth, almost manic.

I edge forward towards them. Trick's staring down at his glass, not looking at me. In an abrupt movement, Lucy stands, and it makes Trick jump. She disappears into the darkness of the far corner of the basement and then returns with another glass, another bottle of whisky.

I take another few steps towards them, not sure what to expect.

"Trick, why did you call me here?" I ask, trying to make him look at me. But he doesn't answer. He doesn't say anything.

"I made him," says Lucy, pouring me a glass, gesturing at me to sit. "I promised him the truth if he got you to come here," she says, smiling. "Now, sit down."

I frown, confused, at the order. I sit anyway and wait for Trick to look at me, but his head stays down, his hands by his sides.

"I… I think I'm the one who needs to tell you the truth," I say, stammering.

Trick looks up then, but there's no question in his eyes. He just looks beaten, like he's given up. His shoulders slump. He looks back down to his glass again.

Lucy reaches across for his hand and grabs it, pulls it up to the table. Her touch makes him look at her, and I see the despair in his eyes when he does. He's so desperate for her to love him it makes my heart ache.

"We already know the truth, Juniper," she says, smiling at Trick and then turning to me. "But thanks for returning the diary. I was wondering when it would show up again. I'll take it back now, please." She lets go of Trick's hand and holds hers out to me. I feel myself passing over the diary even though I don't want to, even though her words are scaring me. *She knows about the diary. She's seen it before. So… she already knows…*

"Thank you," she says, pursing her lips.

She fills up her glass. They're both silent for too long, and after a while, I can't bear it anymore, so I just blurt it out. "I started the fire at the castle nine years ago…"

But I stop. I don't get the reaction I was expecting. Lucy laughs. It's loud and raucous, and it startles me. Even Trick looks up at her, and there's a flicker of horror in his face, but then it's gone. His chin falls to his chest again.

"Oh, Juniper," says Lucy, shaking her head as if I've told her the funniest joke in the world. "Why on earth would you think that?" She smiles at me as she talks, a smile full of immaculate white teeth.

I try to explain myself. "I… I mean, it wasn't Philip. He didn't do it. It was me," I say. My voice trails off as she laughs again.

Why is she laughing like that? Is she delusional? "Trick," I say, willing him to look at me. "I'm sorry. I didn't know. I didn't remember anything. I'd blocked it all out...I'm so sorry." I feel the tears springing to my eyes, but I force myself to continue. "I'm going to tell the truth now. I'll tell the police what happened. I'll tell them I started the fire. Your dad can come back. He can come out of prison..."

But Trick doesn't seem to register my words. He doesn't look up at me once. He takes his whisky and downs it, coughing and spluttering afterwards, and Lucy, still chuckling, pours him another glass.

"Oh, Juniper," she says again. "Even you can't be that stupid. Or maybe you take after your father."

I don't understand what she's saying. I don't understand why this is funny, why Trick isn't looking at me, why he's not relieved at my words.

"So, tell me," she says, her smile turning into a sneer. "If you started that fire, then why did Philip confess to it?" she says, raising her eyebrows.

I go red then. She *has* read the diary. She must know that Kata was having an affair with her husband. And Trick knows too. I wonder if that's why he can't look at me. But I came here to tell the truth, and that's what I'm going to do.

"He was having an affair. With Kata... she... made him do it," I blurt out.

"Wrong!" Lucy roars. She's so loud it startles Trick again, who cowers at her voice. "You really think that pathetic, selfish man would go to prison for Kata? Because they love each other so much? Come on, Juniper. You've read the diary. What did Philip want most in the world?"

I shake my head. I don't understand what she's talking about.

"He wanted a family," she spits out. "He'd already given up on his sons. But when Kata went to him halfway through the trial and told him he also had a daughter, a little *pyromaniac* daughter, Philip saw a way out. He confessed. He told himself it was for you, to cover for you. To protect his bastard daughter. His and Kata's."

My head spins. I feel like I've been punched in the gut.

"Joo," says a voice from behind me. It's Kata. She's here, and she's crying. She's running down the stairs, almost tripping down them, trying to get to me. She grabs my arm, tries to pull me up. "Let's go. Now. Please," she says, taking in our surroundings and tugging at me.

But I pull away from her. She's not the person I thought she was. If what Lucy's saying is true, then she's not my aunt at all. She's... my mother. Waves of nausea rise inside me. It can't be true.

"Hi, Kata," says Lucy, with that strange, bright smile. "I was wondering when you'd show up. Never far behind, are you? Join us. We're having so much fun. I was just telling Juniper here that she's your daughter. Yours and Philip's."

Kata's eyes widen, but she ignores Lucy. She pulls at me again. "Joo, we need to go. Now. Don't listen to her," she's saying.

But I can barely hear her. All I can hear are Lucy's words. All I can see are lies. I shake my head and yank my arm away from Kata.

"Trick," I hear myself saying. "Trick." I want him to look at me. I want to see it in his face.

He raises his head and looks me right in the eye this time. It's a look of pure disgust, and it makes me flinch. "It's true," he says, slurring his words. He's drunk, I realise. "I called the hospital, St. Mary's, in Gilford. I wanted to check out what Kata said, see if they had your birth certificate," he says. "But she lied. There's no record of you at all. James and I were born there. But not you." Trick takes a long drink from his glass, wincing at the taste. He looks up at me again. "Looks like we're family. Hi, Sis," he says, raising his glass at me.

Next to me, Kata's crying. She's still standing there, trying to pull me up, trying to get me to leave, but I can't. I'm glued to the chair, wondering how this is possible, how my whole world has turned on its head. *Kata is my mother. My father is Philip Creed. And Trick... Trick is my half-brother?* I remember Kata's outburst, her loss of control when she found us in bed together.

"Since we're all here," says Lucy, "and clearly you've read this pathetic peace of drivel." She looks at the diary and places her hand on it. "Let's get everything out in the open."

She nods at the fourth chair. "Sit down," she says, looking at Kata. "None of this would have happened if you'd kept your dirty little mitts off my husband."

Kata stays standing, frozen in place.

"He was going to leave me," Lucy continues, with that sneer around her mouth again, twisting her face, making her ugly. "He was going to leave me for you and start a new family, right under my nose, just like my father. They were the same. Both feeble, pathetic idiots. He was disgusting. I couldn't let him do that to me. I couldn't let him leave.

"That fire was never meant for Roger," she says and suddenly her voice is sad. Her face switches from evil to sorrow in an instant. I see how easy it is for her to pretend, to shift from one emotion to another. She's crazy, I realise.

Then her eyes harden, and she turns them back onto Kata. "That fire was meant for you. You and your bastard child here."

My head is reeling from her words. I look up at Kata, and she's in shock, staring back at Lucy, her mouth open wide, her eyes bulging.

Lucy laughs again, that horrible piercing sound that reverberates around the room. "Oh, how I've enjoyed watching you think it was Juniper, all these years!" she says to Kata. "And when Philip confessed, it was all so convenient." She laughs again, looking triumphant, so pleased with herself.

I gasp. *It wasn't me.* It was Lucy who started the fire. It was Lucy who killed them, my family, Papou... It was her all along. I look over at Kata and see her trembling, watch her legs give way as she leans forward onto the table, then grabs the chair behind her and sits, unable to hold herself up anymore.

Lucy gets up and goes into the darkest corner of the basement again, coming back with another whisky glass, another two bottles. She pours another glass and pushes it over to Kata. The silence is thick and heavy around us. I watch, unable to move, as Lucy fills up her own glass.

It's Trick who breaks the silence. "What about James?" he says, looking at me. "What happened to my brother?"

I look over at Kata, who puts her head in her hands and starts to sob. All these years she spent thinking I'd started the fire, covering for me, protecting me. But it was Lucy all along. And James died because of it. Kata thought he was going to find out that I did it, he was going to expose me. So... she killed him.

She looks up at me then, tears streaming down her face. She reaches for my hand, but I snatch it away from her. I'm about to tell them the truth, that Kata did it, but suddenly, Lucy stands up, sending her chair crashing backwards across the room. She grabs one of the bottles of whisky and throws it against the wall behind me. It smashes, sending glass and liquid flying around us.

She's shaking, her face is twisted and red, full of rage. "James," she spits out his name, her nostrils flaring. Then she picks up another bottle, throws it at the stairs this time. I can smell the whisky in the air around us as it leaks into the wood.

She's raging. I've never seen anyone so angry before. It's frightening, and it makes me want to hide. I look over at Kata, who looks shocked, her back stiff. And Trick just sits there, staring at his mother. He's seen this before, I can tell.

"James was just like his father," Lucy says, sending another bottle crashing against the stairs.

"He was going to leave me! He found this blasted diary, this stupid piece of rubbish," she says, throwing her glass against it, covering it in whisky. "I'd done everything for that boy, and he was going to leave me. I couldn't let him. I couldn't let him do it."

I stare at her in horror, her words sinking in. When I look at Trick and Kata, I see the understanding register on their faces at the same time as mine.

"I followed him to your house," Lucy continues. "I heard him tell you he was going to visit Philip in prison. I waited for him to come out, and I tried to talk to him, to tell him not to go. I needed the diary back. We struggled, and… he fell. She starts crying again, sobbing. "My boy" she wails, tears streaming down her face. "My boy… I didn't mean it," she whispers."

I stand, but my legs are shaking. I need to get out of here. Kata grabs my hand, helps me up. There's fear in her eyes as she looks at me, and we turn to run back up the stairs, away from Lucy, away from her crazy, wild fury.

But she's quick. Lucy runs to the stairs ahead of us and

blocks our exit. She pushes Kata with a force I never would have thought she was capable of, and Kata falls to the ground, sending me flying backwards. As I scramble to get up, I watch Lucy stand over Kata, holding the diary over her, tipping a whole bottle of whisky over it, covering Kata in whisky up and down her body. Lucy reaches into her pocket and takes out a lighter, setting fire to the book in her hands. I watch it go up in flames. I watch her drop the diary on Kata. Then the screaming starts.

Everything happens so quickly. I'm moving without thinking, rolling Kata over, pushing myself against her, putting out the flames that are covering her, telling myself she'll be OK; she has to be.

Behind me, Lucy is throwing more whisky at the stairs, I can smell it all around me, and I can hear the clicking sound of her lighter. I feel the heat start to rise, smell the familiar smell of wood just beginning to smoke, to burn.

Kata clambers over to the far corner of the room, whimpering. I watch the room start to come alive, the flames begin licking their way up the stairs. The heat covers me, and the beauty of the flames grabs hold of my eyes. I watch the orange glow begin to twist, hear it whisper at first, then start to rumble, to roar.

I can't look away from it.

It's the sound of Kata's screaming that snaps me out of it. I see Lucy out of the corner of my eye, sitting back at the table next to Trick, flames and smoke rising all round them. I hear her whispering to him, telling him how much she loves him. Her voice is soft and calm now, as she tells him she's always loved him, that he's always been her boy. I tear my eyes away from the flames and look at Trick, at his eyes, his face shining from the heat around us. I see him wavering, unsure of her words. I watch him fall apart inside as she tells him over and over again that she loves him. I get the feeling it's the first time he's ever heard those words, and they're the only words he's ever wanted to hear.

No. I can't let this happen. I can't let her do this. Not now.

"Trick," I say, tearing myself away from the fire that's hogging my eyes. "Trick," I shout, more urgently now. I need to do something. I need to get us out of here. I see a window high up in the corner of the room. I run up to Kata, trying to calm her, but she's terrified of the flames, and she can't stop screaming.

"Trick you can't listen to her," I shout above the growl of the fire. "She doesn't love you, Trick. She never has. Please, help me get us out of here. If everything is true, then you're my brother. We're family. *Real* family."

I keep talking, seeing him waver, seeing him look from his mum to me. "Trick, I'm sorry I chose James over you. He manipulated me just like Lucy's manipulating you now. That's where he learnt it from, Trick. From her. You have to believe me."

"Don't talk to him," screams Lucy as she gets up and staggers towards me. "James was MINE," she roars. "And now he's gone." She starts to cry again as the fire breathes all around us. "He was my child! He was my world," she screams.

She's screaming in my face, cowering over me. I need Trick to hear these words. I need him to understand who she is.

He stands up. I can see from his tears, the hurt and the pain in his face as he roars into his mother, pushes her down, shoves her into the flames. I see the wild look in her eyes as she tries to scramble out, but there's no time. She's covered in fire. Trick looks horrified, terrified for a moment.

I turn him around to face me. "Trick," I beg him. "We need to get out of here. We need to get Kata out."

He nods, that wild look still in his eyes. He keeps trying to look back at his mother as we hear her scream, but I grab him, keep him focused on me, on what we need to do. I know fire, and it knows me. We have a small amount of time before it takes over. I start piling boxes up to the window, and Trick climbs up and smashes the glass. He pushes me through to the outside, and then he goes back for Kata.

"Kata, it's OK," I yell at her, as Trick holds her up to the window. "You're getting out, I promise."

She's coughing and spluttering, but I manage to haul her up while Trick pushes. The smoke is burning my throat, clogging up my lungs as I heave her out. And then, we're outside, Kata and I, on the grass in the garden of the Creed house, surrounded by its fir trees. I hear the faint sound of the sirens in the distance, and then I don't hear anything at all.

CHAPTER FIFTY-ONE

I DREAM of James. I dream of how he was, of how much he loved me. He was my brother. He and Trick, a family I never knew I had. My parents were not who I thought they were. My parents were Kata and Philip.

I dream of Lucy Creed. Of that horrible, evil laugh, that manic smile full of teeth and anger. Of her face twisted with jealousy and cruelty. How she hurt her children, how she drove her husband to despair.

I dream of Rory. Of how safe he is, how different and removed he is from all of this mess, all of these lies. How wonderful and normal his family is. I dream of how I want to be with him, how I want to be like him. I need to tell him I'm sorry. I shouldn't have pushed him away. I should have trusted him. But now it's too late.

CHAPTER FIFTY-TWO

I WAKE up in a bright white room, my body aching, my throat burning. I'm in hospital, I realise, looking at my surroundings. I can see Kata in the bed next to me, lying still on her back. Her eyes are closed, but I'm not sure if she's asleep. There are bandages on her hands and cuts on her face, but other than that, she looks normal. I lift my hands to feel my face, check myself out. I'm OK, I think. I'm not in any pain.

I call out to Kata, but when I try to make my throat work, it feels like I'm going to die. The hot, white heat traps me from inside, and I cough, I splutter, I think my eyes are going to pop out of my face. My lungs fill up with smoke again, and there's no air; there's no air anywhere around us.

People surround me. They do something to me so that I can breathe again. And then I let myself fall back into the safety of deep unconsciousness.

Each time, it's the same thing. I dream, then I wake up, then I remember. When I try to scream, I can't because my body is filled with thick black smoke. Each time, the lucid moments get a little longer. Breathing becomes easier. Kata, next to me, is going through the same thing. It's recovery, I'm told. When I wake up in the middle of the night to sounds of tortured screaming, I can't tell if it's her or me that they're coming from.

Days go by, and they're all the same. Some days, I remember what happened. Others, I forget. After ten days, Kata starts talking to me from her bed next to mine.

When we were outside the Creed house, heaving on the ground, Trick dropped himself back through that window, back into the burning basement of his house. I remember the glow, the orange brightness, thriving, thundering out of the house as

I saw Trick disappear into it again. After everything she did to him, after everything she did to James, he went back to save his mother. Neither of them came out.

Later, when the fire had been put out, two bodies were found amongst the ash. Trick's body was identified fairly quickly. Lucy's body is taking a little longer because it was so badly burnt, and it was found in a different part of the house. She must have escaped that basement somehow, but she didn't manage to get out of the house. In all of this, my heart aches for Trick the most. I miss him as much as I miss James. I didn't just lose my best friend. I lost two brothers I never knew I had.

From our hospital beds, I learn about my real mother, bit by bit. There's a lot of explaining, a lot of apologising. One of the worst things for me to accept is that Kata thought I had killed James. She explained to me what happened when she'd found James in my room the night he disappeared. How she'd never seen me so angry before, how I'd been hitting him, screaming at him, beating him with anything I could find around me. When James had jumped back out of the window, he was bleeding, and Kata was scared. She'd gone out to find him, to check he was OK. She hadn't found him, but she'd found his rucksack in the bushes outside the gatehouse. When she got back, she'd looked in my room, and I was gone. And when James was declared missing, she thought I'd had something to do with it.

When his body was found inside the burning horse, she'd been horrified. She thought it was me, that I'd been the one to kill James and set his body on fire. That's why she continued to lie to the police, to protect me, as always. She was protecting her daughter.

All the time I was walking around suspecting Kata, blaming her, thinking she was a murderer, she was walking around thinking exactly the same thing about me.

Philip Creed's diary burnt in the fire, but I will never forget all his words, all his excuses. He didn't have to take the blame for me. He didn't have to confess. The prosecution didn't have enough evidence to convict him, and I wasn't a suspect. Kata explained to me that when she told him I was his daughter and she told him she suspected me of starting the fire, he'd almost seemed relieved. She'd had no idea he would confess to the fire himself. She'd given him an excuse, a reason to get away. He told her it was to protect me. And she'd believed him.

Kata and I told the truth to the police, that Lucy had started both fires. That she'd killed my family and that James had died in a struggle with her on our very own castle grounds.

I could see the liberation in Kata's face, the freedom of knowing it wasn't me, it was never me. And that wasn't the only thing that was filling her face with hope. It was the fact that Philip would finally be free. She could get him back. This man that she was so desperately in love with would be released from prison, exonerated, and would be able to come back to her, finally. He could tell the truth now; the fire had nothing to do with him. It was all her; it was all Lucy.

But Philip Creed refused to admit that his confession was a lie. He stuck to his story. He wants to stay there, hiding in that prison instead of coming out and facing reality. Prison is easier for him than dealing with the truth.

At first Kata was devastated, but she's beginning to understand. She's starting to see him for who he really is. Lucy may have been crazy and twisted, but she was right about one thing. Philip Creed is pathetic, feeble and weak. He confessed to a crime he didn't commit because he saw it as a way out. And Trick was right too. He's fine there, in his prison. He's not suffering. He's away from it all.

I'll never forget the way he looked at me, at the funeral and when we visited him. It wasn't because he wanted to see his daughter. It was because he couldn't look at his son, the son he left behind. He was too ashamed.

Kata and I are talking to each other, trying to adjust to a new relationship. She struggles with a lot of her feelings, her own guilt over the loss of her sister, her father and Roger. She thinks it was all her fault, that her affair with Philip started everything.

But she can't see that she was only sixteen years old. No matter what she says, she was young, and he was her teacher. People trusted him. It was wrong, and he's to blame. She was seventeen years old when she got pregnant, and she didn't know what to do. She kept it to herself, not daring to tell anyone, especially not Philip. When Lucy announced her own pregnancy, Kata knew she'd lost. She had to leave. She knew that Philip would choose his wife, that he'd always wanted a family, and now he'd get one.

So she never told him about her pregnancy. She kept it a secret. Instead, she told Sofia and Roger and Papou, and together they hatched a plan. Sofia couldn't have children of her own, so she faked her pregnancy, claiming she'd had some miraculous treatment, and a miracle had occurred.

Kata gave birth to me in Greece and then gave me away, let her sister raise me as her own. Roger and Sofia brought me back to Shackleston when I was just a few weeks old and told everyone that Sofia had delivered me whilst on holiday. No one suspected a thing. Or if they did, the people of Shackleston Town never said a word.

Kata tells me that they loved me very much, my pretend-parents. They tried hard to be the best parents they could, and Roger, certainly, was a wonderful father. But Sofia always struggled with the lie. And Kata herself was struggling back in Greece.

She thought it was her penance for having an affair with a married man. But she was so young. And in the end, she couldn't stay away from me, from her family. And she couldn't stay away from Philip.

We didn't tell the police about my real parents. Kata explained to me that it has to be that way, for them, for their memory. They did love me, in their own way, and it's better for the world to remember Roger Slaide as they think of him now, my father, the successful artist. Not a man who lied. Not a man who stole a child from a seventeen-year-old girl and told the world it was his.

While we're in hospital, Kata and I talk about the castle. We spend our afternoons planning how to rebuild it, where to start, how to go about it. It keeps us going, keeps us focused on something, helps us to forget the pain. It helps us to recover. We even talk about opening the castle up to the public again, giving tours around the grounds, showing people the statues. I'm not sure I could do it myself, talking to people in public like that. But maybe I could try.

CHAPTER FIFTY-THREE

AFTER three weeks in hospital, we're told we can go home, and it's Becky Bryan who picks us up and takes us back to the gatehouse. I want to ask her about Rory, about why he didn't visit me in hospital. I think about him being with someone else now, someone normal just like him, not someone messed up like me, and I'm overcome with sadness at the thought of it. In the end, I don't ask his mother anything. I need to see him myself. Either way, I owe him an apology.

Against Kata's advice, I go back to school. I've been given extra time to finish my exams. I can repeat the whole year if I want to. But there are a couple of things I need to do.

I walk to school early, getting there way before everyone else does. I walk straight to the art room, using my keys to get in and going straight to my cupboard. I get out my model, my tools. Medusa is almost finished, but there's something I need to do first.

I mould and fix and carve and chip away until everything is how I want it to be. I hear Mr. Stuart come in, his gasp of surprise as he sees me. I feel him smiling, his presence as he watches me work. He makes noises of approval, starts holding pins in place for me. Whenever the bells ring, he reluctantly teaches his classes, but as soon as he can, he's back by my side, working with me again.

I change the face of my model. Instead of Medusa's face staring back at me, it's Kata's. Her beautiful hair, starting out as snakes then turning back into tresses. It was always Kata, I realise. *She's Medusa.* The beautiful young girl who fell in love with a predator. A predator whose jealous wife turned her into a monster because of it.

Kata. *My Kata*, I smile, as I look at my model. She's my family, the only family I have. I don't care what she's done and how many secrets she's hidden from me.

When I finish, I turn to my tutor. "You can display it," I tell him, looking him in the eyes, my voice confident.

He nods at me, smiling, like he never had any doubt.

Then he walks over to his desk and gets several envelopes. "So," he starts, sheepishly. "You've been accepted at *all* of these schools."

I look at his hands, at what he's giving me. Acceptance letters from all the art academies, the colleges, the best in the world. I look up at him, shocked.

"And they've all deferred your acceptance for a year, in case you don't feel ready to go," he says. "You're that good, Juniper," he adds, seeing the astonishment in my eyes.

I'm incredulous. And then I do something I never thought I was capable of. I stand and step into his arms and hug him.

He returns the hug easily, like it's the most natural thing in the world.

"Thank you," I tell him, meaning it.

"You're welcome," he says, smiling at me.

There's something else I need to do now, something that fills me with far more dread than fixing Medusa. I walk down the school corridor, holding my head up high and letting myself feel the stares, feel the eyes on me, without hiding or running away. I try to keep the panic at bay. I walk with my back straight, and I don't stop until I get to where I'm going.

I open the door to the English classroom, where Ms. Martin is sitting, hunched over her desk. The class hasn't started yet, but I've only got about five minutes before students start tumbling in. She looks up at me, that familiar tight frown on her face.

"Juniper," she says. She's not exactly smiling, but her voice sounds a little warmer than it usually does. "I'm glad to see you're well. I assume that piece of paper in your hands is for me?"

I hold on tightly to the note in my hands, and I shake my head. "No," I say, my voice loud, firm.

"You have a voice, I see," she says. "Well, what is it?" She leans back in her chair, and she smiles at me, properly.

As I try to explain what I need to do, her face softens. She doesn't have time to answer me before the bell rings, and the class starts to fill up.

I turn around and take my seat. I watch Rory come in. He stops when he sees me, and I see the shock in his eyes. Then he recovers and walks on to his desk.

People stare at me. Rob Lewis looks at me and gives me a thumbs up. Carla Jackson asks me if I'm OK. And Natasha Shelby actually smiles at me, a real smile, when she walks past my desk. It just confirms what I need to do.

The lesson starts. I try to follow, but I'm not really with it. Just before the fifty minutes are up, Ms. Martin tells the class to quieten down. Then she says, "Miss Slaide. I believe you have something to read for us today?"

I can't believe I'm doing this, but I get up and walk to the front of the class. There's silence all around me, and everyone's staring. I feel the colour cover my cheeks, but it's not burning me, it's not too hot. It's OK. *I'm OK.*

I look over at Rory, and I begin to read out loud.

My words are honest. I tell the story I want to tell in the simplest way. I say I'm sorry. It's not just an apology to Rory; it's an apology to the whole class. I tell them how sorry I am for the past ten years at this school, about how I froze every time someone tried to talk to me or tried to be my friend. About how I hid from them, how I ran away, how I blocked them all out.

I tell them that I didn't think I deserved any friends other than James. How I was convinced that I was a terrible person, one who starts fires and lets her friends take the blame for them. I tell them about my struggles with anxiety, how the death of my family members affected me, and how James took over my voice. I tell them I shouldn't have let anyone manipulate me into thinking I didn't merit any other friendships.

I apologise for James, for who he was. I'm partly to blame for his behaviour, for how cruel he could be. Every time he bullied one of them, hurt them, or laughed at them, I laughed with him. I was desperate for him not to turn on me, not to make me the butt of his jokes. I tell them how sorry I am that I never stood up to him.

I tell them I'd like to make it up to them. I look at Rory, and I explain my plans for Shackleston Castle, my idea to restore it, to get it back to how it was. I ask them if anyone would like to help, anyone who'd be interested in coming to the castle, visiting the grounds and seeing the statues. If they'd like to be a part of the project, share their ideas, rebuild it together. I tell them that the castle belongs to Shackleston, to all of us. That the gates will always be open, and everyone will always be welcome. And if they could ever imagine being friends with me, I could use that in my life right now.

When I finish talking, everyone is quiet. I'm scared to look up, but I force myself to anyway. I'm shocked to see that all the faces in front of me are smiling. Some of them are nodding at me. I see Natasha Shelby and there are tears in her eyes when she looks at me. I remember a time when we were friends. She was never mean, never cruel. *It was all James,* I think, swallowing back my own tears.

The bell rings. People get up. They smile at me on their way out. Some of them say thank you and that they'd love to help. I nod and smile back and try to be normal.

When Rory walks right up to me, he's got that grin on his face, that wide and mischievous one that I've missed so much. He grabs my hand and pulls me out of the classroom. He starts running down the corridor, pulling me behind after him, out of the school doors and into the sun. And right here, standing on the steps, he kisses me, like it doesn't matter that we're at school, like nothing matters at all except kissing me, right here, right now.

I don't think of James. I don't think of Trick. I don't think of Philip Creed or Kata or my parents who weren't my parents. All I can think about is Rory. And I know that everything will be OK.

CHAPTER FIFTY-FOUR

SOMEWHERE inside me I think I knew, or at least, I should have known. Because later on, when Kata was making dinner singing songs about cats, and I was sitting at the table, making plans for the castle, we heard a car turn up on the gravel outside.

Becky Bryan walked into our kitchen in her uniform. She had a solemn look on her face, and she sat down, quiet and subdued.

After asking us how we were and accepting a cup of tea, she got to the point of her visit. She cleared her throat and told us about the second body, the one that was pulled out of the burning Creed house. The one that was supposed to be Lucy Creed.

I started to feel cold. That fist in my stomach woke up, started flapping around inside me, making me feel sick.

The DNA and the dental records were not a match, Becky explained. The body wasn't Lucy Creed. It was the body of someone who'd been dead for a long time, hidden away in the attic of that house. The body was identified as a reporter who'd gone missing several years before. A reporter called Jenny Mara.

I should have known. Lucy Creed is alive.

I looked at my mother then, my beloved Kata. I saw myself in her face, not just because we look the same but because we wore the same expression. One of fear. One of terror. Lucy Creed is still out there, and she's angry. And there's no doubt in my mind that she'll come back. She'll want to finish what she started.

Kata's eyes locked on mine, both of us hearing the same words in our heads.

No. Everything won't be OK at all.

THE END

ACKNOWLEDGEMENTS

I will always be grateful to Darin, for helping me get here. To Ally, my Doha neighbour and fellow writer, this is really down to you. Thank you so very much for my next thank you: Karen and Rudling House… just… wow. All I can say is that it feels like home.

To Maman, who gave me the love of literature and encouraged the dark, enforced the difference, cultivated the weird. To Dad, who taught me not to dream it, just 'chuffin' get on with it.' To my own naughty Aunt K(C)ata(strophe), well, the ideas have to come from somewhere… Je t'aime. To the Trouts, the most amazingly vile group of friends a girl could wish for, thank you for your unwavering support and belief in me. To my first trout readers, Nicola, Saskia and Cooke, thank you for your encouragement in the early, terrible stages of this book. To Tommy, my best friend and the writer I hope to be as good as one day: I hope you mercilessly destroy everything I ever attempt to write, you make me a better writer and I love you, considerably, always. To my later readers, Helen, Sammy K and Vix, thank you for helping me make this book a more readable one. To everyone whose name I borrowed: if I used your name, it's because you're special to me and you made an impact on my life in some way, thank you. To James: this book started out being about unconditional loyalty between two best friends, and the inspiration for that is the friendship I share with you. (I'm sorry I turned you into a psycho and murdered you.) To Dan…what can I say? It's like you keep an invisible list of my dreams in your head and you're slowly but surely ticking them off one by one. Without you, this book would never have happened. Thank you for putting up with the tempestuous and volatile highs and lows that being married to a writer entails and thank you for always being my first, last, and 'constant' reader. Et pour mon île, mon inspiration, mon rêve... je vous aime. Especially you, especially you, especially you. And finally, to Darcy: I hope one day I make you as proud of me as I am of you.

ABOUT THE AUTHOR

Johanna Handley lives in Qatar with her husband, daughter and an array of rescued animals. She writes with a dog at her feet, two cats on her desk, and three birds in her ear.

For more information about Johanna and her writing, please visit www.johannahandley.com